BROOMSTICK

A. L. HAWKE

PHANTOM HEART, LLC

ISBN: 978-1-7329563-7-7 (ebook)

ISBN: 978-1-953919-05-2 (paperback)

ISBN: 978-1-7329563-6-0 (hardcover)

Library of Congress Control Number: 2020905247

This is a work of fiction. It comes directly from the author's imagination. Witchcraft is included to infuse a sense of realism to the novel, but in no way is it supposed to represent actual practicing witchcraft, witches or the religion of Wicca. The book also includes fictitious names, characters, places, and incidents. Any public names are used solely for creative purposes. Any resemblance to actual people, living or dead, or to companies, institutions, or locales is entirely coincidental or accidental.

Line edited by Stephanie Ward

Proofread by Eliza Dee of Clio Editing Services

Cover Design © 2020 by Regina Wamba of MaeIDesign.com

Published by Phantom Heart, LLC

27702 Crown Valley Pkwy, Suite D4, #201

Ladera Ranch, CA 92694

Printed and bound in the United States of America

First printing April, 2020

Learn more about A.L. Hawke at www.alhawke.com

Correspondence: contact@alhawke.com

 Created with Vellum

In memory of my mother
Your candle shines bright in my heart

1

HER AFFLICTION

I FEEL A CHILL IN THE AIR. BUT THE SUNLIGHT FLICKERS BETWEEN fall leaves warming me as I walk across campus with my best friend, Madison. It will be winter soon, but for now, the last days of autumn in Georgia seem so peaceful. I glimpse at patches of blue through the canopy of trees. The sky is like ... so perfect. I love fall, I really do.

But Maddie doesn't seem interested in Mother Nature. She's been acting like a witch since we got up, which is a bit odd because my BFF is one of the most energetic and cheery girls I know. I already asked her what's wrong, but she won't tell me.

We pass the dorms and climb the grassy hill at the center of campus. At the summit is the tallest building at Hawthorne University: our library. But we're not checking out books. A line of students snakes its way through a bunch of cute tables with burgundy umbrellas to the counter of our university coffee shop. I think the wait takes Maddie over the edge.

She finally starts spitting out the events of her evening. "I went out on a date with Patrick. You know, the guy in my film studies class." She told me about him before, emphasizing how tall and cute he is, but now she looks as if she bit into something sour. "I knew there was trouble the minute he picked me up in that filthy, dilapidated flatbed truck." (I'm not surprised. She's not a very good judge of character, you know). "We had this great tilapia chili dish and lime-green margaritas and everything was going fine until he reached under my skirt and touched my vagina." I look around me, biting my lip nervously. We're still standing in line, and she said the word *vagina* really loud. People are turning to look. Then Maddie tells me she hit him on the head. Patrick, acting like he was the victim, jumped up from their booth, ran, and left her the bill.

Anyway, Maddie's busy telling me this story about her date copping a feel—and saying the word *vagina* real loud—when, right before my eyes, she walks into the store and just grabs a drink off the counter. We haven't ordered anything yet. It looks like a latte, but I'm not sure. I'm not so sure she knows either. Then she grabs my arm and we make a hasty exit. Maddie is like a total kleptomaniac.

As we walk down a cement path paralleling the grassy hill, I stare at her and she flashes a really sweet grin, raising her cup as if in a toast. "Anyway, fuck him."

I'm thinking, *At least she was asked out on a date.*

She looks at the brew in her stolen cup, puzzled. Then she throws her long hair back and cocks her head toward me very earnestly, saying, "Alondra wants to meet you."

I'm still looking at her in shock.

"Why not?" Maddie asks. "It'll be fun."

But I'm not thinking about Alondra. I point at her cup.

"It's really good," she says with a chuckle. "I think it has soy. Want some? I don't usually order soy but...this isn't bad. Look, Katie..." (People call me Katie a lot, even though my name is Cadence.) "Alondra says she wants to meet you outside of class. Just come with me to her house."

"I don't know," I say. "I don't like the look of her."

Now we're dodging bodies on the crowded lawn, heading to

the main hall of the university. The main drag of Hawthorne is a white paved sidewalk surrounded by grass and trees, with brick buildings on both sides—and even more college bodies. The classroom buildings are spread out through the fields and under the tall trees. The leaves are so pretty in red and orange. Fall is my favorite time of year because I love the colors.

Hawthorne University is in Georgia. It's a really nice college, and I'm lucky to have been accepted here. So is Maddie. Everyone has a book tucked under their arm or is carrying a backpack. I have a pink backpack decorated with a unicorn. Maddie has always thought it's a little too cute, but I think it's whimsical. It even has purple swirls around the straps. Maddie's carrying a small book, but I'm pretty sure she won't read it. She's not the best student.

"You should go," Maddie says again, sipping her stolen drink. She runs her free hand through her hair, which is long and black like mine. I reach for my hair and realize I put it in a bun this morning, so I just pat the top of my head like an idiot. Then I think about Maddie's being a poor judge of character and think to myself, *No. No way am I going to Alondra's.*

"Why do you do that?" I point to her cup.

Then she drinks some more with a large grin. Again, she offers me some, but I don't have a chance to taste it because a nerdy-looking boy with glasses sprints between us, nearly knocking down her mysterious drink.

"Hey!" Maddie yells. "Watch where the fuck you're going!" Then she turns back to me. "It's busy, Kate. We should have gone into town like I told you."

I shrug. "I thought we'd just spend the afternoon on the grass studying for midterms."

I must look hurt because Maddie giggles and runs her hand down my back. "Whatever. Whatever you want." Then she leans closer to me. "Just come with me tonight. Please. It'll be a lot of fun. Alondra's really nice. And I have a surprise."

"I don't know."

"Well..." Maddie walks off and stands under a really large tree. "You have to. For the surprise."

"Yeah? What?"

"Bryce will be there."

"So?"

"Whaddaya mean *so?*" she says. "You can't stop talking about him."

Of course Bryce will be there. He's my teaching assistant and is really hot. "You're just scared," I say. "Now you're trying to bribe me."

"I'm not scared, Cadence."

She plops down on the lawn, puts her book on her chest, and closes her eyes. I catch a glimpse of the book's cover. It features a burly man with rippling muscles and the title *Complete Me*. She's not studying.

"Just come," she says with her eyes closed. "I'll meet you back in our dorm at six to get ready."

"Are we eating there?"

"Yeah." Maddie laughs with her eyes still closed. "Alondra always has plenty to eat. Too much. She knows just how to fatten you up."

Dr. Alondra Johansen has a house in the middle of a thick forest, only a couple of miles from the university. It's rumored to have been built during the Civil War. I believe it. It's a white-columned two-story mansion with a large shaded patio and a beautiful paved walkway. It makes me think Scarlett O'Hara from *Gone with the Wind* is going to run down the steps, any minute, to greet us. Surrounding the walkway is a field of grass and tall trees, along with a garden full of white and red lilies. I like lilies. I don't like taking care of them, or any flowers for that matter, but I like looking at them. Especially in the wild. I like the outdoors. Always have.

A small wooden carriage, painted red, sits on a modern paved driveway alongside the property. Parked behind it is Dr. Johansen's dark gray Jaguar XJ. How does she own all this stuff? Some say she's the descendant of an old wealthy family. It can't be from her salary. She's my history professor.

There are others walking up the dirt walkway, mostly girls I recognize from class.

With all the grandeur of the mansion, I'm surprised to see Alondra herself greet us at the door. A long pitch-black cape is draped over a darker black silk shirt and slacks. She has long black hair like mine, hanging loosely in waves. This time I'm wearing my long hair down too. And like the times I've seen her in class, I'm struck by her eyes. Alondra has bright jade eyes, like jewels. Her skin is pale, much paler than mine, and for a moment I imagine that she's a vampire. It would certainly fit her affinity for the nineteenth century.

But her smile isn't sinister; it's sweet. She's always nice—too nice. She has a bright grin and seems thrilled to see me. "Cadence Hawthorne, come in." I'm a little surprised she remembers my name. "I'm so glad you came. Are you considering our project?"

"I'm thinking about it, Dr. Johansen."

Standing beside Alondra is her teaching assistant, the irresistibly yummy guy Maddie used to bribe me to come. Bryce's suit doesn't hide his muscular, athletic physique. He's looking down into my eyes too. But his eyes are blue—gorgeous blue. I'm reminded of the cover of that trashy romance novel my best friend was reading. The model was like a bulkier version of Bryce, but Bryce is the real deal—and incredibly hot.

Now I'm blushing.

"Cadence," Bryce says, taking my hand formally and tipping his head.

I'm cherry red.

Bryce turns to my friend. "Madison."

"Hi, Bryce," Maddie says. Then she looks at me and struggles not to laugh.

I look away.

The foyer is grand. Above me is this amazing chandelier. It's made of a hundred tiny crystals reflecting light. It's the most beautiful chandelier I've ever seen. I almost feel dizzy looking up at the twinkling crystals. But that doesn't do justice to the rest of the house. The hallway, including the wooden-railed stairway, is white, and marble columns frame the front door. Enormous windows extend from the ceilings to the travertine floor. The hallway leads to the kitchen, where everyone has gathered, their voices echoing through the house.

Dr. Johansen greets me as we linger just inside the doorway. "Please, call me Alondra." Oh yeah, my professor is still greeting me. Watching me. She's still looking at me with her mesmerizing green eyes. I completely forgot about her. I'm a little surprised she didn't say hello to Maddie. "You can reserve calling me by my title for when we're in class, Cadence," she says with a nod. "But here, please relax. Call me Alondra."

Oh shit, do I not look relaxed?

My eyes fall on Maddie. My BFF bitch has the largest grimace I've seen in weeks.

"Come in, you two," Alondra says. "Make yourselves at home."

Make yourselves at home. And Alondra really seems to mean it. Bryce leads me to the kitchen, leaving the other two behind.

The kitchen is just as lovely as the entryway, with steel stoves, and marble—like *real* marble—countertops. It's all tidy and neat. About fifteen people are gathered in a small adjoining dining room, talking and laughing, their voices echoing through the large open spaces.

"You can help me with the trays," Bryce says with this

amused smile. I catch his eyes straying along my shoulders and down my elegant black dress. It looks like he's thinking of something other than the trays.

What's on your mind, Bryce? ... Hope it's me.

"Sure," I say.

He collects glasses already full of champagne and places them on two trays. "How do you like our class?" he asks.

"It's good. I especially like ancient history and medieval times."

"Yeah," he says. "You know, I used to be interested in engineering, but that changed when I saw how much math I'd need to know." He chuckles. I ogle his lips and that to-die-for strong jawline as he laughs. I freeze for a second. I fight off a blush and hope he doesn't notice. "I suppose that's what fascinates me about witch trials," he says.

"It's all...fascinating," I say. "You really seem to be into Dr. Johansen's research."

He lifts the tray and places it in my hands. I'm extra careful, because my heart is beating so fast staring at those thick biceps, and the last thing I want to do is drop the tray. But Bryce is so cute.

"Yeah, I am," Bryce says.

"What? Do you like the...subject matter? Or is it all Dr. Johansen's choice?"

"Well, Alondra loves it. I follow whatever she and Bill want me to study." He lifts his tray and gestures for me to follow him. "Come. Let's eat."

We walk into the dining room. Everyone's now sitting, laughing, and talking around a giant antique oak table. Another floor-to-ceiling window looks out onto Alondra's forest acreage. It's another mix of traditional and modern—a classic oak table in an open modern room. And in the center of the table is a series of silver containers, likely holding our dinner. Small candles are lined up on a formal white table mat. Most of them are unlit. The silverware, which looks like real polished silver, is laid out beside the pristine white china. It's so elegant. So classy. So chic.

As I walk in, I nearly step on a small gray cat. It meows and scurries away. That gets Alondra's attention.

"Ah, champagne." Alondra looks at me. "Cadence, would you be a dear and help Bryce hand out the drinks?"

"Sure." *Why does she keep addressing me? Why not Maddie? I came here for Maddie, right? But Alondra practically ignored her when we entered her house. That was weird.*

Maddie and Alondra are the only ones with open seats beside them—a seat for me and a seat for Bryce. Everyone is looking at us. Why? Do I look nervous again?

As we walk along the table, serving drinks, I pass a girl with long black hair, heavy eye shadow, and black lips—the total 1990s goth look. She's wearing a short skirt with black stockings. She has a large silver lip ring with tattoos lining her forearms and neck. The tattoos are creepy red-and-black skeletons and demons—really dark stuff. She sort of rolls her eyes at me when I nod hello.

Then there's an older gentleman dressed in a suit. This must be Dr. Reardon, another history professor at Hawthorne University. I've never met him before. He's wearing a black suit and thin spectacles. He's bald with a goatee on his gaunt, wrinkled face. He's sitting to the left of Alondra. I pass drinks to a few more girls. I see an Asian student, a senior I recognize from class—Jason. He nods. He's a nice guy. I see him talking to Bryce a lot in school. I think he's friends with my Prince Charming.

Prince Charming sits on the other side of Alondra. I catch his eyes wandering toward me. (Or maybe I'm the one who keeps looking at him; I don't know.) I finish making my rounds of the table, and I serve a drink to my best friend and sit down next to her. Maddie touches my arm for a moment. I turn and she seems almost giddy.

What's so funny?

She's probably thinking about Bryce. I told her how good looking I think he is. I remember him handing out assignments on the first day of class. Even on the first day, Tall, Dark, and Handsome was smiling at me.

He's really cute, you know, with really adorable dimples. He always brushes his hair to perfection. If it's early in the morning, he slicks it back with gel. His skin is flawless, with a perfect tan. And those eyes, those bright baby-blue eyes. Sometimes... And, anyway...

"Everyone has their champagne?" Alondra's staring at me again. "Good." I just nod. "Now let's toast." Her voice is commanding and, like in class, everyone is silent before her. "To life."

Everyone sips some champagne. Then Alondra turns to Maddie and me and says, "Can one of you grace us with a blessing before we eat?"

For the first time since walking into Alondra's mansion, Maddie looks uneasy. Her mouth even gapes open for a moment.

Apparently, Dr. Johansen has never met Maddie's family. She doesn't have any parents. She lives with her aunt Jane, who has a house not far from the school. And Jane's atheistic, progressive ways hardly lend themselves to prayer. And as for me ...

"Sure, I'll do it," mutters Maddie.

That prompts many around the table to nod and look down in prayer. But not Professor Reardon. Or Alondra. Alondra tilts her head and squints, seeming to study Maddie. I know Maddie has never said a prayer in her life, and I think Alondra is on to her little secret. Then Alondra looks over at me. So does

Professor Reardon. It's weird; it's like they're examining us. I quickly look down at the table.

"Lord bless us for what we are about to have," says Maddie, her voice echoing in the small room. I try not to laugh at her hypocrisy. It's almost more blasphemous than if she hadn't said anything at all. "We should feel grateful." There. That's it. True enough.

But everyone seems to expect more. They all stare at us. At me.

Maddie falls silent.

"Amen," says Alondra, almost derisively.

"Before we eat," Alondra says, "I want to thank those of you who are new. I know midterm exams will be in a week, and it's time for many of you to start studying." Some people laugh. "So coming to my little party on such short notice is a personal honor to me. Doctor Reardon"—she points at him and he sort of tips his head—"is also really happy you've come. I'd love it if, before we start supper, those of you who are new could just say a word or two about yourselves."

Shit. Shit. SHIT! I hate, absolutely hate, talking in front of people. I'm not the shyest girl, but there's something about talking in front of a group that makes my bowels turn. And just as Dr. Johansen is saying this, Bryce is staring right at me. This time I don't care for his grin. Even my favorite of favorite boys looking at me in encouragement is not enough to relax my stomach. I run my hand through my hair, bite my lip, and look down.

My friend rescues me. "I'm Madison. Call me Maddie. I was born and raised in Atlanta. I'm a diehard Braves fan. I like picnicking under the stars...especially with boys..." People laugh. "I'm a Pisces. I favor Scorpio. I'm also a major sci fi buff. I like *Star Trek*, *Doctor Who*, and all the other nerdy stuff. I also like my share of scary movies, especially in the arms of a handsome man." More laughing. "That's why I like Dr. Johansen's class. Learning about magic and witchcraft mixed with history is totally cool."

"Thank you, Maddie," Alondra says with smile.

"Sure, Professor..." A few more chuckles erupt. "And, I don't know ..." Maddie turns to me. "Let's see..." She puts a finger to her face in thought; then she touches my back. "And my best friend in the whole wide world is sitting here next to me today, Ms. Cadence Hawthorne."

Shit! That's my cue to speak.

"Well, we already know you, Madison," Alondra says reflectively, smiling at my friend. Alondra has a way of putting people in their place with her smile. It's almost worse than if she directly insulted you. "I said those of you who are *new*." Then she looks right at me.

Double shit!

"I'm kinda new, Alondra," retorts Maddie.

"Yes." But Alondra doesn't turn from me.

When I still remain silent, she looks at the rest of the table, disappointed, and nods. "Okay, I suppose I'll go. You all know me as Dr. Johansen from your metaphysical history class. Outside of school I would very much like you to call me Alondra. I have three cats named Whiskers, Pete, and George. I love opera, so if any of you have tickets to a show downtown, please invite me... I like the Braves too, Madison. And...hmm." She laughs and I laugh too. Then she stares at me. "Why don't one of you newer folks tell us about yourself?"

"So we can eat," interrupts the doom-and-gloom goth girl across the table. She offers a wry smile then looks at the window.

"My name is Helen," says a bald black girl at the other side of the table. "I'm new to Hawthorne University—from Phoenix. Just came here this semester. I..."

Helen tells us about herself and I'm relieved. Then a girl named Katelyn speaks up, followed by a girl named Abby.

Finally they circle back to me, and my professor's looking at me with her annoying smile. She's inviting me to speak as if nothing that comes out of my mouth could possibly be wrong, but I don't have the nerve. I don't say a damn word.

Alondra turns away from me. "Why don't you open the trays, Bryce. Mira's right. We should eat."

The food is still steaming in the metallic trays as they're opened. It's a large roast garnished with vegetables and potatoes. There are three of them—plenty for the twenty of us. It looks like a meal fit for a fancy five-star restaurant. And there are rolls and mashed potatoes and salad too.

Maddie whispers into my ear teasingly with a giggle. "I didn't know Bryce would be here."

Fucking bitch.

We eat, talking among ourselves. I start thinking how cool my teacher is. She seems so laid-back, as if she's just happy that we're all together. At times, Professor Reardon leans over and quietly says something to her. Once I even see them looking at me. I don't like that. He's got this sly grin, as if he's up to something. I'm a pretty good judge of character, and I just don't like Reardon. He seems the complete opposite of Alondra. She is so caring and welcoming. He seems to be self-absorbed, aloof, and angry. But the two teachers seem close.

Bryce is looking at me. And it seems every time he does, my BFF nudges me, which is kind of annoying.

By the time we're halfway through dinner, Alondra clicks her wineglass with a fork. There's nothing in it, but she uses it to get everyone's attention. "Now that you're all fattened up, perhaps we can talk a little bit about the project. Many of you are from my class. Others were personally invited by Professor Reardon." She looks at the old man and gestures to him.

Dr. Reardon removes his spectacles, takes his burgundy cloth napkin, and wipes his mouth and his thin gray goatee. Then he waves the napkin in front of him. With a whoosh of red cloth, it bursts into flame. He throws the burning napkin down on his plate, and it remains a bright flame. A couple of students gasp in excitement. He smirks with satisfaction over his stupid parlor trick.

Maddie leans over and whispers in my ear. "I hear he can do a lot more."

I roll my eyes. I figure he put sulfur or something on the napkin. I think I smell it. With his sharp beard and mostly hairless head, shifty eyes, and nasty grin, he'd do well around sulfur and hellfire.

I'm not a stranger to magic, you know. My uncle Ray was a professional magician. He even taught me a trick or two with coins and cards. But this trick is so trivial that it doesn't impress me. It just verifies that the old man is creepy. And he's not done. He tosses something from his hand and the flame changes from red to blue.

"I'm Doctor William Reardon," he says with a dry chuckle. "You're all here because of your interest in magic and sorcery. As you know, Alondra is a history professor whose primary focus is on ancient black magic. Those who are in her class know of her interest in teaching ancient rites, the darker corners of Crowley and Baphomet, and the ancient wizards from ancient Egypt to the Middle Ages. My personal specialty involves the more pleasurable centers of the human body." I squirm at that. He looks like a real pervert too.

I'm thinking Alondra should be saying this. She has a knack for discussing things, in class, that are uncomfortable. But this guy is so mechanical about it. He looks away as he talks, rarely meeting anybody's gaze.

He coughs. Then he turns back and his shifty eyes fall right on me. "We explore our initiates in fine detail."

I slide down in Alondra's uncomfortable wooden dining room chair.

The old man looks out the window for a moment as if he

wasn't talking to anyone. He's pensive for a long time. Everyone at the table is attentively watching him or the blue flame still flickering under him. Then he says, "The nature of our work forces us to set a few rules, of course. If you join, you will have to abide by them. I will explain each as best I can. Number one: you will be safe, but uncomfortable. Be warned. We can assure your physical well-being, but not your emotional well-being. You might even desire to leave or forfeit your position. There are, of course, provisions we can make to allow you to leave, but it's much better that you are committed when you sign. Number two: you will never unveil to others what we do. This is the most binding rule. In fact, if you choose to join us, you will have to sign a confidentiality waiver. Number three: there are..." He pauses for a moment and looks at Alondra. She simply nods reassuringly. "There are things that you will find morally repugnant. I warn you now, this is a study of human behavior. We are applying past theorems to the modern era. If you hold beliefs, religious or otherwise, that are so entrenched that you feel you cannot break with them, do not join us. Please leave now. Dr. Johansen and I have handpicked you because of your free minds."

I'm looking at Maddie and she's looking at me, and I'm thinking, *What the fuck?* Then I'm thinking, *What has she gotten me into?* And of course I'm not going to sign a damn thing—Tall, Dark, and Handsome or not.

Then, would you believe it? Of all the people at the table, shy little me—who wouldn't even introduce myself—finally opens her mouth. "Sir...Dr. Reardon, what do you mean by religious? I was told this project is for a dissertation in the metaphysical techniques of history and our ancient past. What does that have to do with our religious beliefs?"

"Cadence," says Alondra with her now-infamous reassuring smile, "this really doesn't apply to you. This applies to girls who go to church. Who hold superstitious beliefs about God that get in the way of modern views. Magic, black or white, can stir up fears in some who worship the cross. If you are too busy going to church or Sunday school, it is believed—"

"Alondra," Dr. Reardon interrupts, raising his hand. "She has not yet signed."

"It's all right, Bill. She needs to understand." Then she turns back to me. "Our ways may be so distressing that a participant might leave, and that would interfere with the project." Then she smiles. "But I don't think that applies to you, Cadence. You're not very religious. Neither is your friend Maddie."

So I guess she noticed my friend's blessing wasn't very orthodox.

"Am I wrong about this, Cadence?" Then Alondra turns to the rest of the people at the table. "For all of you—am I wrong about this? Are any of you so morally locked in your beliefs that you are unwilling to explore another viewpoint with open minds? Because if you are averse to the metaphysical, we won't let you in."

No one says a word, but Maddie looks at me again. She's really spooked now too, very different from her usual bubbly self.

"Number four," continues Reardon.

There's a number four?

"Those of you who complete your dissertations will be promised high marks from the university. Each of you will write your own thesis, which I will review, and if you are able to complete it, you will be far ahead of your counterparts. Few universities will reject you, upon graduation from any liberal arts graduate school, after completing this project. It's a great honor—not unlike a doctoral dissertation. But you must complete a year with our group. Even after the class is over, you must remain in the program for a year if she is to grant you this special commendation. Some of you, like Mira, are even returning for your second year."

The weird goth bitch nods.

"For those of you who wish to participate in our research, there will be a sign-up sheet at the front door. Please leave your name, phone number, and email so I can contact you. The rest of you, enjoy yourselves. Alondra likes company, and it's her pleasure to entertain you. So...there is no pressure." He coughs again. "What I would suggest is that you talk with those around the table who partook in the experiments last year. And our teaching assistant, Bryce Wallace. They can reassure you about, or recommend against, working with us."

"Good," says Alondra with a big grin. "Thank you, Bill."

The stodgy old man waves a hand over his plate, and the blue flame is doused.

There are a few more *ooh*s and *ah*s. I roll my eyes again. I think he notices.

Then Alondra turns to Bryce. "Now, shall we have dessert?"

2

WORKING OUT

There's something wonderful about sweating your ass off in comfy gray activewear while running as hard as you can, as fast as you can, and staring through floor-to-ceiling windows at the thick wilderness, all the while listening to System of a Down blaring through your cell phone earbuds. Our campus gym has a breathtaking view of the trees. Between the sweat and the view, I find the whole thing exhilarating. Working out is a rush. It's also a good way to put your problems to the side. That's why I exercise so often.

My mother's sick. Well, she's been sick for years. She has MS—multiple sclerosis. It's a demyelinating disease affecting the neurons. First it takes your dignity. (It made her pee on herself at my high school graduation.) Then it takes your mobility and your mental faculties. It's really awful. Dad spends every day he can, back home in Atlanta, caring for her. He keeps telling me that she's not doing well. He's always taking her to the hospital.

So I'm breathing heavily on the treadmill, trying to run a mile in nine minutes, and I'm thinking about Mom.

And then I'm thinking about Bryce. I thought of him last

night, you know. Bryce. All night. I couldn't sleep. I kept imagining that stubble against my cheek. And his short, perfectly kempt brown hair. I can't stop thinking of him. And I think he likes me too. I mean, he was looking at me a lot, and he asked me to help him out in the kitchen. *Me.* Why'd he do that? He must like me, right? I don't know.

Anyway, now I'm moving on to leg lifts. I'm lifting a lot of weight as the music has changed to *"Fuck the System."* Maddie always laughs when she hears the heavy shit I listen to. She's more into Taylor Swift.

I gaze out the window again. I love to get lost looking out at the shadows of the tall trees. I can just make out the shimmering lake through all the foliage.

There are a lot of students walking a dirt path about fifty yards down, leaving campus or coming in, barely visible through the dense woods. They're just shadows through the trees. It's a sunny day outside, but there are so many trees that it's always a bit shadier here. There are bugs out there too—a bit too many for an early October afternoon. They're out with the humidity as it's oddly hot this afternoon. It was sixty yesterday. Birds flutter around the window, obscuring the light of the sun, but I can't hear them with the music blaring in my ears.

So I'm puffing my cheeks and lifting over a hundred pounds when, in the periphery of my view, I glimpse a tall boy wearing a tank top and matching blue shorts. He's standing beside a bench press with a friend, looking over at me. Two other exercisers are on my right, near him, but I notice this boy keeps looking my way. And why wouldn't he? It's Bryce. Bryce and his Asian friend Jason, who I saw the other night.

He walks over. *Holy shit!*

He says something to me. I can't hear, so I pull out an earbud.

"Cadence?" he asks again.

I'm puffing out more air, struggling to lift the weight. I look up and try to act like I didn't see him, but I think he saw me looking over.

"Hi, Bryce."

I pull out the earbud from my other ear and switch off the music.

"It's good seeing you," he says with a grin.

Sixth lift. "Yeah." *Breathe out more. Wipe my mouth to make sure I'm not spitting in front of this Adonis.* "You too. I don't usually see you here," I say. It's late afternoon. I'm not an early riser. I figure maybe he is.

"My head feels like it's gonna explode," he says, rubbing his temples. "That's why I'm exercising this late. I'm usually up at dawn. I had a little too much to drink at a party last night." He smiles again.

Ninth lift. And...tenth. Somehow the weight feels heavier under those gorgeous blue eyes.

I grab a towel and wipe my face. "Maybe you shouldn't drink so much," I say with a shrug. I'm being a little bitchy, but I've learned that boys love that. But I falter a little when I look up into those baby blues again.

"I didn't drink *that* much, Cadence." Then he looks down and chuckles. "Or...maybe I did."

He stands awkwardly over me. The silence is a lot more uncomfortable than it was the other day when we were at Alondra's house, surrounded by chatter. This time, he's hovering over me, and the cling and clang of exercise equipment is the only thing between us. He says quickly, "Listen, you want to go to one of our parties this weekend? It's at the Billington House."

"Hmm?" Of course I want to go. But I can't. I might be traveling back home to see Mom. "I'm not sure I can make it this weekend, Bryce. But I can probably make the next one."

"Well, we're having a party this weekend. It's to celebrate the end of midterms."

"Drinking more? At your haunted house?"

The Billington House is haunted. Everyone knows that. I'm not even sure anymore who told me about it, but you can't be a student at Hawthorne without hearing of the curse surrounding the Billington House. In the very late hours, people say a candle lights by itself before the central window, and some even say the ghost of the voodoo witch Escoba stands by the glass, silhouetted by candlelight and staring wide-eyed outside. But I've been to the house a few times for frat parties and have yet to see a witch or candle by the window.

"Um-hmm." He smiles. "Love to see you. I admit it's kinda creepy there. But the fact that it's haunted makes it a great place around Halloween. We're even planning a séance. I hope you can make it."

"I'll try."

"And...listen, you wouldn't mind if I call you sometime?"

Call me? Are you kidding! Call me anytime, Tall, Dark, and Handsome.

"Ummm...I guess. My number..." I reach down for my bag. I'm so flustered that I can't remember my own phone number. Then I can't find my phone.

"I know your number, Cadence."

"I gave it to you?" I can't remember.

"Alondra gave it to me."

3

THE FRAT PARTY

MADDIE AND I ARE TREKKING UP A FOREST PATH TO AN OLD HOUSE sitting by its lonesome atop a hill of witchgrass and weeds. It's on the highest summit of Hawthorne. Surrounded by dead twigs and hollowed-out branches, it looms above thousands of trees, making it seem isolated. Turning back and looking down through the oaks and elms, I can still make out the evening lights of the university. The Billington House is the oldest house on campus. It's even older than Alondra's. Probably older than anything in a five-hundred-mile radius. Maddie and I are walking hand in hand. I'm not sure if it's out of affection or because the dark path up to the haunted house is giving me the heebie-jeebies.

I feel silly being so scared, but the tree branches tap each other and the wind howls under moonlight. I hear the evening creatures scurrying—probably squirrels—and the distinct sound of an owl. It's like right out of a horror movie. I think that's part of the house's charm, especially around Halloween.

"I don't like it," I say as we walk. I'm really just making conversation, trying to get my mind off the surroundings.

"Whatcha mean, Katie?" Maddie asks. She seems calm.

"It's dark and creepy."

"It's haunted," Maddie says with a chuckle. She winks at me.

She's acting like it's a joke, but she isn't fooling me. I know her well enough to know she's nervous too.

"Can you blame Abigail for consulting a witch?" I ask. "It's sad in a way."

"Yeah, I probably would have fucking cut Josiah's balls off," she says with a nod. "But I don't think it's sad. Abigail deserved it."

Honestly, I could care less about the Billingtons' curse, but talking about it, talking about something—anything right now —gets my mind off the dreary hilltop.

Let me tell you what I've gathered about the curse, attending Hawthorne University over the past year. I think it's a real sad story.

Josiah Billington, a Quaker from Scotland, was married to Abigail, a lovely girl from Tallahassee with long dark hair and pretty green eyes. They built their haunted house on the highest hilltop in the forest—the one we're climbing now. They lived a normal, mundane life until Josiah fell in love with another woman living on the neighbor's plantation. Then rumor claimed that there was an illegitimate child, Maverick— and not only was the baby illegitimate, he was brown-skinned. Josiah tried to cover it up and forget the disgrace, but the girl from Tallahassee could never forget.

Abigail consulted a witch named Escoba Hawthorne, a local voodoo queen who had recently moved from New Orleans. After agreeing on payment, Escoba asked Abigail to get some-thing from Mr. Billington that only he possessed. Abigail cut a lock of her husband's brown hair. Then the witch cooked a foul-smelling bloody stew outside her shack while chanting magic charms. Only Escoba didn't curse Josiah—she cursed Abigail. Because Josiah was Escoba's lover.

"Escoba didn't really do anything," I say to Maddie. "Spells aren't real."

"The two boys died from consumption." Maddie lets go of my hand—I wish she hadn't—and then she touches her fingers as if relating a list. "The girl died from the school roof falling on her head. And Josiah was rammed by a bull. Everyone died a month after the witch brewed Abigail's hex. I'd say that proves curses *are* real, Cadence."

I hear something in the bushes and grab her hand again. She chuckles but doesn't pull away. She's acting all brave, but I know she's creeped out. As I look back, we're far enough from the campus lights that it's only getting darker, except for occasional strobing lights emanating from the house at the top of the hill.

"It's a hex, Katie," Maddie insists.

The story goes that while Abigail was busy walking around the witch's house of mysteries, touching her shrunken heads, shells, gems, and cauldrons, Escoba cut a lock from Abigail's long hair. She didn't add Josiah's hair to the cauldron—she added Abigail's.

"Well, Escoba didn't cast a spell because spells aren't real. Maybe she just killed them. Then she stole the house."

"Fine, Kate," Maddie says. "But if it that's true, we should still be scared of the house. A murderer makes a pretty evil ghost too."

Right. Exactly. And that's not making me feel any better.

We walk up to the front door alone, and I'm shaking a little from the cold, or maybe from the Billington curse. Actually, I'm still seriously creeped out, even with strobe lights flashing through the central window, reminding us of the party inside. The full moon is shining above us, lighting the path up to the door. Flies are buzzing around, and I swat at one near my face. Maddie clutches my other hand a little more tightly. I knew she was scared. I don't think she likes the look of the front of the house in the darkness either. When we reach a wooden gate, I put my hand on the latch. That's when Maddie touches my hand and screams in my ear.

"Fucking stop!" I yell.

Maddie bursts into laughter and embraces me more tightly. "Happy Halloween, bitch," she says, still lost in uncontrollable laughter.

When the front door creaks open, this tall, geeky redhead with pimples, carrying a red plastic cup of beer, gestures for us to enter, and all my ghostly fears leave me. The sound of music helps break the spell. But my stomach is still turning—in a good sort of way, because I'm thinking of Bryce.

The inside of the Billington House is much different than the creepy exterior. It's a typical frat house with boys sitting in recliners and beanbag chairs drinking beer, ladies swaying to music, and boys playing pool. Posters of half-naked girls are spoiling the classy antique walls, and lots of leftover antique furniture, frosty glass windowpanes, and vases fill the house.

I'm looking for Bryce, but he's not there. Nick is. Nick rushes over, hugs Maddie, and plants a long kiss on her cheek. That doesn't surprise me. Then he says hi to me. Hi, Nick.

I've known him since we took an anthropology course together last year. For a while he and my BFF were just friends. But apparently, since her fallout with Patrick, they're getting closer.

Nick has on a simple white button-down and black slacks. He's in a really good mood. He always is. He starts introducing me to all sorts of friends. I kind of get lost in the shuffle.

Soon I even lose Maddie. I pick up a beer from an ice chest and sit myself down on a beat-up leather recliner in the living room. A few girls are drunk, practically drooling or comatose, on a nearby sofa. The music is loud. It's some kind of heavy shit; I'm not sure what. But I like it.

There before me is a large frosted-glass window, probably

from the nineteenth century, overlooking the fields. I can barely see the university buildings through the trees, but I know they're down the hill. This must be the infamous window at the center of the house where Escoba stands at night. I look for the candle but don't see it. And I remember the story as I'm sipping my beer by my lonesome.

That's when Bryce walks over. He always dresses so nicely. He's wearing a black silk shirt with jeans. He has a little bit of brown stubble along his cheeks, which looks really yummy, but his dark brown hair is combed back perfectly. I nervously run my hand through my own hair.

"Hi, Cadence."

"Hi." I'm trying to act really cool and nonchalant.

He sips his beer and looks at me with his famous wry smile. It's like he's always amused by me. That's kind of annoying. But those bright blue eyes looking down at me make it worth it. I'm sinking into them.

"Sucks you decided not to join us," he says.

"I'm just so busy with studies, you know," I lie.

"Well, I can tell you personally that Alondra was really disappointed."

"She seems to be," I say with a nod. "She seems so distant lately."

"She is." He nods and sips again. "She's busy too. We're busy. And...I think she's disappointed. You would have done well in our honors program."

We both turn to the window. He seems uncomfortable with the silence between us, but I don't really mind, I like just sitting beside him.

"But we welcome you anytime you change your mind, Cadence."

"Thanks."

"Well, enjoy the party." He starts to walk away.

Wait! That's it?

"Are you a member of Psi Kappa Psi?" I blurt out like a stupid child. That's the chapter that lives here at the Billington House.

It stops him.

"Was," he replies. Then he stiffens and gestures to his chest. "Before I graduated. I'm an honoree, Cadence. Since I graduated, I come by once in a while. Especially for annual back-to-school parties."

"I...I didn't know I'd ever get to meet an *honoree*," I say sarcastically. Then I resume sucking my beer bottle.

He smiles.

He doesn't go. He hovers over me hesitantly.

Then we're both staring at that infamous window again. I'm wondering if, after the party, candlelight will be shining.

He drinks more beer. So do I.

I like sitting beside him. I really do. Even though we don't say anything, I like just being near him. It sort of sends tingles down my back, you know, like in a lovesick schoolgirl sort of way. I know, it's stupid. But I also know that I'm starting to like him. I wonder if he likes me.

I turn for a moment and catch Maddie. She's talking with Nick but flashing me a huge grin.

Bitch!

"You stayed in this house?" I ask Bryce, trying to break our silence.

He nods. He pulls over a large beanbag chair and plops down near me. "Yeah. When I was a student. What's wrong with it?"

"Nothing. It's haunted. That window..." I point with a beer bottle in my hand. "It's lit up every night by a ghost. Escoba's ghost. You know the story."

"Yeah." He chuckles. "I know the tale, Cadence. But, between you and me, it's just a ghost story. And it's not Escoba who haunts that window. It's Abigail."

"Huh?"

"Who told you it was Escoba?" Bryce asks, furrowing his brow. "Escoba's been seen in the halls, but Abigail likes the window. Don't you know what Abigail did to Escoba?"

Honestly, looking into his mesmerizing eyes, I really don't care.

"You don't know about Abigail's ghost?" Bryce repeats. "After the Billington family was cursed, Escoba and Maverick took up residence in this house."

"I know."

He shakes his head and, with the hand holding his beer, he points to the window. "But Abigail began showing up with a lit candle by that window every night. It shone in the evening, even when Escoba didn't have company." He looks at me incredulously. "You really don't know about Abigail's ghost, Cadence? That's the best part of the story."

"I just know that Escoba got rid of Abigail and her whole family so she and Maverick could get the town."

"No, she didn't get rid of Abigail." He shakes his head. He seems to get more excited at the prospect of telling me more. It's like he's teaching me again and he loves it. "After the Billington family died, Escoba's eight-year-old son, Maverick—Josiah's illegitimate son—started seeing Abigail's ghost. One night the boy saw her standing here in the living room, with her back turned toward him, by the window. She was just sort of staring out into the woods. And Maverick began seeing repeated visions of her, screaming every night, waking Escoba from her sleep."

"So the house was haunted even before Escoba died?" I ask.

"Yeah. Abigail."

"I thought the ghost was Escoba," I say with a shrug.

"No. One day, Escoba saw Abigail's ghost too. In the middle of the night—when all was quiet and dark in her bedroom, as her son slept calmly beside her—Escoba turned and looked with one eye at an open window. The drapes were moving, as if in a slow breeze. But there was no wind. Perhaps the shutters had moved. So Escoba closed her eyes. But then she heard a noise from the side of the bed her son slept on.

"In the doorway to the hall stood an apparition. It was a pale woman with long black hair. She held a curved knife in one hand and a candle in the other. She stood over Maverick with malice as he slept calmly. Escoba screamed. Holding the candle over the child, the ghost did not move or lose her smile.

"The next morning, Escoba consulted her grimoire in order to oust the apparition from their home. She used items the Billingtons had left behind, in a chest in the basement, to serve as a connection with the ghost. Then she concocted another brew, in the grassy field around the home, spewing curses and spitting in a cauldron.

"Escoba's body was found three days later, sitting in a rocking chair, upstairs in her bedroom. She was holding a crucifix, and a knife had been stuck into her chest. Even in death her eyes were wide open, staring toward the hallway in terror. It was assumed that her death was from suicide."

"Then the ghost at the window could still be Escoba?"

"Abigail was found a year later," he says, shaking his head, "on neighbor Jesse M. Davis's farm, grazing naked like an animal, still catatonic, not saying a word. Everyone was over-joyed to know she was alive, but it's said that she never spoke a word again. Some say she was committed to the local sani-tarium—at the time, a fate not much better than death. Others say she committed suicide in the forest. And others claim her spirit still haunts the halls of the Billington House today.

"And many still see a candle burning in the downstairs window, in the middle of the night, along with Abigail, *not* Escoba. Cadence, *Abigail* holds a long curved knife, staring out the window with wild eyes. Abigail."

God, that's even creepier than the original story.

I lean back in the old recliner. We both sip more beer and look out the window together. I hear the music again. It's really loud and comforting because it's not scary. I really don't want to hear any more ghost stories.

"It's just a story," he says with a chuckle. But he's totally creeping me out again.

"It sounds like a true story," I say. "I've seen their graves."

"Well, if it really happened, just like the story said, then the house really isn't haunted, is it? It was just occupied by a witch and a madwoman. But you know, you should come here next week. We have a great party on Halloween every year. The stories only make it more fun."

"Yeah, I know." I shrug. "I was here last year on Halloween." I look up at him, tapping my beer bottle with a fingernail.

"Want a tour of our haunted house?" he asks.

Uh...yeah.

He laughs, gets up, and reaches out toward me. I jump up and grab his hand, probably a little too eagerly. He laughs again. I feel like I've lost my cool act and am now acting really geeky. Then I find myself about two inches from his face.

Holy shit!

I can't breathe. I even feel the breath from his mouth. And for a moment, just a moment, Mr. Calm looks nervous too. He runs a hand gently through my hair. Then he grins and tugs my hand. "Come on, I'll show you around our haunted house." Meanwhile, I'm probably looking like a total buffoon, staring into those dreamy blue eyes.

"Yeah, okay," I say, trying to act cool again.

Show me. I'd love a tour of your run-down ghost shack.

And he does. He shows me everything, from the basement to a creaky wooden hallway leading to a room with a balcony. We're alone, but we're not alone. It feels intimate even though every room of the house is crawling with frat boys and their dates.

I love the way he incorporates history into every room. It actually feels like my history TA is teaching. He talks about the Civil War and how the house was occupied by the Confederate army before the Battle of Atlanta. It was on one of the highest peaks for miles and was a perfect lookout for the military. Then he shows me a bed warmer that's still stowed away in one of the rickety wooden closets. I love it.

"And there is the master bedroom," he says, gesturing to the end of the hallway. He's got a gaping smile and is still holding my hand. His hand feels so warm. It makes me tingle all over. We're dodging bodies along the hallway to get there. I see a couple lying in each other's arms on the floor, either comatose or too drunk to move.

When we get to the bedroom, I'm disappointed. From the tale, I was expecting to see a great big antique bed and large windows. Now I'm picturing Bryce's story of Abigail standing over Maverick with her curved knife, dressed in a white gown, with a wild stare. But there are three bunkbeds, using every bit of space possible in the large room. The walls still have white plaster. "I wonder if this is the same color it was two hundred years ago." I touch a wall.

Bryce tells me it is.

There are two desks in the room and, like in the rest of the house, the walls are decorated with posters of ladies in G-strings holding up beer.

"This is where Abigail stood over her victim," says Bryce with pride. Then he turns to one of the desks. "And there, according to legend"—he points to a wall—"is where Escoba sat for days with a curved dagger in the center of her chest."

How the hell does he know where Escoba sat? But I love how he acts so sure of himself.

"Doesn't look that way anymore," I reply with a stupid smile.

"Grisly isn't it?"

Bryce is still holding my hand. He refuses to let go, even when we're weaving around people in the crowd. We're sweating a little, but neither of us lets go. That's so cute.

"I stayed in this very room last year," he says.

"Really?"

"Yeah." Then he gently touches my chin and looks down into my eyes again. "When the wind blows and it's dark, I can swear I hear screams. I think it's Escoba."

I'm waiting for him to yell into my ears stupidly, like Maddie did at the fence, but he doesn't. He just grimaces. But, honestly, we're more lost in each other's eyes than giving a fuck about poor Abigail and any ghosts.

I raise an eyelid. "You said...you thought it wasn't real." I force myself to sip some beer and find it difficult to swallow.

He shrugs and we walk on. "Let me show you something."
Okay.

We walk back down the stairs, across a room full of drunken dancers, and through a creaky door. It leads down a flight of wooden stairs into the basement. This is where we're finally truly alone.

I'm a little apprehensive as we walk down the steps of the old wooden stairwell. The wood creaks terribly with every step, and I'm scared it's going to crack under my feet. But we make it to the bottom.

He takes out a lighter and lights a candle on the wall. It's dim, but it casts shadows throughout the small room. The wooden walls and rafters are dank and dusty. And now I'm beginning to freak out. Bryce's candle barely lights the room.

I sneeze.

Bryce tightens his grip around my fingers, almost as if he knew I'd be afraid. He leads me to a large chest.

"Perhaps we should go back," I say.

He chuckles. "Don't worry, Cadence. You have to see this. I

found it last year when I was at a party like tonight's. It's really cool. You're gonna love this."

He lets go of my hand. I really don't like that. In the shadows, it was his hand that comforted me. But he needs both hands to open the heavy wooden chest. It reminds me of something you'd find in a pirate ship. Then he flashes the candlelight over the opening. The yellow light outlines his face, which looks a little spooky in the darkness. His hard jawline and those bushy eyebrows. His blue eyes, now flickering in the candlelight, looking down at the chest and staring back at me. He smiles. Damn, he's so hot.

I sneeze again.

"Go ahead," he says. He moves the candle closer to the chest and gestures for me to explore.

Inside the chest are a bunch of old things with thick dust covering most of them. There's a portrait the size of my hand. I pick it up and he shines the flickering light over it. It's a drawing of a girl. I'm guessing it's Abigail's daughter? Or Abigail? Or a friend? Or...who knows? It could be anyone. But her dress is long and formal and appears to be from the early nineteenth century. There's also a very beautiful necklace and a small mirror. It reflects a shadow of me in the flickering light, which really creeps me out, and I quickly put it back. There's also a pile of very old clothing at the bottom. I rummage through a scarf, a light coat, and a dress. It's all caked in dust. Then I see a drawing of a woman wearing a bandana, bright gold rings on her fingers and ears, and a long black dress—Escoba? I don't know.

While I'm exploring the contents of the chest, I catch Bryce staring at me. I look up at him, and he places a hand on my shoulder and smiles.

"I found this last year. Great, isn't it?"

"Sure."

"I knew you'd appreciate it because you love history so

much, Cadence. It's never left the room. I don't think it's worth much, but it's history, you know? I was gonna show Alondra...if she doesn't already know. You like it?"

"Yeah." I do. I love it. It's like looking in a museum.

I take out the scarf. I think it's purple, but it's so covered with dust that I'm not sure. Then I start sneezing terribly.

"Sorry... Sorry, Bryce. I'm allergic to dust."

"Oh." He gently moves me away. "I'll close it then." He closes the heavy chest and takes my hand again. A cloud of dust forms, and my nose becomes worse. I just can't stop sneezing.

"This might sound silly, but you always seem so interested in class. I think you have a love for history more than most students."

"I've always liked it." I sneeze again. "It's like peering through a window into the past. It's like a journey, you know. Their story. Their journey. But a real story."

"Yes, I know. That's why I like it too."

Somehow it sounds to me like he said, *That's why I like you too.*

He brings my hand up to his lips and kisses it. I don't see much of him. Only a hint of his hard chin and kind smile under the flickering light. But I feel the whiskers of his unshaven skin. That makes me giggle a little. I giggle nervously. Then I sneeze again.

"Can I kiss you on the lips, Cadence?"

KISS? Hell yeah!

I giggle again. I sneeze halfway through the giggle.

"Okay. But you...better...hurry before I"—I sneeze again— "can't stand still for you."

In a flash, Bryce has his lips on mine. I can't see much. It's like the whole world is literally Bryce and me. His hands move from holding mine to embracing my body. My fear of being alone in the dark in the haunted house is lifted. All I think of is Bryce, his strong arms squeezing me tightly. I'm sort of lost in him. I inhale the scent of his cologne and rub my fingers along his short hair. He pushes his lips more firmly against mine, then gently moves his tongue into my mouth, tasting me. I let him.

But then I sneeze again, ruining everything.

"I think," he says, pulling back slowly, "that I need to take you back upstairs."

Gallant Bryce. I'm really starting to like this guy.

"Yeah," I say, his voice having a hypnotic effect on me. But I really don't want to.

He takes my hand.

I sneeze again.

The insulation in the basement is thick, and I can't hear much music until we open the rickety wooden door again. Then the party is louder than ever. Bryce leads me toward the kitchen. He's finally forced to let go of my hand when Maddie grabs me by the arm.

"Katie, come on!" She points to the living room. "We're playing a game."

"All right."

I look back, but Bryce is gone, lost in bodies. I'm not sure what happened to him.

Now it's Maddie who's taking my arm and guiding me, around frat boys, to the living room. I see a few girls from Kappa Alpha Kappa. Maddie sees them too and gives them a dirty look. They stupidly sit around on couches and chairs wearing matching red T-shirts, with their Greek letters in gold, and matching pants: elegant black slacks. If they didn't act so snooty, it might be cute. Well, Maddie and I never liked their chapter.

There are only four fraternity chapters and one sorority at

Hawthorne University. Sororities never caught on for one reason or another, and only the most affluent kids end up in it. Maddie and I never even tried—well, Maddie's forbidden to join after joining Dr. Johansen's honor club. Anyway, the only fraternity worth its weight, to me, is Psi Kappa Psi, and that's only because of Tall, Dark, and Handsome.

So we pass the sorority snoots and walk into a large, dimly lit room. About twenty people are standing around a dining room table covered with an elegant red cloth. In the center of the table is a crystal ball—yeah, an actual crystal ball—illuminated by a row of candles. That's pretty cool.

I sneeze again. The room is obviously full of dusty antique stuff. I look toward the door, and there's a wood cabinet about the age of the house and some dusty lamps.

People are sitting at the table holding unlit candles. The windows are covered in thick dark drapes. All we see is the yellow light emanating from the candles on the table.

Next to the crystal ball is a large board. And on top of that is a white plastic triangular-shaped thing with a central opening. It's a Ouija board. It looks like it's new, from Mattel. Maddie sits with me next to the board, and another five boys sit near us. I look at the large crystal ball again and even touch it. It's covered with dust.

"We're gonna play with the Ouija board." Maddie seems excited. Across from her is Nick, who seems equally enthusiastic. "Have you ever played, Katie?" Maddie asks.

"Yeah, when I was a little girl."

"Well, Cadence," says Nick, "we've been playing with it for a few weeks now, and I promise you it's nothing like you've ever played before. There's a vital energy here. This house has so much paranormal energy from the spirit realm. There's—"

Some girl shushes him. "Place your fingers over the planchette."

I'm still staring at the magnificent crystal ball. I can see reflections of everybody in it. It looks old. I wonder if it was Escoba's. I run my finger along the glass. It's so cold.

"Place your fingers over the planchette," the girl snaps at me.

I look up and am surprised to see that I recognize this girl. It's that weird goth girl I saw at Dr. Johansen's party. She's wearing a long black cloak, black lace gloves, and a very tight black dress showing a lot of cleavage. The candlelight is reflected by her large metallic nose ring, and her skeleton and serpent tattoos seem to dance in the light. She creeps me out.

I shrug, thinking this whole thing is stupid. Then I place a couple of fingers over the central device and look at the board.

"Spirit," the goth girl says, closing her eyes. Her face is serious. "Spirit, we call on you. Here in the house of Escoba and Abigail. Spirit, if you are here, please answer us."

Six people have a finger or two on this central device, the *planchette*: the goth freak, who's leading this Mattel séance, Nick, Maddie, a few boys I don't know, and me. But nothing is happening. I turn from the board and look at the crystal ball again. I marvel at it. I'm taken by it, just like the time I went to the Smithsonian and gazed at the Hope Diamond. It must be expensive. It looks expensive.

"Cadence!" hisses Goth Girl. "You have to concentrate! You're messing up the energy. Either concentrate or get the fuck out!"

"Hey!" cries Maddie. "If Katie goes, I go."

"It's all right," I say with a chuckle. "I'll play."

So I'm back to touching the *planchette*, as the goth girl calls it. Then the goth girl starts acting weird—really weird. She starts swaying and moving up and down while touching the white piece of plastic, closing her eyes really hard. She's so focused. I look at her, then at the boys, then back at her again. I realize her movements, up and down, up and down, actually appear lewd. It's as if she's orgasming over the table. The boys love it. They can't take their eyes off her. And being overweight, her tight clothes put her large breasts on display. I think the boys are more focused on her bosom than the board.

"Come to us, spirits! Come and join us in this room. Talk to us through the board. Enter from the spirit world and speak to us. We are here to speak with you."

The white plastic thingy, the *planchette*, seems to move a little. With my other hand, I take my half-drunk beer and take a sip. Goth bitch opens her eyes and stares right at me with venom. "Focus! I say focus or leave us, Cadence!" she hisses at me.

"Christ, Mira!" cries my best friend. "Leave Katie alone!"

Mira lets go of the planchette and slams her hands on the table. "You wanted her to be here, Maddie! If she's here, she joins. Otherwise..." She turns to me. "She needs to get the fuck out!"

I get up, embarrassed. All the others look up, feeling pity for me. That makes me angrier.

"It's okay, Cadence." Maddie smiles, grabbing my arms and pulling me back down. Then she glares at Mira. "Mira can be a real bitch, Katie, but she's nice when you get to know her. Sometimes. Forget her. Come, come play with us."

I sit back down, irate. I'm staying for my friend, and only for her, but I scowl at goth bitch. Mira takes a deep breath and touches the white plastic thingy again. She closes her eyes. With one hand, I drink more beer. She opens a sliver of an eye, but then she closes her eyes tightly again, ignoring my transgression.

"Spirits," she says. Then she takes a few deep breaths and opens her eyes. They seem wild. Then she looks at each of us. "Repeat after me. Spirits." We repeat it. "Spirits, come to us. In this house." She speaks slowly, and we repeat every word. I play along, but I still take a swig or two of beer in rebellion. "Spirits, move the planchette and show us you are here. If you have come to us, move the planchette to *YES*. You who remain in the spirit world. You who preside with the witch Escoba and the ghost Abigail. Come to us. Come to us, Escoba and Abigail. Show that you are with us tonight." She starts doing that up-and-down motion again, with her eyes closed. The boys are staring at her again.

And then...the plastic thingy moves. It moves slowly over the word *YES*.

We all smile, and I hear murmuring, for the first time, from the spectators behind us. There must be ten to twenty people gathered in the room. But everyone is quiet. Everyone is here for Mira's séance.

Mira is ecstatic. "Good. Good! Now, tell us, spirit. Tell us. Send us a message."

The plastic thingy moves to the letter *I*. It sort of vibrates under my hand. I wonder if Mira is moving it, or maybe Maddie. It moves again. First it circles around the board; then it slides over another letter: *L*.

"Excellent," cries Mira. "Excellent. I ... L ..."

The planchette moves to the letter *U*. And then *V*. And then *U*.

Nick mouths the letters. He writes them on a notepad. Then he chuckles and says, "I love you. It says *I love you!*"

I'm rolling my eyes. Maddie catches me and gestures for me to shut it.

"All right," says Mira. "You love us. Who? Who are you? Identify yourself, spirit."

The planchette moves again. It circles around and around the board. Then it lands on letters. It starts moving faster, and now I'm sure someone is moving it.

The next letters come down in a fury. Nick jots down each letter on a piece of paper:

E M I L Y H A W T H O R N E

I lift my fingers and stare at my best friend with rage. *Emily*

Hawthorne. Emily. Emily is my mother's name. The only one in the room who knows that is Maddie.

"What are you doing!" I yell.

"Nothing," Maddie says innocently.

I jump up. "What kind of a joke is this!" I cry, hitting the table with a fist. "It's not funny!"

"Sit down, Cadence!" shouts Mira. "You're disrupting the energy!"

I'm not amused. Maddie shakes her head again.

The rest of the goth bohemians stupidly believe they've stumbled on Abigail's family tree. They're excited. But no one except my best friend knows the name of my mother—and why I'm beyond pissed—my dear mother who is very ill at the moment and in the hospital. I don't get it. It's not like Madison to play such a sick practical joke.

"Is this a fucking joke?" I snap at Maddie. "What are you doing?"

"Katie, no! It's not me. I swear." She's shaking her head desperately. I'm ready to deck her. My own best friend. I want to kill her for this.

"Then who is it?" I'm pointing at her. I'm accusing her, and I'm only getting angrier that she's playing dumb.

"It's just a game," Maddie says. "I didn't do anything, Kate. I swear."

"Will you sit down!" shouts Mira.

"Forget you and your game!" I shout at Mira. "You're all a bunch of creeps!" Then I turn to my so-called best friend. "And you... it's not funny!"

I storm out of the room.

"What's the matter with her?" Nick asks as I leave.

I'm set on walking back to my dorm when Bryce, of all people, stops me by the exit. He's holding a red plastic cup. "Got you one," he says with a big smile. He tries to hand the drink to me, but I don't take it. He looks in the direction I'm heading and watches me throw on my long black coat. He looks disappointed. "Going somewhere?"

"I have to go, Bryce. I... I forgot I have a paper due Monday." But now that Mr. Handsome is here, I falter in my resolve.

"Oh, all right. Well, it was really great seeing you, Cadence."

"You too."

And he touches my hand. His hand. For a flash, it reminds me of the basement, but my feet sort of push me toward the door. I just nod and smile at him as best I can.

I'm not only angry and confused as to why my BFF would spoil the little Mattel séance for me; I'm also totally freaked out. The whole thing was super creepy. And now, as I walk down the hill alone, under the full moon, I'm even more spooked. I hear an owl and imagine a wolf's howl. The trees cast shadows in the moonlight all the way down the path back to the university and my dormitory.

Then my cell phone rings. It's my mom and dad's number.

"What?" I snap.

"Cadence," says my father. He sounds terrible.

"Yeah, Dad?"

"Cadence...your mother... She's...she died."

4

FALL LEAVES

IN EVERY MOVIE I'VE EVER SEEN, WHEN A LOVED ONE HAS DIED, it's a gloomy, cloudy day with a mist blowing and all these morose mourners walking in single file, wiping tears from their eyes with white laced handkerchiefs and shaky white-gloved fingers—and black umbrellas; people usually have black umbrellas too. They're dressed in dark double-breasted suits or lovely flowing black dresses. Everyone's hugging each other and looking down at the ground, bawling their eyes out. But they all look beautiful for the dead.

Why? She's dead. Get over it.

I don't look pretty. I'm not even wearing makeup.

I'm too dainty and thin to carry the mahogany casket—or maybe I just don't care to. Instead I walk beside it while my brother, uncle, and mom's older friends, wearing T-shirts and shorts, carry the casket. It's hot outside. Fall's coming late this year.

I don't cry. I never cry. I never do.

It's raining. But it's figurative rain, you know, water dripping inside my brain. It's not actually raining. Outside, on the fields of the cemetery, it's hot and muggy. It's a lovely day in Atlanta.

The sky is a beautiful cerulean blue. The bluebirds are singing. It's not raining at all. Only in my heart. In my chest. There it feels tight and constricted, and it kind of weighs me down as I walk beside the coffin. Inside is where the tears are. Inside there's this fog, shrouding all the pretty birds and lovely trees, and the scene looks just like those funerals in the movies.

But water actually does drip down my face. Sweat is dripping down my forehead.

I have on a lovely black dress. It once belonged to Mother. I liked it even before she died.

I don't want to mourn. Just like I don't want to cry.

The thing is, I have to get back to school.

The ceremony is really short. My brother and I say a lovely eulogy. He wrote it, and I nervously intone a couple of sentences from a sheet of paper I'm holding with a shaky hand.

Then it's over. I get in my cheap twenty-year-old Honda Accord and drive the one hundred miles back to Hawthorne University.

You see, Mom was dying anyway. And I think everyone saw it coming.

I could be sad. I see a bumper sticker and it says *CRY*. That finally makes me cry a little on my drive back to Hawthorne.

I can't concentrate in class. I study. I'm really smart, you know. I always get good grades. But I can't drop the images of the hot and sweaty funeral from my mind. Such a lovely day. Such a fucked-up lovely day. Such an awful feeling. I still feel it. That tightness. I want it to leave me, but it won't.

In Alondra's metaphysical history class, I take an exam on the various torture techniques utilized throughout the Middle Ages. I know I'm gonna get an A, because I studied all the required reading and even the optional materials before I left for the weekend.

5

AFTER CLASS

"I need a week off from school, Dr. Johansen."

Alondra is stuffing a MacBook laptop and a folder full of papers into her black bag. She seems in a real pissy mood.

"All right, Cadence," she says with disinterest.

We're at the front of the lecture hall, and all the students are leaving. I know Maddie is waiting for me outside.

Alondra has been aloof over the last few weeks. She used to smile at me a lot. Now it seems she doesn't want to give me the time of day. Of course I didn't sign up for her research freak show. Maddie did. Maybe that's it?

"You did well on the test, Cadence." Alondra stuffs a laser pointer into her bag.

"Thanks. I thought the witch hunts were interesting. Particularly the method of judging the witches. It seems so stupid."

"It proves how stupid men are," Alondra says with a shrug and a faint smile.

"Will we be getting our papers back soon, Dr. Johansen?"

"Excuse me, Cadence, but I really have to go," she says rudely, practically hitting my shoulder with her bag. "If you need a week off, you can just let Administration know. You needn't tell me."

"I know, but my mother died, Alondra."

I don't know why I said it. I tried to avoid saying it. Then I just said it.

Alondra stops in her tracks for a moment. I watch her pale hand rest on the podium, and she nods and cocks her head back. "How terrible. I'm sure you were close, right?"

And that's just as awkward.

"She was like my mother." It was meant as a joke, but it sounds like I'm mocking my teacher. I chuckle stupidly but Alondra doesn't laugh. She looks down. She seems genuinely upset.

"I'm sorry for you," she says.

I feel that tightness again. Somehow, it seems even worse in front of her.

"That's why I need time. I need to, you know, mourn, I guess."

Isn't that what people do? How should I know? My granddad died when I was four. I never knew him. That's all I knew about death—until Mom. People need time—right?—to feel shitty and sad.

Dr. Johansen turns around with a sad smile. She lays down her heavy bag for a moment.

"I'm so sorry for you, Cadence."

A tear runs down my cheek. I don't know why. I haven't cried at all since I saw that stupid bumper sticker but, somehow, for someone to acknowledge me makes me feel awful. Particularly Alondra, whose sweet smile always puts me at ease. Her kindness hurts.

"I'm so sorry," she says again. "You know, I really hoped I could work more closely with you. You're at the top of your class. That was the other reason you were invited for dinner."

"I thought it was because I'm an atheist," I say with a stupid grin. I'm still trying to be funny, but it's even more awkward now. I'm brushing tears from my cheek.

"Are you an atheist?" she says, surprised. I don't know why it surprises her. "That's not the profile I was looking for."

"I think I am."

"I don't think you're an atheist, Cadence... I'm so sorry to hear about your mother." She looks down for a moment; then she looks deeply into my eyes and puts a hand on my shoulder. "It is this pain that I study. It's this thing that we all turn from: pain. But it's an energy, just like joy, that we carry with us all our lives. I research nature's energy. Pain and pleasure. Even pain is a part of nature. But your ghosts are always so deep..." She looks down for a moment; then she nods. "Of course, of course you can have a week...but I can't speak for your other professors. You should let the provost know."

"I already have."

"That's good."

Alondra gently raises my chin and smiles. Her green eyes seem to pierce right through my soul. Then she brushes her hand along my hair like...like my mother. This reminder almost puts me over the edge.

"Please, don't worry about a thing. If you'd like, it would please me if you can come again to my house this Friday. I know you haven't signed up, but you can come for our initiation meeting. I want to make an exception for you. I think you will find it's not as scary as you might have believed. And our coven always honors those who have recently passed. I think it will help you through this. I'd really like to do this for you, Cadence."

"I'll see."

"Come if you wish. Anyway, I'm so fortunate to have someone as bright as you in class, whatever you decide."

"Thanks, Dr. Johansen," I reply with a smile. She's so nice.

"Please. Call me Alondra."

6

———

THE CEREMONY

I take Alondra up on her offer and ride back to her house alone, in my beat-up Honda, on Friday night. I'm very late. I made a tactful decision earlier not to tell Maddie I was coming. I didn't want her to know. We've made up since the party—I can't stay mad at Maddie for long—but I warned her never to mention the séance again.

Anyway, I'm crossing Alondra's gorgeous manicured front lawn, meandering along the dirt path to the door. It's a drab, gloomy day, and there's not much visibility. Looking back, I can't even make out my car. It's too foggy. In front of me the fog seems to amplify the yellow light coming from Alondra's old mansion. I shiver in my thin black cotton sweater; I forgot my coat at the dorm. Winter is coming. Soon the trees will turn their lovely red and yellow autumn colors to brown and it will be cold.

I knock on her door. She has a large antique metal knocker. I smile at its old-fashioned look. It's very Alondra.

Then I wait. I wait a long time, staring out at the trees under the mist.

"Hey, Cadence." It's Bryce. Normally I'd be shy, but I'm not in the mood for shyness.

"Hi, Bryce."

He gives me a gentle hug. "I heard about your mom," he says. "I'm so sorry."

"She's dead."

He loses his smile for a moment.

Well, she is dead, so get over it. Is dwelling on it going to make things better?

He places his hand gently on my shoulder. I think he would have preferred to hold my hand, but he's cautious. Then, just as he did many weeks ago, he walks beside me down Alondra's gorgeous hall. I expect to head straight to the kitchen like last time, but we don't. Instead we head into a room that looks like a den, with a sliding glass door.

I'm admiring her home. It's so chic. As much as she adores history, the interior is ultramodern. As Bryce works the lock to the glass door, I look at the stonemasonry on the chimney. Everything is in sharp angles and very chic. The white leather sofas surround a soft, furry white carpet with white wood around its perimeter. A flat-screen TV is mounted to one of the walls, which are painted light coffee-brown. How can she afford all this stuff?

Bryce finally yanks open the sliding door. "I told her she should have left it open. It keeps jamming. Anyway, come on, we're waiting for you."

Waiting for me?

Everyone is gathered around a blazing bonfire, the height of a person, in the center of Alondra's huge backyard. It's in a large open field of wild grass, like that surrounding the Billington House, with giant trees. Unlike the front yard, none of her back-yard is manicured. In fact, it blends in with the surrounding forest.

Eleven people are gathered around the flames, surrounded by a circle of large white stones. They're all wearing these weird black hooded cloaks, like the clothes ancient druids wore. Alondra's hood is down, and her long black hair is hanging over it. Beside Alondra is my friend Maddie. I can't make out Maddie's face under her cloak, but I recognize her pants underneath. Dr. Reardon is there. He's wearing a button-down and slacks. His cloak is over his face, but I recognize him from his old-person clothes. Then I recognize Mira and a shy girl, Hannah, who I met at Alondra's party.

Bryce and I approach the circle around the fire and, for some reason, the walk seems to take a long time. It's like everything is in slow motion. As we draw closer, I realize they're all holding hands and chanting quietly. It's not English.

"They're waiting for you," Bryce repeats. "Don't be afraid."

I look up into his eyes. He smiles sweetly. Then his hand tightens over mine.

I'm not afraid. I'd never be afraid in those hands.

All right, I'm a little afraid. But the tightness in my chest has been lifted. Now I feel butterflies rather than dread, but I'm still nervous. What is this freak club all about? I'm thinking of walking out.

"Cadence, you made it." Alondra gets up. She has that infamous smile of hers. "We built this fire for you. Please, sit."

She looks weird. Under her cloak, her pants are old-fashioned. It looks like she found them in the basement of the Billington home. And she has on really thick black makeup. Her mascara's like Mira's everyday dark makeup.

I sit down next to Bryce.

We're all sitting in cheap white plastic chairs around Alondra's bonfire. The odd thing that strikes me—aside from my professor's attire, and everything else—is the fire. There's no outdoor pit. Just a pile of wood thrown down on her lawn and ignited into a big conflagration. That's weird. Well, the whole thing is weird.

"Everyone knows what's happened to your mother, Cadence," says Alondra. She looks creepy, but with her gentle smile, it seems okay. She sits back down. Her face turns grave, and her speech is slow and measured. "I would like to perform a ceremony in her honor. If you let us, it might ease some of your pain. But more importantly, it will benefit your mother. It's up to you. If, at any time, you feel uncomfortable, we can stop. The coven is just happy to have the opportunity to be with you tonight. And...it is a special night because we are initiating Hannah, Tammy, and your friend Madison."

"Okay," I say. But I don't know if it's okay. And Alondra pauses for a moment to check if I'm sure. I don't say anything else. I just sit there watching everybody stare at me.

"We are here to pray for you," Alondra says with another comforting grin. "It is our hope that your mother passes swiftly to the higher realm. I, and many of the others here, believe the spirit moves to the Summerland. Then the soul moves on to inhabit another body in another place. With this ceremony, we can help her on her journey. Without our efforts, sometimes the soul can get stuck. Then it can become a ghost."

"Like Abigail," Maddie says.

"No," Alondra says with a chuckle. Then she turns grave. "This is quite serious, Madison. I'm not talking ghost stories."

"Okay," Maddie says. Then she gives me a comforting smile. It's a pitying smile, and knowing my BFF so well, it makes me a little sad.

Alondra reaches under her plastic chair and picks up a photograph and a candle. "We have this memorial candle. And your friend Maddie brought me a picture of your mother. We'd like to light the candle in memory of her, if you will permit us."

"Sure. All right." *I'm game. Why the hell not?*

I turn to Maddie. She surprises me. I expected to see her whimsical, fun face, but she's very serious.

"Katie," Alondra says to me, calling me by my nickname. "If you can hold hands, we will all begin."

I laugh. No one else does. "All right, but...I really don't believe in any of this," I say. "But thanks for all your trouble."

"It doesn't matter if you believe, Cadence," Bryce says. He grabs my hand. "What matters is that you are here. And we are here for you."

"Exactly, Bryce," says Alondra.

My left hand is holding Maddie's, and my right is holding my handsome TA's. I look at Alondra again and she nods, trying to comfort me, and closes her eyes. She closes them tightly, just like Mira did. Then I look over at Mira. The girl's copying Alondra, and I suddenly realize how her mannerisms seem to mimic my professor's. Then I think about the Ouija board, and for a moment I get a little upset and unnerved. I confronted Maddie about the incident, and she swears that she never told anyone my mother's name.

Everyone bows their heads down. I don't. I just gaze at the flickering flames.

I like the touch of my best friend's and boyfriend's hands. Their closeness is comforting. I also like that all these people are doing whatever they're doing for me. But I still feel uneasy.

Then Dr. Reardon speaks. I had forgotten all about him. "We who have been taught to follow a false god, taught to love all people, even those who hurt us, to listen to fools, to follow those who are misaligned or stupid, to live in guilt over our pleasures and live in pain—you who sit in this circle need do this no longer. None of us in the circle need do this any longer. We are protected, just as the darkness shades light. By Baphomet, the holy one. Through darkness roams the hunter. Through the hunter comes the sacrifice. We follow truth and believe in shadows, under the embrace of Gaia, that shall guide us toward our salvation."

"Atman," says Alondra.

"Atman," say the others.

"And for Emily." Dr. Reardon looks at me. I shudder. His goatee is shadowed by the dancing flames. He looks almost like a demon. "Allow her to pass over. Allow Cadence's mother to pass over to the Summerland and then beyond. Let her not remain as a ghost or vapor. Let her move on to her next life."

"Atman," says Alondra.

"Atman," say the others.

"So eloquently said," Alondra says, addressing Dr. Reardon.

I look up at the moon. The clouds have dispersed, and I can even see glimpses of stars. If the fog completely lifts, it will be a beautiful night. With the fire, it's the perfect temperature. It warms me and I think about removing my black sweater, but I'm reminded of Mira. I think that any such move will break the weird spell surrounding me, so I do nothing. I sit quietly. Then I look around the fire.

The others begin to raise their hands, and some of them say similar words. Many of their speeches are cloaked in this weird quasireligious shit. I'm not sure what they're referring to. Alondra seems to understand. Hope, one of the older initiates from last year—she stayed, just like Mira—recites a long dirge in a strange language. As she speaks, everyone looks down as if in prayer. Everyone except Alondra. Alondra is staring at me. And when I see her, she nods reassuringly.

I look into the fire. The red and yellow dances and the wood crackles.

Alondra rises. She lifts up her hands to the sky and gazes at the stars. All the fog has lifted. Then Alondra stands before us, addressing us, like she would do in class. Her smile has left her. Everyone opens their eyes, and Bryce and Maddie let go of my hands.

"We are here," Alondra says, "to mourn the passing of Cadence Hawthorne's mother, Emily. We know that her passing was timely. I thank the stars for that. Emily suffered terribly the last years of her life with a debilitating disease. No one should suffer pain. We, here in the circle, are here for the pleasure given to us by the earth. Emily's ailments caused her problems with vision and hearing. She couldn't walk. Because she couldn't see, she even suffered a terrible fall. She finally succumbed to a heart attack. We mourn the death of Cadence's mother, for we know how it has affected our sister Cadence so terribly. And we know how that love, though the bond may not ever be truly severed by death—the greatest illusion—has disturbed Cadence. Please take Emily and have her pass to a happier plane."

"Atman," says Professor Reardon.

"Atman," say the others in unison.

Alondra walks over to me and hands me the candle.

"Cadence," she says, smiling again, "can you light your candle by the fire, please? After you light it, take it back home with you. Let it stay lit as long as it will. Then one day it will burn out. If you wish, you may light it again whenever you feel pain over the loss of your mother. Know that she loved you and that the light from this candle not only represents her, but is her. It's the energy of her in you that shall never burn out. It resides within you, and unlike fire in the physical realm, it will never die. Ultimately, you control where and when such energy will manifest itself. Her love now resides in you and always will. The power of her flame lies in your soul. When you discover that light within, through love and hate, through black and white magic, you shall finally be reborn in full wisdom."

For the first time, I think of the Ouija board. And I think of the words *I luv u.* At the time I shuddered. Now, looking into Alondra's mesmerizing eyes, I think how beautiful the message was. Particularly, I think of how it was meant for me. If it actually was my mother, it was beautiful. It was a message to me right after her death.

And with that, I falter over the fire. Bryce grabs me before I fall. I open up and start crying terribly.

So does the rest of the circle. My grief seems to spread around the fire, and everyone starts crying. Even Mira, who I always thought hated me, bursts into tears. Even stoic and dark Dr. Reardon sheds tears. There are tears from everyone.

Bryce and Maddie help me slowly back to my seat. They hold the candle over my fingers.

Alondra walks over and kneels beside me. She gently lifts my chin and says, "Release your pain, Cadence. There is no reason to be sad any longer. Your mother has been freed to the Summerland. Your love just freed her."

I look up at her. She seems so sure of her words. Then I'm touched by the tears that have streamed down her face.

"Thank you," I say quietly. "Thank you."

Alondra smiles sweetly. "The rest of the evening is secret. You have not signed on. I'm afraid you need to return home... But know that the coven prays for you, Cadence. We are here for you, our sister."

"Thank you," I say softly again.

Everyone looks at me. They all smile sweetly.

I turn and leave.

No one escorts me out. As I reach the sliding glass door, I look back. Once again, around the circle, the group is holding hands. They're chanting something that I cannot understand. Even Bryce is completely immersed in the moment. And this time it's Doctor Reardon, not Alondra, who leads the group. The fire eerily dies down and, in shadows, the group dances around it, following Reardon, circling as if in a trance, mesmerized by the dying flames. I try to close the glass door. A few times. But it won't budge.

I walk back to my car alone. And then I drive home.

7

______

CRYING

I'M CURLED UP IN A BALL, IN BED, CRYING MY EYES OUT. IT'S THE middle of the night when I hear the lock turn and Maddie walk in. She's initially cautious not to wake me, creeping slowly to her side of the room, but when she hears me crying, she kneels beside the head of my bed. I feel her fingers run through my hair and rub my neck and back.

"Oh, Cadence."

I don't say anything. I just cry. It seems strange that I didn't do this before. And as much as I liked crying at Alondra's house, I really don't like it now.

"Oh, Kate."

Maddie can't really say much more. She just runs her hand along my dark hair.

I catch a whiff from her arm. It smells strange. It's an outdoor smell of juniper mixed with lavender. And there's an earthen smell. I turn quietly and look at my friend. Only the sliver of light from the door shines over us—she hasn't closed the door yet, nor has she turned on the light. I jump at the sight of her hair. Her hair is a complete mess. And the black mascara from her eyes is running. Her face is smudged with dirt, and there are small leaves stuck in her hair.

"What...what the hell happened to you?" I ask. Even her clothes, the formal black dress and stockings she's wearing, are torn up. Then I catch a few scratches and scrapes at the nape of her neck. "Maddie, what happened?"

I forget all about me. My friend looks like she was assaulted. Then I'm even more surprised when Maddie chuckles.

"Nothing, Cadence. Don't worry. I'm fine. I'm more worried about you."

Now I've spent time with Madison every day since first year orientation. There has never been a secret between us. Now there plainly is. Something did happen to her, but it's clear that she has no intention of telling me. And yet, as awful as she looks, it doesn't seem to bother her.

"Don't worry 'bout me, Cadence. I'm fine. What about you? How are you holding up?"

"Terrible," I say, turning away from her into my pillow. I suppress another sob. "I was so proud of myself for not crying. Now, ever since Alondra's little ceremony, the tears won't fucking stop flowing."

"But that's good, Katie," she says, rubbing my back. "You need to mourn. You'll feel better later."

I shrug. "That's shit, Maddie. That's complete bullshit. There's no reason I need to cry for anything. I just feel miserable."

"I thought you seemed relieved at the candle ceremony."

Did I? I don't even know.

She runs a hand along my cheek. Then she says, "You want me to sit here with you tonight? Or in bed? I can hold you."

It's not gay. It sounds gay, but from her tone I know it isn't. The funny thing is her affection suddenly makes me start crying more.

I don't know how long I cry, but it seems like hours. And all the while, my friend lies beside me. She's trying to sleep in my arms. That's cute. The funny thing is, I think her affection only makes me cry harder.

By morning, Maddie is sleeping like a log, impossible to disturb. Unlike Yours Truly, who feels like crap and has had no interest in sleeping since I got the news about Mom. I move out of my friend's arms and slip on some slippers. I marvel that she hasn't woken up due to our cheap, creaky bedsprings. It's cold and the window is frosted. The morning dew has formed icicles on the leaves on the bushes and trees outside my window.

I walk to the dresser and take out a shirt and pants to change from my white negligee. Then I turn on the Keurig and brew two cups of coffee, one for me and one for Maddie.

Maddie is still sleeping like death on my bed. I've never seen her look so awful. It looks as if she was attacked, and I'm not going to let her get out of it as easily as she did last night. I'm gonna find out who did it, where it happened, and why. It looks like I should call the police or something. And yet, besides her disheveled brown hair and dirty, torn-up dress, she looks completely at peace. Her smile is angelic.

The Keurig is loud enough to wake my roommate. She stirs, draws out her arms, and yawns. Then she opens her eyes and smiles at me.

I sip some hot coffee, then walk to her with her Donald Duck mug.

"Morning," Maddie says.

"Hi."

I lean against the wall and look at her. Maddie stretches again and sits up in bed.

"You feeling better?" she asks.

I'm still staring at her. And no, I have no interest in crying anymore. I've had quite enough of that. I just look at her and don't say a word.

"What?" Maddie asks. She sips some coffee. "What is it? ...

You know, this shit sucks. What happened to those pods Nick gave me?"

"Drank 'em all," I reply with a shrug.

"Oh. Well, this tastes like water. Water mixed with a faint flavor of coffee."

But she still drinks it.

"So?" I ask.

"Hmm? So what? It's water." Maddie sips more. She leans her forehead against her hand, and light shines on her and all her train-wrecked glory.

"No. I mean, what *the fuck* happened to you?"

"I told you not to worry about it." Then Maddie laughs. "But you know..." She looks down at her tattered dress. "I really should change."

I'm staring at her. She avoids my gaze as she gets up, walks to her dresser, and pulls out some clothes. "I suppose this will have to be disposed of. Pity, it was my best dress."

"Tell me. Tell me now."

"Don't start, Cadence," she warns, pulling off her mud-laden, torn-up dress. It angers me to think she was wearing that in bed with me. Not because she dirtied up the sheets, but because something was obviously wrong. I was too messed up last night to address it. Now I feel better. A little.

Something's wrong. Really wrong.

"Just forget it, okay?" Maddie says.

"Tell me right *now*, Maddie. Tell me, or I'll call the cops."

"Stop it, Cadence," she says, waving a hand. She changes into a campus sweatshirt and jeans. Then she walks back to my bed and pulls on her socks and shoes. "Just forget it, Cadence. I'm just happy you seem better."

Maddie's tying her shoes. I sit next to her and lift her face—as she's been known to do to me, many times before—but she pulls away.

"Cadence, forget it."

"No. We're friends. Tell me what happened."

"I can't," she says, shaking her head. "You know I can't."

"What do you mean, you can't?"

"I'm sworn," she says, averting her eyes from mine. She just raises her eyebrows and figures that's enough. Then she resumes pulling on her shoes.

"It looks as if someone hurt you."

"Nobody hurt me, Cadence," she says with her head turned down.

"Your clothes say otherwise."

"Katie." She looks back at me with a sad smile. "Katie," she says again. "It was the initiation. Nobody hurt me. No one hurts anyone there without consent. Everything is done with consent. I promise. You must believe me."

"The initiation? What the hell do they do at the initiation?"

"I can't tell you that."

I give up. Or rather, my body gives up. I feel like a chair has landed on me, and I sort of fall on the bed. I'm exhausted. I haven't slept in days.

"Katie, don't worry about me. Take care of yourself. Just rest." She pats my back again. "I tell you what. I'll go to your professors today and get your homework, 'kay? You can just stay in bed today and get some sleep."

"All right." How can I argue with that? I can barely keep my eyes open.

"Great."

"Swell," I say sarcastically.

"Keen," she adds.

I laugh at her mockery of my fifties language. The situation isn't funny, but exchanging dumb words is. Just being friends together, you know.

But I want to know. I want to know what happened to her. I'm worried about her.

I felt good after leaving Alondra's mansion. I felt like her heart was there for me. I felt so good that I even considered joining their club. But not now. Not after seeing what she did to my friend.

And what's so good about some charm to make you cry all night, anyway?

"You want me to get you breakfast at the dining commons?" Maddie says.

"No. I'll try to go."

"Sure?"

I nod.

Then she puts her finger to her chin for a moment. She looks around and finds something on the dresser beside the door. It's the mourning candle from last night.

"You forgot this. Alondra wanted to make sure you got it."

It was only partially lit last night. It's still a fully lightable candle.

"Thanks." I touch her arm and look at her very seriously. "But please tell me, Maddie, is everything all right? Please. Are you okay?"

"Cadence, believe me, I've never been happier."

8
———

THE T.A.

A FEW DAYS AFTER ALONDRA'S CEREMONY, MADDIE FINALLY convinces me to go to class. It's early in the morning, and she knows I'm not a morning person. But I think it was after I laughed at her stupid comment, "Bryce'll be there," that I capitulated. Of course Bryce will be there. It's his class.

I'm majorly behind in my studies. The point of TA classes is to brush up on things, not to teach. Bryce usually just reviews Alondra's lectures and I, being the stellar super-smart gal that I am, often raises my hand just to regurgitate information both of us already know, just to see Mr. Handsome's infamous wry smile. But today I actually have to pay attention. At eight in the morning.

We walk through the quad. It's empty. Everyone is sleeping or recovering from their weekend hangovers, but I know Bryce's ancient history class will be full. It's one of the most popular classes in school. Apparently, that's why he can meet so early. At eight in the morning. As Maddie leans on my shoulder, telling me how she just dumped that dickhead playboy Nick (she's been telling me all week), I yawn and struggle to move forward to my boyfriend's class.

Just as I thought, the class is full. It's small, like a high school classroom, with about twenty people. Mr. Handsome is pulling out his laptop from a brown leather briefcase on the desk at the front. He's wearing pressed slacks, loafers, and a button-down shirt—left open ever so slightly to show the stud's chest hairs. Who dresses him? His clothes are to die for.

We sit in the back since the room is already full. Then Maddie pulls out her laptop from her bag. I forgot mine.

We wait. For a moment, I recall why I haven't slept in over a week. I feel that constricting feeling in my chest. But then I'm saved by the vision at the front of the class.

"Let's talk about Amarna," says my tall hunk. He looks down the rows and sees me. I win that smile, and I feel my heart bounce a little. "Ancient Egypt. Dr. Johansen spoke of Nefertiti and Akhenaten. This is, of course, well into the time of the pyramids. Do you know the son of this famous couple?"

"Tut," says a redheaded girl in the front row.

"Right. King Tut. Know that. And know of the mystery of his father, Akhenaten. Dr. Johansen will not want you to tell me what every kindergartener knows of Tut. She will want you to give me information on his parents. What's important here is Akhenaten, Amenhotep IV of the Eighteenth Dynasty, who changed his name to Akhenaten and created a religion based on monotheism, worshipping the sun disk. Have you seen statues of Akhenaten?" It's a rhetorical question. Bryce doesn't wait for an answer. "They're grotesque. The man has some of the weirdest features of any pharaoh. He doesn't look human. His wife, too, has been depicted in statues and hieroglyphs that look odd. But then there is also a famous bust that many believe to be the true bust of the Egyptian queen. She is beautiful—*nefer*, meaning, in ancient Egyptian, beauty."

He looks around the room. Everyone is intently focused on him. Then his eyes fall on me, and I can swear he flashes that smile again. At me. That irresistible smile. *Holy shit, he's hot!*

Then Maddie ruins it by hitting my shoulder. I turn and she has the exact same wry smile, making fun of me.

Bitch.

"You all need to know of Amarna," continues Bryce. "You see Akhenaten, not only being from another world, in my opinion..." I hear a lot of murmuring over that. "See, Akhenaten started a revolution. It was only upon his death that statues and paintings were defaced in order to cover up his rule and return to the ways of the past...because this is what people do to the unknown. People cannot deal with mysteries, and their fear and prejudice make them eliminate them."

Bryce looks at his PC. He moves the cursor around and types a little. The room is silent until he gathers his thoughts.

"Those of you who brought your computer or have access on your phone, open the file on our website on mummification. For others, I'll write the most important steps on the board. Know the following and memorize it. It will be on the test. If Dr. Johansen doesn't see them on your essays, know that you're not going to squeak by with much more than a C. She grades tough, but you already know that. "

"The following is done to the dead in the mummification process." He starts writing on the whiteboard:

1. *The brain is removed in pieces by a hook through the nostrils.*
2. *The organs are removed through a cut in the chest at the left side of the abdomen (sparing the heart) and placed in jars later buried with the mummy.*
3. *The body is dried out with natron, a salt substance. NATRON. Remember that.*
4. *The body is wrapped.*
5. *The mummy is placed in a coffin in an ornate tomb.*

"The whole process takes up to two months. Know the steps. But if you want an A, Dr. Johansen will want to know the details."

"How detailed?" asks a guy in the front row.

Bryce leans against his desk and recites, as if reading from a book:

"*The first step in preparing the dead is embalming, after which a hole is punched into the ethmoid bone of the skull not far from the nose. It is hammered in with pieces of the brain, meninges, and spinal fluid, adhering to a stick, as the priest thrusts in and out. In and out. After many thrusts—in and out—the fatty goo flows from the hole. But this never removes the entire brain. As much as possible is scooped out...* That detailed. Got it?"

The boy nods.

"Know your steps. Know your instruments. If you were in class, you would have seen the pictures." There are a few groans from the students. I'm sorry I missed it. "Now let's move on to Babylon and Hammurabi."

I start doing what I really shouldn't be doing in Bryce's class: daydreaming. The problem is, Bryce doesn't hold my attention the way Alondra does. He sort of spits out information. That's great for getting As on exams, but it won't work well for keeping me awake at eight in the morning after a restless sleep. I'm drifting off, getting some much-needed rest, when I suddenly hear my name.

"Cadence, can you expound on the Code of Hammurabi relating to witchcraft?"

I can. I learned this a couple of weeks ago, when we were learning of Salem and witchcraft in medieval times. He knew this, the sneaky, irresistible fucker.

"Yeah." I sit up, clearing my throat. He flashes that infamous grin. It irritates me a little this time. "The code is one of the first of its kind throughout history," I continue with pride. "It states that if someone accuses a witch of a harmful spell, the witch shall be thrown in a sacred river. If the witch dies, the accuser shall know she was guilty and take her possessions. But if the witch lives, the accuser shall be put to death, and the witch shall obtain all their possessions... It's stupid, and I can see why the dunking of witches has been made the butt of jokes ever since."

The class laughs and I pat my ego on the back. Bryce knew I would know the answer. I really like this guy.

"Right," he says. "Except the law is not stupid, Cadence, if you believe in the sacred river. I suppose, if you don't believe in magic, then it may seem stupid. But I think you're being stupid if you make fun of a law just because you don't believe in witchcraft."

Oh.

"And also, the law pertains to men, not just women. You said *she.* What makes you think witches can't be men?"

I'm sinking in my seat. It sounds like he's reprimanding me. It's like he's challenging me in front of the whole class, and I'm really embarrassed. Maybe he's not such a swell guy after all.

After I don't answer him, he goes back to Babylon, and the rest of the class is a complete blur. I'm pretty sure I sleep through most of it. But I need sleep. And I decide that if he calls on me again, I'll ignore him.

At the end of class, Maddie gets up and takes me by the arm. I'm not sure what she's up to until she plops me right in front of Mr. Handsome.

"I'm so glad you came, Cadence," Bryce says, stuffing his computer in his bag.

"Well, you didn't have to embarrass her," Maddie snaps.

"He didn't embarrass me," I say.

"Did I?" he asks surprised. He picks up his bag. "Don't be silly. I knew Cadence would know that." He turns to me. "You did outstandingly, as you always do. I just didn't agree with your mockery of magic and witchcraft."

"I wasn't making fun of magic. I was explaining—"

"You don't believe in it. If you did, the law wouldn't seem so ridiculous to you."

"I think she's just upset over how you corrected her in front of the whole class," Maddie says, chiming in. I look at her. She's not smiling. She's defending me, as always.

"I'm not upset," I say.

"You two are quite a pair," he says. "You fit so well. You're like sisters."

"That's why I know when she's hurt," Maddie adds.

And that pisses me off. Nobody's hurt. Maddie is going too far.

"Cadence," he says, hauling his man-bag over his shoulder, "I would love to be of assistance to you during these hard times. I can review the lesson plan further with you—"

"So you can prepare to embarrass her more?" quips my friend.

"Can you leave us for a second, Maddie?" I ask.

Maddie looks confused. "Yeah...all right," she says. Then she turns back to Bryce before she goes. "Take better care of my best friend next time, okay?"

Bryce doesn't say anything. He just stares at me with those baby-blue eyes.

"I would love to review the *lesson plan*," I say, knowing full well he intends to do much more.

Maddie's gone.

"Great, Cadence," he says with a glowing dimple-laden smile. Then he turns serious and touches my shoulder. "How about Wednesday in the library?"

"Okay."

He nods and walks with me to the exit. The classroom's empty now. Maddie's slipped out of sight, knowing when to leave us alone. I'm kinda cheerier walking beside Bryce. Or maybe I'm just more awake. I'm laughing inside about how my BFF was defending me.

Bryce seems preoccupied. He loses his smile. I'm thinking maybe he's still a little mad about Maddie's accusation. He cocks his head as we walk and says, "Look, Cadence, we all really care about you. The whole circle. Alondra wants you to know that. You have our heart and our blessing."

"Huh?"

He chuckles.

"Oh," I say when his words register in my sluggish head. "I don't care much for your circle, whatever the hell the *circle* is. But thanks, Bryce."

He nods. We walk down a cement walkway between two buildings, near the main drag of campus. There are a lot more students out now, carrying their backpacks, laughing, or walking alone to their next classes. Bryce is oddly quiet, but I don't mind. I just like walking beside him.

It's funny because neither of us knows where the other one is going. But somehow, the minute one of us drifts, the other follows. So we're kinda just dancing our way to the main walkway in the center of campus together.

"Incidentally, why Nefertiti?" I ask, fishing for something to say. "I don't get it. Why is Alondra teaching about Nefertiti and Aken...whatever his name is? It has nothing to do with mummification, does it?"

"Alondra and I are fascinated with his sun disk cult. That's one reason."

We reach the quad together. I suddenly realize what's happening. I'm walking with my teacher, but not because he's my teacher. It's just to be with him. And he's here to be with me. And there's still no push or pull for us to go our separate ways. For a moment, I consider meeting with him *now* in the library. I wouldn't mind his company for the rest of the day, "studying."

"The other," he continues, holding me back from being run over by an idiot on a bike, "is the lesson plan. As much as Alondra would love to teach the arts and the paranormal, the university expects us to actually teach ancient history too. And anyway, you find Nefertiti fascinating, don't you?"

"Sure, I guess."

"I don't doubt it. Because her name stands for beauty. I would think you'd be very familiar with that, Cadence."

Ooh, I didn't know you could be suave, Bryce. You're full of surprises, aren't you?

"Are you trying to say you find me pretty?" I ask casually, twirling a strand of my hair like a complete idiot.

He takes my hand and pulls me closer to him, and we stop for a moment. There's a lot of traffic back and forth, but I cease to notice. It's just me and him.

When I looked in the mirror this morning, I thought the glass would crack. My skin looked chapped and the skin beneath my eyes was sagging. My hair looked like a bird's nest. But judging from the way Bryce is looking at me, what he sees is quite different.

"Well?" I swallow a lump in my throat. "What are you trying to say, Bryce?"

"If we weren't on campus right now," he mutters almost in a whisper, looking into my eyes, "I would swoop down and lose complete control of myself, Ms. Cadence Hawthorne. You are very, very pretty. In fact, I would say quite irresistible."

I giggle nervously. It breaks his stare.

"My ..." I say. "Well, then, perhaps we need to meet outside of school instead of in the library."

"No," he says, mustering a chuckle. "The library's safer."

Safer?

He smiles and takes my hand. He rubs my fingers, and I feel shocks through my whole body.

We're walking again; now we're holding hands. I truly

believe he refrained before because he was worried about rumors spreading throughout the school, but he doesn't seem to care anymore.

We're near a cement stage. During the summer, plays are performed here. Today, it's just a beautiful sitting area where a few students have their eyes glued to their phones or laptops. Everyone's wearing jackets or coats. I'm not. I've been so flustered lately that I forgot one. I try to hold back a shiver as I walk with my favorite TA.

He pats my hand with his other palm as we walk. "How about seven on Wednesday?"

"Seven in the morning?" I quip stupidly.

"Seven at night, Cadence," he says. "I'll see you at seven in the library?"

"I will be wearing my best T-shirt and jeans."

"Wear whatever you'd like." He runs his hand over my cheek, and I just about die. Then he says very seriously, "Take care of yourself, all right, Cadence? I mean it. We're worried about you."

"Okay."

"Bye."

"Bye, Bryce. Bye."

My hearts races as I watch him dip through another pathway and behind a building. *Aren't I supposed to be upset about something?* My conscience answers, *Cadence, your mother just died.* Oh yeah. *But, Mom, you need to meet Bryce. He is sooo hot! You'd like him.*

If Mom were alive, I would call her and tell her.

But she isn't. So I just walk a few long arcs around campus thinking of him. Then, when I want to snap out of it, I just think of Mom again.

I'm...confused. So confused. The tightness in my chest has grown, and I don't even know what it means anymore.

I need sleep—desperately.

I go back home, lie in my bed, and close my eyes. I think of the funeral and the rain. Did it rain at Mom's funeral? I can't remember anymore.

Then I think of Bryce. He said he can't control himself around me. He said I'm irresistible. Well, he obviously likes me. No, he loves me. I think I'm in love.

9

———

THE GIFT

The Jonathan Brewster Taylor Library, better known as the Taylor Building, is the most modern building on the entire campus. It was built a few years ago, replacing a very old, ugly three-story brick building. The old building had small rooms with low ceilings. The only modern feature was an escalator in the back. The new Taylor Building has floor-to-ceiling windows, two mall-like escalators, and tall vaulted ceilings. And it has five stories, not three. There is plenty of room to study, and there's even a coffee shop that opens onto an outside court —where Maddie stole her latte a month ago.

So I'm on the escalator, heading to one of the study lounges upstairs, when Nick, of all people, walks up to me. I like Nick. I always have, ever since we had an astronomy class together last year. He's a nice guy. He's kind of like Bryce, but he's more flamboyant and brash. "Hey, Cadence."

He's dressed in a Hawthorne basketball T-shirt. He was on the team last year. His pants are tacky. They're gray sweatpants.

"Hi, Nick," I say, cocking my head his way. I stay planted, waiting to exit.

"How is she?"

"How is who?" I ask, acting dumb.

"How is she? Tell me. She won't return my calls."

"Maybe you should forget about her," I say with a shrug. Then I walk away, and he follows me.

"Look...can you send her a message? Just tell her I miss her. Tell her I'm sorry about her car. She was right. I'd had too much to drink. I was stupid."

I start thinking about the night I went to Alondra's. Maddie looked like she'd been manhandled. Was it Nick? A car accident? Maddie never told me why she suddenly hated Nick, but she did tell me she was having car trouble.

"I think you should just leave her alone."

"Wait...Cadence, just give her a message."

I stop at the top of the stairs and throw my hair back. For a moment, in the silence, I look out the windows. They span both floors, and I can see the half-moon in the distance. The autumn leaves have fallen from the trees, leaving bare branches. It might be cold, but it's a clear night.

I sigh and look at Nick. "What?" I can't help but be mad at him. I don't know why, but Maddie and I are just that close. We have some sort of unwritten pact that if one of us is hurt by someone, the other responds the same way.

"Just...please ask her to call me," he pleads. "Please. Or...tell her I'll call her and ask that she just picks up. Ask her to give me another chance. Damn it, I miss her."

He's falling apart. It makes me smile and, for a second, the old Nick is back. He smiles too. That seems to reenergize his normal manic self.

"I'll tell her."

"Promise?"

"Promise."

"Look, if she stays mad, maybe...you know, you and I can hang out and—"

"I'll talk to her," I snap. Then I think of changing my mind. The nerve of that bastard!

Nick finally leaves, and I make my way into the study room. It has the same floor-to-ceiling windows and is furnished with thick carpets and brown leather couches. There's no one there. Why would there be? Everyone waits until finals to study.

I sit on a couch facing the large window. I take out my laptop from my unicorn backpack. Then I sit and look at the half-moon and the view of campus. A few people are traipsing along the walkways, lined by quaint streetlamps.

I take my iPhone from my pocket. It's 7:10 p.m. I thought *I* was late.

I don't want to read. I don't even really want to study. I know in my heart that I'm not here to learn anything. I'm waiting to see Mr. Handsome and enjoy his company.

But what if he stands me up? What if he never comes?

He comes.

He's wearing the same clothes he wore during his class on Monday. I'm not. I'm wearing a short, tight black skirt. My hair is up in a rather elaborate chignon. Maddie helped me with it. I have on dark mascara and burgundy lipstick. I'm wearing high heels. I look like I'm dressed for a steak restaurant. Well, at least I'm being honest. Bryce isn't gonna teach me anything tonight —not related to ancient Egyptian history anyway.

I stand up.

"Hi, Cadence."

"Hi." I wave, acting all suave like I did at the party.

He cracks a grin and sits in a brown leather recliner beside my couch. We're both facing the window. He puts down his large leather bag and hands me a small white box with a pink bow. My heart leaps a few times in my chest.

"What's this?" I ask.

"A gift. Something for us." He smiles his infamous smile. "I know we're here to study, but I want you to have this."

I start to open it, but he stops me.

"Not yet. Open it at home. Read the instructions and try it. I think you'll like it."

I look at him oddly, but then I just nod.

"I know we're here to go over what you've missed," he says with a chuckle, "but I couldn't help giving you something. It's a gift. Think of me when you use it."

"All right."

Here's an idea: how 'bout we dispense with the lesson and move on to the gift and us?

"Now, with everything going on with you, Cadence, have you even had time to read the passages in the handouts?"

I guess we're dispensing with us *at the moment.*

"Yeah. I read them. Maddie showed me where we are. I went through it."

"Great."

I'm a week behind in my studies. But the fact is, between you and me, most of the other students are always a week behind. In fact, many are ten weeks behind, planning to cram before their finals. Maddie's like this, except when it comes to Alondra's class. Her involvement in Alondra's club makes her an A student. This is a change for my BFF. She's really a C student.

So I know, and Bryce knows, that this study session is all a bunch of bullshit. But I play along and nod at him again. He leans forward, more intent. "All right. Well, I'm not Alondra, but I'll try to add facts that she's given us in class. 'Kay?"

"Sure."

I'm looking at his large hands. He's folding them, but he keeps twitching a finger or two. I want to hold them. But then I look at his eyes again. He's in his serious teacher mode.

"The pyramid structure is a marvel in construction. Cadence, even in today's age, we could not replicate the perfect measurements involved in the hallways of these structures." He points at me. "Know about the Sphinx—and the new one. A new one was recently discovered. Know that for the test. And know about ..."

I cease listening to a word my TA is saying. Instead, I just look at his mouth. And his lips. I want to touch those soft lips, and I can't help but believe he's thinking the same about mine. I know I look gorgeous. It was intentional.

I feel so good around him. I look at his short, wavy dark hair. There are curls near his ears, and I want to straighten them. Then I look at his shirt. There are buttons I want to unbutton. He's also wearing these well-worn brown loafers. That's cute. And his face is a little unshaven. Oh, how I'd love to touch the stubble on his chin.

He doesn't stop talking. I've already read the notes, and he's not telling me much about ancient Egypt that I don't already know, but far be it from me to stop him. I love his intense eyes. And his posture. He's sitting forward, so intent on teaching me. I just watch him.

"Cadence, are you listening?"

"Aha."

"No, you're not," he says, leaning back in his chair.

"I know most of this stuff already, Bryce," I say with a chuckle.

"Okay, then there's no reason to be here."

"Right." But then I flash a sly smile, and he chuckles again. He grabs my hand and strokes it.

"Cadence... I..."

"Yes, Bryce?"

He laughs again. I'm not sure what's so funny.

I look around the room. We're the only ones here. Then I turn back to him. He's leaning toward me again. I want to kiss his lips—just like I did at his frat house. I really want to just lean into him. But he grasps my hand in both of his and says, "Open my gift when you get home, all right?"

I nod.

"I think I should go."

What! No, wait.

He gets up.

"So soon?"

"Cadence, we've covered most of the lecture."

"You just got here."

He pulls out his cell phone and shakes his head. "I've been talking to you for half an hour. I think you know enough for class now."

"Oh." *Shit, has it already been a half an hour? It felt like three minutes.*

"Are you gonna make it to her lecture tomorrow?"

"Yeah," I say. But I really haven't thought about it. Alondra's lectures are at ten in the morning. I've really started getting used to getting up at eleven.

"Okay... Then can I have a goodbye hug?" he asks.

Of course you can have a hug.

We embrace ... for a very long time, and he touches my cheek. The room is still vacant. I suppose if there were students studying, they'd be looking at us. Then he finally lets me go. He heaves his bag over his shoulder and turns hesitantly toward the exit. I can't believe he's leaving. I'm actually a little hurt. Even if this wasn't technically a date, I figured he'd buy me a latte or something.

"I'll see you tomorrow, Cadence."

"Um-hmm."

He looks down into my eyes and kisses me gently on the lips. I almost fall. He holds me with a chuckle. Then he holds me tighter and kisses me once more. I feel him enter my mouth with his tongue, gliding it around mine and then sucking on my top lip. He leans into me, and the erection in his pants brushes against my leg. I yearn for him. I want him.

He lets go of me.

"Tomorrow."

"Yeah," I whisper. "Sure. Tomorrow."

~

"What a fucking tease," says Maddie, back at our dorm. We're sitting together on my bed. I'm still decked out in my dress clothes. I'm frowning a little.

"He's nice."

"Sure. So was Nick."

"Yeah," I say, "what happened to Nick? You know I saw him. He's desperate to talk to you."

Maddie's face lights up a little, but then she turns sour. "Nick, my dear, has the opposite problem as Bryce."

"Oh...seems you have that effect on a lot of boys." I regret saying that the moment it comes out of my mouth. It's like I just accused my BFF of being a whore. I cover my mouth and turn away.

"Well, this isn't about me," Maddie says with a laugh. "So... tell me, what was the kiss like?"

"Good."

We laugh again, like stupid grade school girls.

"He's really cute," Maddie says. She looks me over. I see her in my periphery, but my eyes are focused on the foot of my bed. "And...did he...touch you anywhere else?"

"No!" I snap.

"I'm just asking," Maddie says with a chuckle. "You don't have to get so defensive." Then she touches my hands. "Anyway, it's good to see you're back in the game, Cadence." Maddie knows I haven't really dated anyone since high school. I've been on a handful of dates at Hawthorne, but they always seem to fall flat. Somehow my library "date" was the best one so far.

In high school, I had a boyfriend for a year and a half. His name was Albert Selzer. He was Jewish and was one of the student leaders at our school. He had a really good heart. He was really shy, like me, and unlike Bryce, he rarely even tried to kiss me. He usually just gave me a peck on the lips. I liked him a lot, but after prom, we sort of went our separate ways. Then he moved and I never saw him again. I never scored with Al. It got hot and heavy in the back of his car once, but never a home run. Maddie knows all that. That's why she has this stupid smirk on her face at this very moment.

"Well, I'd be careful with Bryce, Cadence." Maddie leans back on the mattress.

"Why?"

"Because he's obviously an idiot. Anyone meeting a single, available girl looking as hot as you and not doing much more than kissing you on the lips must have a screw loose."

"Shut up, Maddie."

We giggle stupidly again.

Maddie picks up his gift. "Can I open it?"

"Sure. Why not."

Maddie pulls off the pink lace bow and opens the box on her lap. There's a handwritten two-page note inside. Then there are various herbs. I smell the odor from Maddie's lap.

"What the hell?" I say. I snatch the note from my friend.

Dearest Cadence,

Thank you for taking time out of your evening to spend with me. If you are reading this, it means things did not go so badly. I am well aware that our meeting was for us to get to know each other on a different level from a student/teacher relationship. But if, somehow, I have misread you on this, please do not read any further...

Good. If I still have your attention, I would like you to try an incantation for me. I think it will rejuvenate you.

"What does he say?" Maddie asks.

"Shh! He wrote to me. Just shut up!"

"Obviously. A bit too overdone, don't you think? What does it say?"

"Shut up, Maddie!"

Allow me to introduce you to an ancient method of communing with someone of the opposite sex. It involves bathing. If you follow the steps below, I think you will be pleased at the end. The one thing I ask is that you meditate on your memory of me. Remember my appearance and my presence. Remember me always as you follow these steps. But DO NOT do this during menstruation.

1. *Wash your bathtub with white vinegar. Ensure it is completely clean.*
2. *Draw a warm bath, not too hot but not too cold.*
3. *Cover up your mirrors. Your reflection could ruin everything.*
4. *Empty the contents of this bag, containing damiana, jasmine, and red and pink flower petals, into the water. Mix it rapidly with your fingers.*
5. *Undress yourself. Do it slowly and methodically, paying close attention to touching each part of your body.*
6. *Slowly enter the tub naked and face the moon. (But DO NOT do this if it is a full moon.)*
7. *Lean back against the tub and try to relax. Take three deep breaths. Try to rid yourself of all thoughts. Meditate on nothing except me. Remember me. Remember me in complete relaxation as you breathe. Imagine that my very presence is with you, Cadence.*
8. *Relax. When you are fully relaxed, repeat the following mantra addressing the goddess Venus:*

EGO SUM VENUS; EGO SUM VENUS; EGO SUM VENUS.

If you must, repeat it out loud. Repeat it again and again, feeling the goddess Venus enter you. If you do all these elaborate steps, you won't regret it. Let me know. I await the results of my gift!

Your not-so-secret admirer, Bryce.

Maddie is standing over me, trying to read over my shoulder. I turn to her and drop the sheet of paper by the box.

"You all are so fucking weird," I say. She laughs. I don't. "Why can't I find a normal man, Maddie?"

"I think it's cute."

I jump up and shove the small box at my friend. "You go do this shit, then. You like it, right? It's like a part of your cult, right?"

"Cadence, if you'd only seen what I've seen," she says with wide-open eyes.

"What? What have you seen?"

Maddie is smiling at me. I'm getting upset with that smirk.

I had been looking forward to this "date" with Bryce for days. Now I'm left disappointed. All I have to show for it is a "spell."

"Are you going to do it?" Maddie asks.

"Why don't you do it?" I ask, pushing the box at her again.

"I can't," Maddie says with a shrug. "It's not a spell for me."

"Oh, come on! Be serious."

"Guess your man isn't such a tease after all." Maddie jumps up and pats my back. "You've got nothing to lose, Katie. I think you should try it."

I just lift an eyebrow. I take a deep breath and stare at the floor. Then I cock my head up. "Where do we even have a tub?" We don't have a tub—not for ourselves anyway. The bathroom in the dormitory has communal showers.

"Well," Maddie says, "Alondra has a tub."

"Oh, come on!" I snap, whirling around. "Be serious."

"Now, wait..." She raises her hand. "Hear me out, Katie. I know Alondra. She cares about you. I know for a fact she wouldn't mind."

"*No*," I say with my eyes wide.

"All right," Maddie says with a shrug.

"You take it," I say again. "You go take a bath at Alondra's."

"Katie," Maddie says, falling back on my bed, "this is a love spell. It's for you. Why would I want it? Bryce gave it to you. He obviously likes you—*a lot*."

"I don't believe in this shit."

"Well, you'll never know unless you try. I got it!" Maddie says, hitting her leg excitedly. "The Billington House. You can use one of their spare bathrooms."

I shake my head like crazy. "Creepy."

"Come on, Katie. Give it a try."

"Well...I could try your aunt Jane's house. It's not too far from here." Maddie was raised by her aunt Jane ever since she was a little girl. Their house is about thirty miles from campus. She's basically her mom, but Maddie's been known to call her "aunt Jane" to her friends.

"Great idea! You can come to our house tomorrow night."

She's ecstatic. I'm not. I have that same sinking feeling I get whenever I visit Alondra's house. "Wonderful," I say sarcastically.

She gives me a tight hug and laughs.

Maddie decorates the hallway bathroom of her house with scented jasmine candles in red glass candleholders. She also strews red rose petals in and around the sinks. Since Jane doesn't have a shower curtain, a long black curtain has been hung over the mirror. A statue of a naked woman adorns an altar between the two sinks. Maddie says it's Venus.

Jane's not even home. She's visiting her grandchildren in Omaha, Nebraska. So we have the house to ourselves. It's frigid outside and we've just had the first snowfall. I'm thankful for Jane's central heating. Her house is always more climate-controlled than our dorm.

I stand by the door to the bathroom. Everything is ready. Maddie even helped me draw the bath.

"You'll have to add the herbs," she says with a smile. She's giddy over the whole thing. I'm not. I'm kind of freaked out. But I'm glad I thought of Madison's house. The haunted Billington House would have taken me over the edge.

"This is stupid. I feel like an idiot."

"Okay, I have to go." Maddie hugs me, ignoring my comment. I'm in my bathrobe; Maddie is dressed and still wearing a jacket.

"Wait! Where are you going?"

"I have to go, Katie," she says with a chuckle. "The spell will be broken if I'm here."

"How do you know that? The instructions didn't say anything about company."

"I just know."

Maddie doesn't wait any longer. She closes the door behind her, and I'm left in the flickering red light. I feel like an absolute idiot. I pick up Bryce's instructions and read them again. *"Empty the contents with your fingers. Mix them rapidly."*

I follow the instructions, mixing the herbs. Then I try to think of Bryce, but it's hard. I can't stop feeling stupid.

I prepare to just drop my robe on the floor, but then I recall the instructions. *"Undress slowly and methodically."* I really don't like this part. It feels perverted—wait, the whole thing feels perverted—but I let the robe slowly slide from my shoulders. The cotton glides along the nape of my neck and over my naked breasts. Then I untie it and push it slowly over my belly button and down over my hips. I'm not wearing panties or shoes. I am now completely naked. Then I put my finger to my chin, trying to remember where the moon is tonight.

Maddie already told me. She told me to face away from the door.

I enter the tub. It feels sooo good. Thanks to my friend, the temperature is perfect. There aren't any bubbles, so I can see my naked feet and legs. I readjust and lean back on the white porcelain. Then I try to relax. That's the hard part. I haven't relaxed in two weeks. Not since my mother passed.

I try to remember Bryce. That's not so hard now, as I close my eyes. I recall his hard jawline and his bright blue eyes. I think of the stubble along his chin and cheeks. Then I think of his chest.

I think of how I wanted to unfasten a button. Just one. I imagine doing it.

I lean back. The red glow of the room soothes me. The aroma of the herbs intoxicates me, making my skin more attentive to the warm water. It's so relaxing.

What were the words I have to chant? I can't recall. I should have brought the paper over.

EGO ... SUM ... VENUS; EGO SUM ... VENUS; EGO SUM VENUS.

I start saying the words out loud. I'm not ashamed and I no longer feel it's weird. I seem to have accepted the spell—it would be ridiculous not to. I'm committed. And I know Maddie left. She promised. I know she's devious, but she'd never be deceptive about her witchcraft. I know I'm alone.

EGO SUM VENUS.

I look at my naked feet. Then I run my right hand along my arm and stomach. I slowly move it over to my breast, cupping it. I feel my hard nipples, and I'm aroused. But nothing special is happening.

I think of Bryce again. I lean back and sink further, feeling my long hair float behind me. I'm supposed to think of him. My mind starts swooning, and I think of Bryce and speak the enchantment. I think of Bryce's hands. Those strong fingers. The touch of his fingers. His eyes. It's not so hard to think of him, actually. I can picture his blue eyes hypnotizing me and entering my mind. Then I remember his body and his warmth. And I think about the bulge I felt down there. I think of him. And soon my skin seems to feel him.

I don't know if I fall asleep. I seem to. But the mantra keeps being repeated, whether it's from my lips or my mind, over and over again.

Then something really weird happens. Smoke starts filling the room. It's as if the water in the bathtub were scalding hot, but it isn't. I imagine that if I hadn't covered the mirrors, they'd be covered in mist now.

In time, I hear the door. It doesn't bother me. I don't even turn. It just creaks open. And I know who's there.

He's wearing the same clothes he wore in class and at the library. He walks to the tub and kneels before me. His eyes are a little glassy, as if he's in a trance, but those blues look right at me. Then he reaches out for my hand and kisses the back of it.

"Cadence," Bryce says. "Cadence."

I don't respond. I keep repeating my mantra.

He's still holding my hand, but I turn from him, repeating the words.

EGO SUM VENUS.

"Cadence. Cadence."

He says my name while I say my incantation. I feel as if we're saying the same thing.

I reach over and run my palm along his fingers. I feel tingly all over. Then I feel tightness between my legs. I look up at his eyes. He has his famous grin, but he looks hungry.

I move him closer and pull at his top button. I unbutton it, like I've been meaning to do for weeks. Then I reach down to unbutton the others. Just like I did with my robe, he ever so slowly pulls off his navy-blue button-down; then he lifts his T-shirt. I run my hand along the brown hairs at the center of his hard chest. Then I wander down over his well-developed abs. I look into his glorious blue eyes and he smiles again.

He reaches down and kisses me, just like at the library, but it's less guarded and more intimate. He sucks at my lower lip this time and runs his tongue over mine. Then he grabs my wet hair from behind, tugs it a little hard, then slowly, gently runs his fingers down my mane while massaging my back. It feels sooo good as he presses his fingers against my upper back muscles and the back of my neck, licking and sucking with his mouth again and again.

Then, after a time, he stands up straight. He pulls down his pants and underwear. Apparently, there's no delay anymore and I don't mind. His long, hard penis is throbbing before me. I touch the tip. It's wet. I've never seen a man's penis before. Not like this. I rub the tip and he closes his eyes and moans.

After I touch him, he reaches down into the water and touches my legs. He gently glides his fingers over my pubic hair and slowly rubs up and down my clitoris. I know under the water I'm wet. I want him. I want him sooo bad.

But then he releases me. He grabs a large yellow sponge from the edge of the tub and rubs it along my cheek, squeezing the scented water over my lips. I stick out my tongue and taste it as if it's a magical elixir of the gods. But the elixir is me. It's my body. I'm touching my lips to myself. Like my inner goddess or something.

EGO SUM VENUS.

I'm not saying it anymore. At least I don't think I am. The words seem to be echoing around us from someplace else.

He slowly makes his way around the curves of my breasts and rubs the sponge over the tips of my nipples. Then he follows the curves of my breasts again and trails down my back to the crack of my ass. It's like he's washing me, and it's unbelievably erotic. I lurch up just from the touch of his hand. He strokes and touches from behind too.

I look at his penis again. I want to taste it. I've never done that before, but I want it in my mouth. I want to suck his dick. Yes, I know it's wrong, but I want to try it. Somehow, knowing it's wrong drives me even more crazy.

He seems to know, and he moves closer to my face. Soon I have his penis fully in my mouth, exploring it with my tongue, just as I sucked his tongue when I French-kissed him. I bob up and down on his dick, sucking and pressing my mouth against it. He moans again. Up and down, I touch and lick him. But I want him. And now I want him inside me. I reach down and touch my groin again as I suck. He moans more and I chuckle.

I want him to jump into the tub with me. I so desire this! I want him to fall in and join me, but he won't. Every time I pull him, he shakes his head, refusing.

I close my eyes. I feel him touching me down below again. He's pressing up and down along my pussy with one hand, and I'm shaking in joy. Then, with two fingers, he enters me. At first it hurts. There's a sharp pain. But the pain only takes me over the edge. I come in the water. But he doesn't stop. I feel him pressing in and out, in and out. He keeps doing this with ever-increasing intensity. I so want him in the tub with me, but he keeps pushing me away. I want him inside me. He refuses. Instead he keeps pressing in and out with his fingers.

I come again. The water splashes around me like a wave.

EGO SUM VENUS!!!

The words shout out like a clap of thunder, literally shaking the whole room. The room quakes, knocking down candles and causing the statue of Venus to fall off its altar and hit the tile floor. I lurch back with a shot of ecstasy, splashing in the tub. I feel spent, but so satisfied.

Then the spell ends. I know it's all over. Bryce is gone. I'm alone inside the tub. And the only evidence I have of the magic is the small statue now lying on the floor.

I look down at my groin. There's a little blood around my vagina in the water.

I jump up from the tub. I feel ashamed and a little violated. I've never even touched myself like that before.

10

RUN CADENCE

I'm running.

I'm feeling alone.

As I dodge a couple of branches that nearly poke my eyes out, I push the leaves away and leap over a mud puddle. I look up at the canopy of trees surrounding me. The red and yellow leaves arch over me like a domed ceiling, and I feel small, like an insignificant bug. That's really not such a bad feeling right now. I feel unimportant and that's a good escape for me. I wish I could just shrink down to nothing.

The clouds above are shifting, with white and gray mixing over the misty sky. A stream meanders near my dirt path. The water trails along with me, rushing over rocks, as I run. I feel one with nature. That's good. I like the forest—always have. I don't have much company otherwise.

I nearly twist my leg on some uneven ground, but it doesn't slow me down.

I start puffing a bit harder, climbing up an incline.

I know this trail. It wanders far into the nearby mountains. Some say it even connects to caves, but here I can still catch a glimpse of the brick buildings of Hawthorne University.

I stop to catch a breath. There's a brown bird with a red breast—don't know what kind, maybe a robin—on a nearby branch, singing. I reach out a finger and it lets me touch its feathers. I'm surprised. I thought it would fly away before I could touch it. I run my finger over its head. Touching the bird puts me at ease. Then my finger brushes its wing, and it finally takes off.

I kneel down beside the rushing water. It smells clean.

I think of taking out my cell phone and calling Dad. He'd welcome the call. I've already made out the whole conversation in my head. It would go something like this:

"Hi, Dad."

"Hi, squirt." His voice has energy, but I can still hear his depression over Mom.

"I'm leaving."

"Hmm? What do you mean?"

"Hawthorne University." I start crying. It's the right moment, you know. "I'm leaving."

"Why? What's the matter?" he asks.

"It's...it's really weird here. Everyone's so weird. I don't feel like I fit in. I want to go home."

There's a pause. Dad's thinking of what to say. I keep whimpering.

"You can come home anytime you like," he says, but he sounds really down.

"I'm sorry. I know so much—"

"Baby, I just want you to be all right," he says.

Of course he'd say something like that. And he'd mean it. He really loves me.

I brush some sweat from my forehead and lean against a thick tree trunk. Of course I don't reach for my phone. I know the conversation would be something like that, but I'm more the kind of girl who will just drive home if I want to.

That I could do. I could drive home. I could take my

battered Honda and just head home. It's only two hours. It seems so far away, but it's close enough. Still, it's not the right time. It would be unfair to Dad.

I could also just cry. But I'm not the crying type either (except that night at Alondra's—I'm not sure what the hell got into me there).

I start running again.

There aren't many people out today. It snowed a few days ago and rained the other night. But today, bundled up in a thick jacket, I can run.

I'm not sleeping during the day anymore. I guess that's better. Instead, I'm working out incessantly. I go to the gym twice a day now, once in the late morning and again after dinner. I'm running so much that I worry my calves are gonna look too big.

The path winds back so I'm approaching a hilltop close to campus. It's the highest point in Hawthorne aside from the outlook at the Billington House. I reach a plateau, covered in weeds, where several dirt paths converge. It's quite beautiful. Trees form a ring around a grassy knoll, and I feel at home here.

I run to the hilltop and look down at the surrounding forests. In the very far distance, I can see the mountains. In the other direction, I just see trees. And more trees. I also see the nearby river meandering into the lake. If I followed the river, it would take me down into the valley and over to Dr. Johansen's house. Alondra has prime real estate. Then, on the other side, at the other tallest peak, I can see the Billington House. Campus is not far below. I put my hands on my hips, breathing heavily, just looking at all this stuff.

The sky is heavy with the sort of dark clouds that look ready to open up in a downpour. I wouldn't mind so much. A little cold mist would do me some good. It's humid enough already that a calm wind brushes a cold vapor against my cheeks and wet hair.

My eyes wander along the wild grass. That's when I notice something very odd in the weeds: a pile of charred logs. I walk closer. A slightly torn black cloak is lying nearby. I step back. I know this cloak. It's part of Alondra's freaky "honors club." They were all wearing them at the initiation. Did they come here too? It's not that far from the other side of campus, maybe a ten-minute walk.

So they were here. They were on this hilltop. Why? I suppose they came at night; this hilltop must offer a spectacular view of the town in the moonlight—and a better view of the stars. They must have been worshipping, doing their hedonistic pleasure shit under the moonlight. That's what they were doing. Then I shudder. I remember Maddie. Perhaps she was wearing this torn cloak.

I walk back down the hill on a meandering dirt trail. Near a stream, the trail converges with a paved path leading me back to campus. I jog past classrooms and, even though it's Saturday, pass a few people carrying backpacks. The clouds are thick enough that I can see some light coming from the central library. I pass Tammy, another girl from Alondra's club. She waves and gives me a genuinely kind smile. I just keep running. They're always smiling. What do all of them find so amusing about me?

When I return to my dorm room, I unlock the door and walk in. Then I throw my drenched sweatshirt and pants in the hamper and head for the communal showers.

As I stand under the soothing hot water, my mind wanders to fantasy again. I'm thinking of the cloak. I'm picturing Alondra and my best friend and the others walking up to the knoll and bowing to the moon. Fucking weirdos.

I shower—fast (not slowly as my pervert TA might instruct me to do). Then I get in a skirt and sweater, preparing to head to the library. I switch off the light, and before I close the door, I stop cold. I turn and see a dim light. It's the candle that Alondra gave me. I placed it near the window a week ago. It's lit. It doesn't look much smaller than it did when Alondra gave it to me, so it must have just been relit.

Boy, Maddie's gonna get it. This is really not funny.

I turn to leave. I think of snuffing it out, but who cares—it's on Maddie's side of the room anyway.

I turn back to the room. The yellow candlelight still flickers.

I feel scared. My chest tightens like it did that night with the Ouija board. What if Maddie didn't light it?

11

DINNER

It's Taco Tuesday and the college always puts out a taco bar in the dining commons. It's my favorite. The food isn't half-bad, and I can put lots of shredded cheese all over the shredded beef and tortillas. And now that I'm working out incessantly, I don't have to worry about my waistline—well, not as much. So I can add sour cream too.

It's six o'clock, peak rush hour, so the dining room is crowded. I sit down alone, and a few girls give me snooty looks. I feel a little lonely, but I'm hungry so I really don't care.

I empty a packet of sugar into my iced tea. It's my ritual, you know—cafeteria food washed down with a glass of iced tea. Usually I'm eating with Maddie. Not now. Not today. We're fighting again.

"Cadence?" I don't recognize the voice. I look up. Standing over me is an overweight goth girl with thick black makeup, her hair tied up in ugly curls, wearing a giant metal nose ring. I stare at the red-and-black demon skeletons along her neck and arms. It's Mira. Mira just sort of squints at me with a deadpan expression. "Is this seat taken?"

Are you serious?

I look around, still surprised that she's talking to me. My table for four is empty.

"No... Have a seat."

"Thanks." She sits down across from me.

Mira has a healthy plate of lettuce, carrots and tomatoes. It makes me feel a little guilty about the tacos. She's even drinking orange juice.

But she looks like death. She leans her head in her hands and rubs her temples, her thick black eyeliner, mascara, and squinting eyes exuding a dismal aura. She seems to be constantly squinting in contempt at everybody around her.

"So..." Mira stabs her fork into the lettuce. It doesn't look like she wants to eat. "How you holding up, Cadence?"

I really don't think it's any of her business, but I offer a fake smile. "Mom's dead," I say with a shrug.

Mira puts her hand on my arm between shoveling a few leaves and, without looking at me, says, "Sorry."

"Yeah." I bite into a taco. It's really good. I gain some satisfaction knowing that my meal is much tastier than hers.

Then she raises her fork, holding a long strip of lettuce, and points it at me. "I don't usually eat here. I try to go out and eat healthier food."

"Oh, all right." *So can you, like, leave?*

"Yeah, but I figured you'd be here ... I mean, you're really cute and all." She throws more leaves in her mouth and continues with her mouth full. "But, if you really knew me, Katie, you'd know that I don't really like joining anybody for dinner. Even someone pretty like you."

I don't like her calling me Katie. And I really don't like her calling me pretty. I'm getting annoyed that I'm eating my taco in the company of such a gloomy goth bitch. Then I nearly lose my appetite when she actually winks at me.

"I'm here for you, Little Bo-Peep," she adds, "but I don't really give a shit what others think of me. I say fuck 'em, you know? So…" She shrugs and tries a smile again. "Don't think I'm here to have dinner with you. I don't really like eating with anyone."

O-kay??

On that note, I pick up my taco and eat again, watching a music video on the TV screen. I try my best to ignore her… because, after all, she doesn't really care about anybody anyway.

"So the real question, Cadence, is why am I here?"

"Yeah, why are you here?"

"To warn you."

I put my taco down and wipe my face with a paper napkin. "What?"

"A lot of changes are coming, Katie. Be ready."

"Please don't call me that."

"What?"

"Katie."

"Why?" She seems amused. "Isn't that what your friends call you?"

"Yeah, but—"

"I'm not your friend," she says dismally. "I understand."

She's so depressing!

"Okay, Cadence, or whatever the fuck people call you." She points her fork at me again. "Now that Madison's one with the coven, you need to know that she won't be your friend either."

"What do you mean?"

Mira smiles again with this mischievous, almost lewd, gaze into my eyes, and I can't help but think that her lips are curling in a way that seems more sensual than kind. I feel sick again.

"Madison answers to Alondra now," she explains. "That's more important than your friendship." She examines me as if trying to be sure what she's saying is sinking in. Then she shakes her head. "Don't look at me like that. You're acting like I'm full of shit. I guarantee you, Little Bo-Peep, that I know, after being a member longer than most, what I'm talking about with regard to the coven. I know you two were close, but you have to accept now that Maddie's a member of our family, not just your friend."

"I don't see how my friend is your business."

"She is"—she takes a swig of her orange juice—"when she's my sister."

I go back to eating my taco and staring up at the TV.

Mira chuckles contemptuously. "And Bryce. Bryce is our family too."

I nearly spit out my food. This is getting personal.

"Perhaps I should go," I snap, getting up. "Sorry, but I'm really not interested in talking to you."

"How rude," she says with a smirk. But there's actually a hint of offense in her voice.

"I just don't like people talking about my business."

"Bryce? He's *our* business, Cadence." She stabs more leaves, staring at her salad. "You need to join. If you join the coven, all this will make sense."

"I don't think my friends are any of your business."

"Sit down, will you?" She looks up at me curiously. "I said, they are when they're my brother and sister. They're members of the coven."

I reluctantly sit.

"You know I don't really care what you think about me," Mira says. Then she chews on more lettuce with an empty expression, almost to prove it. "Bryce ..." she finally mutters with her mouth full.

"What about him?" I snap. "Bryce is my teacher. So what?"

"Your *teacher*?" she says with a cackle. "Seriously? Is that all? He's part of the coven. When he came to you as an incubus, he broke our pact."

"Incubus?"

She rolls her eyes at me. "If you were one with the coven,

you'd know. All you have to do is join. If you don't, you'll suffer...but you liked it when he came to you, didn't you, Cadence? He made you feel good?" She smiles that wicked smile again. Then she whispers, "When you sucked his dick."

I jump up. "Enough!" People turn, startled by my outburst. "Just stay away from me."

"Sorry," she says, raising a hand. "But you asked what an incubus is. An incubus is a demon spirit that comes to fuck you. Bryce came to you as a spirit that night to fuck you. That black magic shit actually kinda pissed Alondra off. Wizard Reardon taught him how to do that. He came as a demon spirit to fuck you, Cadence. He's quite smitten by you."

"You're really disgusting, you know that?" I snap. It doesn't seem to faze her. Even all the students still staring at us don't seem to bother her much. She chuckles. Then she gets up too.

"I'll go. I've said enough. I'm just warning you, that's all. If you don't join, things will stay confused. If you enter our circle, it will be a lot clearer."

"Why are *you* telling me all this?"

She picks up her tray, stands up, and cocks her head. Then she nods. "Because Alondra asked me to."

12

SHOPPING

MADDIE'S WITH ME, SHOPLIFTING AT VICTORIA'S SECRET IN downtown Atlanta. She has a list of outfits she needs to get and a bunch of things she aims to stow away in her pockets. When I snatch the note from her hand, I gasp in disbelief.

1. *Burgundy pair of lace stockings*
2. *Burgundy lace bras*
3. *Burgundy panties*
4. *Burgundy silk scarf or tie*

Burgundy this, burgundy that; what's with burgundy?

1. *A black or white silk negligee with a matching bra and panties*
2. *Four G-strings (color is unimportant)*

Maddie grabs a pair of purple panties from the shelf and quickly sticks it in her pants pocket. I think she was only a few seconds away from being spotted by the clerk at the desk, but she's a pro.

"What's this?" I say in a forced whisper, shoving the paper into her chest.

Maddie grabs it and laughs.

"Is it kinky shit for Nick?"

"Yeah," Maddie responds sarcastically. "For Nick." Then she steals another pair of panties and closes a small wooden drawer. Of course it's not for Nick. Why would Nick need four G-strings?

I'm thinking she's preparing for a pornographic movie or something. Maddie has a basket of items in one hand and a few other things in the inside pockets of her jeans.

"I can't tell you," she says. "Just don't worry 'bout it, Katie."

"What can't you tell me?"

We're BFFs, you know. There's nothing we've ever kept from each other. But I back off a little. It's been good to be with my friend again, and I don't want to spoil our peace.

"Can't tell you," Maddie says and browses some more.

I lean against another white oak table covered with underwear. I've got nothing slutty to buy in this place. The only boy I can even think of is Bryce, and I haven't been thinking much of him either as of late.

"If it's for another frat party, count me out."

"Okay," Maddie says with a chuckle. Then she resumes her whore attire hunt.

She's looking at a pretty black silk negligee. She's picks it up and touches the material. It looks expensive. She's probably thinking about how she can stow it in her pocket without being caught and realizing it's too big. Especially since, by now, her pockets are pretty full. She lays it over my chest and says, "Can you try this on for me, Katie?"

"What? Why?"

"Try it on, Cadence. I want to see what it looks like on you. I want to see it on someone else before I buy it."

It feels soft. It's silky smooth. The black is as black as you can get.

"I think it'd look better on you. I can wait here if you want me to."

"Come on. Try it on, Katie. I've got some other stuff for you to try on too."

So we head over to the changing room, and I'm trying on this black negligee, but it's really not a negligee. It reminds me of something an S&M pervert would wear with tight leather clothes and boots while holding a whip. But Maddie's looking very earnestly at my get-up.

"Hurry," I say, rolling my eyes.

She chuckles. Then she starts tying these laces, which I didn't even know existed, on my back.

"You're kinda scaring me." *Is she turning gay? Maybe that's what Mira meant when she talked about their "coven."* "Why do you want me to try it on for you?"

"Looks good," Maddie says with a nod, ignoring my question. "Here's another." She pushes a burgundy one to me and then, before I can try the red one on, she presses a black silk bra over my chest.

"We're not here for me," I say with a sigh.

Maddie laughs. "It's the last one."

It's not the last one. She hands me another, but this silk negligee is white. There's something even more sinful about that. Being white, it looks like it fits under a wedding dress.

"So why are you getting all this kinky shit, anyway?" I ask, trying on the last garment.

But she's ignoring me. She's looking me over really carefully for some reason.

"You buying this for me?" I ask. "You want me to wear this when we're spending a nice quiet night at home alone together watching a movie?"

"Shh ..." Maddie says. "Don't be stupid, Cadence." She's so

focused. She raises an eyebrow. Then she shakes her head. "Not bad. White. Goes well with your darker complexion. Definitely not burgundy. Nor the black one. Only white."

"Okay. Then I can take it off?"

"Sure," she says with a laugh.

"So," I say as I quickly untie the laces, "how's Nick? You two hit a home run yet?"

"A long time ago, Katie," she says, shaking her head contemptuously.

I don't like that. I don't like how my friend always acts like I'm so prudish. She's only six months older than me. And anyway, it's just sexual intercourse. What's so special? It's just sex. It's no big deal.

I've never had sex before. Maddie knows that. But she acts like it's some special accomplishment that makes her more mature than me.

I did have that weird encounter with Bryce. It seemed so sinful and wrong. The whole thing makes me uncomfortable when I think about it. It's why I've been avoiding Bryce ever since.

I start throwing on my blue cotton T-shirt and hand silk panties back to Maddie. She wanted me to try it on with the white outfit. There was no way I was gonna do that.

She finally turns away.

"You becoming a perv, Maddie?"

"Fuck off, Katie. But thanks for trying it on. I needed to shop for someone about your size."

"For Alondra's club? You having an orgy?"

"Fuck off again."

She swings open the dressing room door.

"Did you two find everything you were looking for?" asks the salesclerk, who's been waiting for us. She's got a warm smile. She seems nice.

"Sure did," I say. Then I stick my tongue out at Maddie when the girl takes the articles of clothing we don't want.

We walk to the cashier. Maddie somehow manages to pay for most of it, but she stows away the rest. Then she turns to me. She has a big grin and hooks my arm into hers.

"Come on, girlfriend. Let's have lunch before your boring dad comes."

"Okay."

So, we're eating fast-food hamburgers together, and I'm savoring a tasty hot fry when I notice that my friend's ordered a Caesar salad. That's odd. She usually eats unhealthier food than I do.

Red and green are all over the food court because it's the yuletide season. Christmas is coming, and I reflect on how odd Hawthorne University is. Everywhere in this mall there are pictures of Santa Claus and his helpers, Christmas trees, stockings, sleds, fake snow—everything that tells everybody that Christmas is coming. But not at Hawthorne. Our college pushes Christmas to the side. I've been told it's for political reasons. In order not to offend people, the university chose not to celebrate anything tied to religion. They could have celebrated Hanukkah, Kwanzaa, and everything else during December, but instead they chose to celebrate nothing. That's probably why Halloween is always such a big hit at the Billington House. Anyway, Mother Nature tells you when it's the yuletide season in Hawthorne with leafless branches and frigid weather.

It was the same way last year. But not in Atlanta. Here, especially at the shopping center, Christmas is all over the place.

"Want one?" I ask, offering a French fry.

"No."

"They're good."

"Sorry, can't."

Maddie turns on her iPhone and starts texting somebody. She's typing quickly.

"I really should be shopping for something for your aunt Jane."

"Huh?" she asks.

"Jane. Your mom."

"What?" she asks again, staring at her phone irritably. She keeps typing away.

I look around the food court. Few of the tables and chairs are empty. If it weren't for the holiday season, it would probably be a ghost town this time of the week.

A large glass dome provides light to all the fast food restaurants. I look up at the cloudy sky. I think it might rain today. Maybe snow again.

"Shit!" Maddie says.

"What's the matter?"

"Hmm?" Maddie asks with a fake smile. "Nothing."

I unwrap my burger and take a giant bite. Maddie's still staring at her phone, not too interested in her salad. It reminds me of Mira. Obviously, their weird sex cult involves eating leaves. I find it funny how much they seem to hate doing it.

"Want some?" I offer my burger.

She just shoos me away with her hand. She's glued to her phone.

"Who are you texting?"

"Jesus, Cadence," Maddie says, looking up. "You're so nosy."

"Just wondering. And...what's with you not liking fresh, hot French fries? You know they're the best food in the world."

"Alondra..." Maddie shakes her head and looks back down at her phone. "Now please, leave me alone so I can send this important message."

"Can I ask you a question?"

"Hmm?" But she's still texting.

"Can I ask you a question?"

"What?"

"Can you stop lighting my mother's candle? I wish you wouldn't do that. I'd rather leave it unlit. When it's lit, it reminds me of losing her. I don't like that."

Maddie's still looking down at her phone. She shakes her head. "I haven't. I haven't lit your candle, Katie."

"What?"

"Hmm?" Maddie's pressing in all the letters carefully now. I look over her shoulder, mostly as a joke, but that really pisses her off. She jumps back. "Stop it, Cadence!"

"What do you mean you haven't lit it? Then who has?"

"What are you talking about?" Maddie asks. "I've never seen it lit, Kate." Then she hits the table. "Shit!"

"What's the matter?"

"Cadence," she snaps. "I..." She wavers for a moment. "There's just things I can't tell you, 'kay? I've sworn. I told you this before."

She puts her phone down and gives me a pouty face. "Don't look like that, Katie. You know I've joined Alondra's coven." There's that word again. "I swore secrecy."

"We've never kept anything from one another before." I'm surprised at how sad those words sound.

"You're so cute," she says, touching my arm. "But that was before I signed."

"And what happens if you disobey? You die?"

"No." But then she smiles and touches my arm again. "Don't worry 'bout it."

"Okay. But...what about my candle? If you didn't light it, then who did?"

Maddie shrugs. She presses a few more buttons and then stuffs some lettuce into her mouth. "Where's your dad, anyway?"

13

DAD

My dad doesn't look any better than when I left him at the funeral. He's thin and gaunt. Mom did that to him, even before she passed. And he looks depressing as hell, but I know when he interacts with people he hides it. I see him hiding it when he spots Maddie from across the mall. But even with his fake smile, he still looks sad. It reminds me a little bit of Mira, but that makes me hate Mira, because she doesn't have any reason for her depression. Dad does.

When our paths finally merge, Dad loses his melancholy and lights up at the sight of me. And his smile is real. He walks up and gives me a tight hug.

"Cadence."

"Hi, Dad."

Dad turns to my friend. "Hi, Madison."

"Hi, Mr. Hawthorne."

"You're looking good, Madison."

Madison's holding the pink Victoria Secret bag. Dad glances at it curiously. Thank God *she's* holding it.

No matter how much he smiles, I can feel his pain. And I think Maddie can too.

"I thought we'd meet for lunch," he says.

"We just ate," I say.

"Oh," he says. And for a moment, under his bushy eyebrows, his forlorn gray eyes nearly reveal his sadness. But then he recovers with a smile. "Well, I can just grab something. Perhaps we can go shopping?"

"I need to get back to school, Mr. Hawthorne," Maddie says.

"Oh. You're welcome to come with us and stay in our house," Dad says.

"That's okay. I really have to get back."

I wonder if it has something to do with Alondra's club. For a moment, Maddie flashes a disapproving glance, probably guessing my thoughts. I don't want her to go yet. The fact is, now that we're back to being friends, I haven't even begun to drill her regarding Alondra's mysteries.

"All right. Well, thanks for taking care of my baby." Dad gives Maddie a hug. But no one takes care of me. That kind of pisses me off.

"Bye, Maddie. I'll see you Monday," I say.

"All right, Katie." Then she winks and says, "Thanks for helping me with my shopping."

Bitch.

Maddie pecks me on my cheek and gives me a hug. Then she's off, turning her iPhone on again and texting as she walks briskly away.

"Nice friend," Dad says.

"Yeah."

"She's always been good to you, Cadence. She's a keeper."

"Sure is."

As we're heading outside to the parking lot, Dad cocks his head and says seriously, "I thought you'd want to take a break from school for a while. It will be good for me to have some company this weekend. And it'll give you time to think. And... rest... now that Mom's gone. I've made your bed in your room."

I don't know why, but everything—from seeing him walking toward me and Maddie with his head down to his holding my hand and circling the parking lot under the dark, cloudy sky—strikes me as really fucking depressing. I don't like it. I suddenly have an urge to call Maddie to pick me up and rescue me. But then my sweet dad looks right into my eyes with those gray eyes and says, "Whatever you need, whatever you want, squirt, I'll get you. You and your brother are what's important now. I think Mom passed too early. And it makes me angry that she had to go."

"I know."

"She shouldn't have left us so soon," he adds, clenching his teeth.

"I know. I don't want to talk about it."

"Oh...sure, Cadence. Neither do I."

Dad drives me home in silence.

Home isn't home. It's a mausoleum for Mom. Mom's favorite scented candles and the perfume she wore every day of my life linger in the halls. And it's the last thing I want. Really. I want to just forget the whole thing.

So I leave as early as I can on Saturday. And then I feel guilty. I feel bad for Dad. He's so lonely. But I can't stay in that house. Not with the smells. Not with the pictures and the memories. Not with the memories of Mom.

I call Maddie. She drives me home. But she lets me drive most of the way back while she texts on her iPhone.

14

———

THE SACRIFICE

I'm walking to my English lit class, passing a few bodies along a covered sidewalk—it's raining, so everybody's crowded under the ugly metal awning—and somebody taps me on the back of my shoulder. I turn and it's a boy wearing a white T-shirt and gray slacks and carrying a large brown leather bag. His hair is brushed back, and he looks too clean to be one of the students. It's Bryce. He comes up to me as the walkway descends down a few stairs.

"Cadence," he says, sounding a little desperate, "I called, but you didn't answer." We dodge some more bodies. Not only is it raining, it's around 11:30 rush hour. Most of the other students are like me and don't go to school in the wee hours of the morning. I haven't been to Bryce's class in two weeks.

"Just busy," I say with a fake grin. "How are you, Bryce?"

"Great." After being a gentleman and waiting for an elderly woman with a cane to walk down the stairs, he jumps over the last steps to keep up with me. "Did I do something wrong?"

I look at his eyes. Damn, those baby blues! How could he ever do anything wrong? I could get lost in those blues. But I don't. I won't. I don't want to be a part of his hedonistic shit. And my best friend's coven. But...he's...so...cute.

I'm not mad. Or am I? I don't even know. All I know is that after the strange bath ceremony, I really don't want to see him anymore.

"Nor have you come to class," he says.

Damn, he's persistent. And he's referring to *his* class. I never miss Alondra's.

It's pouring rain, and we're at the end of the antique steel awning. I take out an umbrella. He grabs it out of my hand, saying, "Allow me."

I snatch it back. "It's all right," I say. "I'm fine."

"Well, I was hoping we could meet again," he says. Now he's getting wet while I'm shielded by my giant red umbrella. He doesn't give up. "Well? Did I do something?"

Yeah, you had sex with me under a magical demon spell. And... What was it Mira called it? ...an incubus.

I finally stop at just the right moment to watch him getting drenched. Then we just stand there together.

"This is really weird, Bryce," I say after some uncomfortable silence.

"What? Weird?"

"The package you gave me. It was really weird."

"Oh. Sorry. But is that why you're not answering your calls?"

Uhh...yeah. I roll my eyes.

"Wait," he says, gripping my arm like a vise. "Did you...try it, then?"

I would have thought he knew, being that he was there. I look at him as if to say, *Are you for real?* What does he mean, did I try it? It was his hands rubbing my naked ass. Indeed, there's a hint of deception in his gaze. I smile back at him, on to his lie. All the while, his nicely combed hair is dripping.

To be honest with you, I actually like how he's acting

desperate to see me. I'm being a real bitch, but I can't help but be mad.

"Don't play with me," I say. But I don't pull away my arm or walk away. I look down. That gets me madder because it feels weak. But we're alone now. And as much as I'm acting pissed, I don't want him to go.

People pass us, leaving the shelter of the awning, walking fast. We're the only ones standing out in the rain getting drenched.

He doesn't respond. But he doesn't move away either.

"I don't want to play with spells or voodoo shit," I explain finally, forcing my eyes to meet his.

"All right," he says. "No more spells. I promise." And then that infernal handsome smile.

"If you want to spend time with me, don't do that again," I add.

"Sure."

"Right."

I'm searching his eyes. Shit, I'm hooked! I'm mesmerized. He is too. He's just letting the water drip down his forehead, and he doesn't even care about the rain. We're just staring at each other like high school sweethearts. And neither one of us wants to go.

"Here," I say, putting my umbrella over him. "You're really getting wet."

"It's okay. As long as you're talking to me." *Damn, don't say stuff like that!*

He gives me a stupid smile. I finally walk toward the quad and he follows.

"May I ask you out to dinner, Cadence?" he asks. He's so suave about it. I laugh, and it seems to hurt his feelings a little.

"Why not?" I say with a nod. I'm trying to cover him with my umbrella. "Where?"

"How about Lacey's?" Lacey's is a quaint steak house a few miles from campus.

"'Kay."

"Great, I'll pick you up tonight at seven." He's super excited and it's cute.

"Wait! *Tonight?*"

"Yeah. Why not?"

How rude. Who asks someone out on a date on the same night? How arrogant. Then again, who has sex in a bathtub using devil spells?

"I have a test tomorrow," I lie.

"Then we can make it Thursday."

"Hmm...I'd rather see you on the weekend. I'm freer, without any tests from my teachers or...*you.*"

He chuckles. "I can't this weekend. There's a meeting with the coven at Alondra's on Friday and Saturday. Unless you're referring to Sunday. But Sunday is before Monday, isn't it? You probably have a test then, you little bookworm."

"Okay, I'll call you when I'm free, then. Bye, Bryce."

And then I rush away, leaving him in the pouring rain. I look back. The poor boy's drenched.

Why did I do that? I don't know. He creeps me out, I suppose. But it gives me time to think about him. Maybe talk it over with Maddie. No, she's a part of their voodoo club too.

Do I want to spend time with him? I don't know.

He's so hot. Yeah, of course I want to see him.

I do what I really shouldn't do. I go to Alondra's house Friday evening. It's not because I've been invited to some sort of party or initiation or because I've finally decided to sign Dr. Reardon's consent forms to join their pagan club. And it isn't because I plan on seeing Bryce there—though I know he'll be there. It's because of my friend Maddie. Maddie's been missing for the past two days.

She's been coming home late lately, but her not showing up at all really upsets me. I figure she'll be at Alondra's, or at least Alondra has some idea of where my best friend's gone.

I walk up the familiar path. It's still raining and cold, and I have a thick coat and my giant red umbrella. I think of how wet Bryce was and how he was trying to woo me—just like Nick did for Maddie in the library. That was cute. But I still haven't called him.

I rap on the door using that huge knocker. Then I close my umbrella under the ancient white wooden awning of Alondra's mansion. No one answers. But I hear them. Or I hear something. There's singing or chanting and the clanging of tambourines and drums. It's coming from the backyard. I force myself to swallow and walk around the house to sneak a peek.

From behind a thick tree beside the wall, I crouch down and watch. There's a bonfire in the backyard, but this time the group, or *coven* as they call themselves, is dancing around the flames. And they're naked. They've left those black cloaks on the ground, and they're dancing and chanting in the nude. They must be freezing under the icy rain, but it doesn't seem to bother them. I turn away. But then I recall why I've come. I'm looking for Maddie.

In some ways, I don't want to find her. I'd rather tell myself that she's not involved in this weird stuff. But I see her. At least, I think I see her. A woman about her size, wearing camouflage paint on her face and body, is dancing naked with her eyes rolled back. She seems drugged. It's very frightening. I've never seen Maddie in such a state.

I don't recognize the girl standing in front of Maddie, but I recognize the black-skinned girl behind her: Tammy. And then I see Mira. Mira's also naked, but with all her tattoos it's hard to tell. She seems to be leading the circle.

I try not to look, but my eyes are glued to them. Then I see men. Two men, one old and one young, dancing together in the circle. The older one is Dr. Reardon, and the young man is Bryce. They're naked too, with their privates flapping about, as they dance with the women. And, like the women, they're wearing thick camouflage makeup.

Another figure emerges from the back of the house. I glimpse long hair under the hood of her black cloak. She pulls a cart by a rope toward the circle. On the cart is an animal, squirming, tied down with ropes. It looks like a young calf or sheep, or maybe a dog. I can't tell from this distance. The woman stops before the fire and raises her palm to the sky, a large metal charm dangling from her hand. An old man, I'm guessing Reardon, falls to the ground before the charm with his arms wide, dancing on his knees. The others seem to come more alive, like ants suddenly stirred into a frenzy, raising their arms as they circle around the Reardon and the woman in the cloak. It's like they're worshipping.

Then the woman unsheathes a long curved knife inside her cloak. I see her profile as she turns, and I can clearly spot her breasts, hips, and legs. She's naked too, under the cloak. The woman raises her knife and thrusts it into the animal, which utters a terrible cry. Then the circle cries out too, and their voices echo throughout the grounds. I nearly fall back into the bush in a panic.

The woman in the cloak turns and looks straight at me. The others are totally oblivious, lost in their drugged furor, but the leader seems to see me. Then she smiles. A shiver runs down my back as I realize not only have I been found by their leader, but the leader who's found me is Alondra. I would recognize that smug smile anywhere. My legs move against my will and I almost run, but I'm afraid the others will see me. So I'm left frozen, still watching the bizarre spectacle before me.

With the knife, Alondra slices the back of her arm. She

allows the blood to slowly drip over the animal while the others circle around her, with their eyes rolled back, flinging their bodies about in drugged revelry. But Alondra seems sober. She moves with her usual grace and focus as she looks down at the animal. She runs a bloody hand—her blood—over the creature. Then she thrusts the knife into the animal again. She thrusts again and again. The naked worshippers cry out along with the animal until it stops moving. I hear one last scream— an odd animal scream. And when it's done, one of the ladies from the circle hands Alondra a towel. She wipes her bloody hands.

Then Alondra turns and looks at me. She smiles her infamous smile once more. It's all too much for me. I run for it.

15

OFFICE HOURS

Dr. Johansen's office hours are Mondays and Fridays between seven and nine in the morning. Her office is always packed with students, despite the early hours, because her class is so popular. I never go, but after the events of the weekend, I force myself to go now. I'm determined to confront her. I want to know what this is all about, not just for myself but for my friend. Maddie was upsettingly tight-lipped when she returned home yesterday. She even denied having been there on Friday, even though I'm sure I saw her.

I'm one of the last students in line. (You can't expect me to get up this early in the morning, can you?) There are still three students ahead of me. Alondra walks out in her formal white silk blouse, leather jacket, and slacks and looks at the three of us.

"Sorry, guys," Alondra says. "If it's short, you can see me after class and ask...or next week."

Everyone's disappointed. Then she closes the door on me. I'm enraged. She didn't even acknowledge my presence, though I'm sure she saw me.

Everybody leaves the hallway. I don't. I knock. Nothing. I knock again. Still nothing.

I'm resolved not to move. She'll either have to make an exit out her window or run into me. I wait nearly thirty minutes, knocking intermittently. Then she opens the door.

"Oh, hi, Cadence," she says, acting as if she didn't see or hear me.

"I need to speak with you, Dr. Johansen."

"Is it regarding the Inquisition? Egypt?" Her evasiveness is almost sarcastic. Before, I always found her smile endearing; today it seems so fake and infuriating.

"What's going on?" I snap. "What have you done to my friend! What—"

"Keep your voice down," she hollers back. Her anger surprises me. I've never seen her angry, and her voice is commanding. Then she looks down the hall, impatiently shakes her head, and opens the door wider. "Come in." It's not a suggestion; it's a demand.

Dr. Johansen's office is very small but immaculate. Two cheap red suede chairs face a dark mahogany desk. We're on the second floor, and there's a really nice view of the quad. I sit on one of the red suede chairs. Alondra drapes her leather jacket on the large leather chair, sits down, and leans back. She puts her finger to her chin. Then she says—nothing.

"I saw you," I say. "I saw all of you dancing naked around the fire."

"Close the door," she says impassively.

I had forgotten about the door. I get up and oblige; then I sit down. I'm uneasy before her. I'm not accustomed to an angry Alondra. I'm used to her sweet professor persona.

"What did you say?" Alondra is deadpan, still leaning back in her chair, making me feel stupid.

"I saw you and the honors students dancing naked around a fire." Again I feel really weird hearing it come out of my mouth.

She squints and leans forward. "Do you have any idea how ridiculous that sounds?"

"What's happening? What's going on with my friend? Maddie was gone for days last week."

"I don't know what you're talking about, Cadence. How should I know?"

"I saw you. And I know you saw me."

She looks up for a moment. "Well, I'm very busy, Ms. Hawthorne. I have to review quizzes. If this isn't a question about class, I would prefer you leave."

I stand up. "I can tell Administration. There are a lot of weird things going on at your house. Who knows, you could even be abusing the students."

"There's nothing hurtful going on at my house. I can assure you of that."

"Tell that to the animal you killed."

Alondra smiles. It's a sly, wicked smile. "Please leave."

"No. Tell me what you're doing. You looked right at me! Stop acting like nothing happened, because I know it did. I saw you with my own eyes."

"If you believe your eyes, then something indeed happened, Cadence. I'm not refuting that. You saw what you saw, but that has nothing to do with you leaving my office. Office hours are over. Get out."

"What does that mean?"

"It means what I said."

Tears start streaming from my eyes, surprising both of us. I'm not one to cry, but I'm furious. "I trusted you," I mutter. I jump up and make my way to the door.

"I trusted you, Cadence," she says as my hand touches the doorknob. "I asked you to join, but you refused. Do you think I can tell you anything? Even if I want to?"

I'm frozen, with my hand still on the doorknob, looking down at her drab brown carpet.

"Mira told me you sent her." I'm still looking down at the floor. "Is that true? Can you at least tell me that?"

"Yes. I sent her to speak to you." I whirl around, and she doesn't have that infernal self-assured smirk on her lips anymore. She looks concerned.

"Why?"

"Because I wanted you to join. You're a smart girl, and now that your best friend is one with the coven, I thought things would be easier if you joined. Things like this would not be so hard on you."

"You're all witches, aren't you ... Like Wicca?"

She smiles and gestures for me to sit, but I remain standing. Then she shakes her head. "Not Wicca. I see you've learned from class. But I don't affiliate myself with any formal group, Cadence."

"But you are a witch?"

"Yes, Cadence, I am a witch."

"A good witch or a bad witch?"

She laughs, and for the first time the tension in the room is lifted. "I think I'm a pretty good person. Don't you?"

"It didn't look that way last night."

"Sit down, Cadence." She gestures with a broad sweep of her arm. I feel like she's about to cast a spell. I sit back down, anxious.

"Where did you see me and this animal I supposedly killed?"

"At your house. In your yard."

"What were you doing in my yard, Cadence?"

She's not accusing me. She's giving me a welcoming smile, and I have to admit I feel better. I brush the tears from my eyes.

"Maddie's been missing. So has Bryce. So I figured they'd be at your house. I knocked on your door, but no one answered, so I walked around. That's where I saw the fire—"

"The bonfire?" she asks. "The pyre, like you saw when we honored your mother?"

"Yeah."

"And what was I doing with—"

"Don't play games with me."

"I'm not playing games." She earnestly shakes her head. Then she opens a desk drawer and takes out a very large metal object. It's a five-pointed star with a circle around it, the size of her palm. It's the charm she cast over the animal before killing it. She puts it on the desk and leans back, waiting to hear more from me.

"What's that?" I ask.

"A pentagram."

"Why do you have it...in your desk?" *What the hell?* But I'm actually not that surprised.

She smiles again. I wish she'd stop doing that. "Does it frighten you? You're not a practicing Christian. Christians fear it as a sign of the devil. Of Satan. But if I recall, you told me you were an atheist. And anyway, the pentagram was used by early Christians to symbolize the five wounds of Christ. But if I turn it"—she turns it so that one point is pointing downward—"it becomes the symbol for Satan and for devil worshippers. Just as if I turned a cross over. All it takes is one turn." She turns the pentagram back. "There, now it's back to being safe again. This is good, and this"—once again, she turns it backward—"is evil. Good Christian faith, bad Satanic worship. That is how quickly one can turn. Perhaps a construct, perhaps not?"

I can't help but feel like she's teaching again. I almost have an idiotic urge to open my backpack and take notes.

"I can teach you a lot more than history," Alondra says, her face now quite serious, "but you have to swear secrecy. If you can't do that, then I can't allay your suspicions regarding your friends. Or me. I told Mira to tell you that."

"And which way do you prefer?" I ask with my own sly

smile. I turn the pentagram back. Facing her, it is evil; facing me, it is good.

"You won't know until you join, Cadence. Until you can trust me."

"I told you, I don't want to join."

"Why are you afraid?" She turns the medallion around again. "They say in the Buddhist religion, evil is ignorance. The word *witch* means wisdom. Perhaps if you will allow me to impart wisdom, you will not see me as evil anymore."

"I don't think you're evil." But after I mutter the words, I'm unsure.

"Then why not join?"

"I...I don't know."

I bite my lip. She's staring at me, seeing my frizzled morning hair, the bags under my eyes, and my casual attire: a university sweatshirt and jeans. I look outside the window to avoid her penetrating green eyes. It's like she could hypnotize me with one look. And now that she admits to being a witch, I wonder if she can cast a spell just looking at me with those jade eyes.

"I will deny everything," Alondra says, finally averting her gaze. "I have to in order to protect the coven... Did you record this spectacle you say you saw? Perhaps record it with your phone?"

"No."

"Then you have no proof," she says. "And every member of the coven will deny it. We have all sworn to maintain secrecy and protect each other."

"Why?"

"Because people are just as scared as you are, Cadence." Alondra takes a deep breath. "People fear the unknown. And they persecute those who are different. They have been doing that since Salem. Since before Salem."

I merely nod.

"Do you know what happened twenty years ago to a daycare

teacher?" she asks. "It was like Salem. There was a man who practiced witchcraft in Minnesota. One of the kids he was caring for told her parents that he'd touched her. Authorities investigated. Then another student claimed wrongdoing. Then another. One said that the teacher was forcing them to eat their own shit." I don't like it when Dr. Johansen cusses. She seems to notice and pauses for a second. Then she looks back into my eyes and makes it worse. "Another claimed he touched her vagina and rammed a pencil up it. There was no proof, but when it was found out that the teacher was a practitioner of Wicca, it was all over. The teacher was arrested. He was actually jailed for a couple of years, until it was found that he was completely innocent."

"I wouldn't tell anybody anything about you."

"Cadence," she says, leaning forward and raising her eyebrows, "you said a minute ago that you were gonna tell Administration on me."

Oops.

"Cadence," she says, recovering her smile, "I know you're under tremendous stress right now. I respect that. I told you how sorry I was to hear about your mother. But you have to understand my position. As much as I care about you, and you are one of my favorite students, I can't risk everything and tell you our secrets. Unless you join."

I nod.

"I think you should give us a try. All your friends have joined. Why don't you?"

"Can I leave? Can I leave once I join?"

Alondra nods, and there's a sudden look of triumph on her face. "If you swear secrecy, you can return to your normal life at any time. I don't think you'll want to. It's just that you must never tell anyone about us if you go."

"I only care about Maddie. I want to join to help her."

"All right." But Alondra didn't believe that was the only reason. And I wasn't sure I believed it myself.

"What if I tell?" I ask.

She turns the pentagram backwards in front of me, but her face is impassive. The meaning is clear enough.

"Why do you want me to join so badly?"

She shrugs. "Your best friend and boyfriend are members."

"Bryce isn't my boyfriend," I say with a chuckle.

"He gave you a love spell. He sure seems to think there's something between you."

He does? Of course he does. He was so anxious to see me again. And I haven't answered one call or text.

How does Alondra know? Of course she knows. It was a spell. She must know everything about her group. Her *coven*.

I look at her bookshelves. All her books are on ancient cultures, many regarding magic. It all makes sense. She's a witch. She's teaching all this stuff about history and magic because it's a part of what she does, her real job. Her work as a professor is just cover. Outside school she's a bona fide witch.

"I can leave at any time?"

She nods.

"Will I have to dance naked around a fire?"

She laughs. "Only if you want to."

16

———

A DATE

Bryce is taking out a confidentiality agreement for me to sign, but even in the dimly lit restaurant, I'm distracted by those bushy eyebrows, well-kempt hair, and baby-blue eyes. He's so excited that I'm signing. I'm not. I still have my reservations about Alondra's cult. But I'm also really curious. And I keep telling myself that Maddie needs me to save her. She doesn't, but I keep telling myself that.

I'm wearing a really pretty blue dress with a golden brooch pinned to the shoulder. It kind of makes me look like a goddess—like Diana or something. I even braided my hair all formal and Greek-like. But I don't think Bryce can see much. Lacey's is a small steak house encompassing one very dark room. Either they're trying to save on their electric bill or they think pitch-black darkness is romantic. There are booths on the side and candles lighting every table, so I can see Bryce in the flickering flame. He's wearing a T-shirt and jeans. He looks way underdressed, but he's so clean shaven and neat that it doesn't matter. And anyway, I can see those pecs and I'm reminded of what lies underneath his clothes.

"Just sign the last three pages, okay?" he says with a smile.

He butters some bread and hands it to me. That's so adorable. "Got it?"

"Aha."

"I think it's a good decision, Katie. You won't be out of the loop anymore."

I sigh and raise my glass of wine as if in a toast. It's a really big glass. It tastes sweet and quite lovely.

"So...it might snow next week," I say. "Are you guys still going to get on your brooms and fly around naked?" I often try to be funny when I'm nervous.

He smiles. "You'll know after you sign," he says, waving his hand over the document.

I pick up a pen. I'm surprised at how much legal jargon there is. It's actually a bit intimidating.

I look up. "So...you sue me if I tell?" Then I'm staring back down at the document. I turn two pages because there's no way I'm actually going to read it.

"It's a formality, Cadence. It's more binding through magic than by law. But the secrecy is quite real for the coven."

I sign the document. He takes it from me, looking elated. Then I feel regret. I feel like I just signed away my soul to the devil.

"On Friday, Cadence, we'll initiate you."

"Great." That seemed simple enough. I sip more wine.

The waitress comes and takes our order. She's wearing a formal suit. I can barely see the suit because it's so dark. Then I take a bite of the sourdough bread and wonder if it has mold on it. I'd never know because it's so dark, but it tastes quite warm and fresh.

We order steaks, cooked medium, with baked potatoes. Then I sit back with my wineglass and smile at my hunk of a date. I'm amused by the fact that we've been chasing each other back and forth for the last couple of months, but this is our first actual date. And then I wonder if that's my prime reason for joining.

"Well, now that that's over." Bryce raises his wineglass and looks up thoughtfully. "You know it's not often I take my students out to dinner."

"It's not often I go out on dates with my teachers."

Then we're quiet. I butter more bread and turn to the windows, which are draped in red and impossible to see out of.

What I really want to ask him about is our encounter, but I don't know how to broach the subject. It was so weird, and I'm worried that bringing it up will just spook me again. But if we ever want to go beyond our date tonight, I should bring it up. But then I think about the contract again, and I wonder if I'm a complete idiot for signing it.

"You're such a mystery, Cadence," he says with a chuckle.

"What do you mean?"

"You're always thinking. What're you thinking about right now?"

"That I shouldn't have signed my soul away to the devil."

He laughs. "I can tear it up."

And now's my chance. What a perfect time to ask him about—

"Why don't you tell me about your mother," he says. "Whenever we mourn for someone, in a way that person becomes a part of us, or at the very least, a part of our family. Emily's now a part of the coven. What was she like?"

I don't want to talk about my mother. He seems to sense it, and he puts a hand up. "I'm just—"

"No, Bryce. Tell me about yourself. Did you grow up in Georgia?"

"I grew up in Missouri...Springfield, Missouri. My family has a farm out there."

"How'd you get interested in history?"

"For the same reason as you." He sips his wine. "I love

stories. And I love learning of the past. Ever since I was a child. I used to play with Civil War soldiers. I learned about all the battles."

I smile, imagining Bryce as an adorable little boy.

"I imagined I was fighting the Battle of Bull Run or Gettysburg. So even in elementary school I read books about the nineteenth century. I came to Hawthorne University because of its emphasis on historical studies. Then I was as mesmerized as you probably were with Dr. Johansen. I loved her passion for her work. Her subject matter—the dark arts—put me off at first —as it probably did you—but then I understood the reason for it. She studies it because she seeks to cure evil. She's a very bright blue light, Cadence. Her personality is of the clearest water. She is good, but so many misunderstand her. She's probably better than anyone I know. But of course she creeped me out at first too—you know, her obsession with shadowy dark magic."

"Which you can now tell me all about, since I signed that stupid document, right?"

"Sure." He leans forward. "But it's just a legal document. Your agreement—with your blood, at your initiation—will be more binding."

I gulp my wine down harder.

"What would you like to know?" he asks, amused by my reaction.

"Blood?"

"Alondra will take a dagger to your arm." I'm remembering when I saw her do it to herself. I find myself shaking my head, and my eyes are probably bulging. I'm picturing myself as their sacrificial animal.

Bryce grabs my hand. "Don't worry, Cadence. Everything will go slow. Alondra is the greatest leader any coven could ever have."

"I don't want anyone to stab my arm."

"You will," he says reassuringly. "When you see the rewards, you'll bear all the costs. Just as a pregnant woman bears pain."

Shit. Now I'm about ready to ask for the documents back.

"Cadence," he says, rubbing my hand, "there's nothing anyone will ever force you to do against your will. You'll have every right to refuse the blood sacrifice."

"I can't even get my blood drawn at the doctor's office."

He laughs and I laugh too. Then he looks around. "There are herbs that Alondra will give you. Some will let you see more clearly than you've ever seen before. Some ..."

He keeps talking, and I'm struck by his passion for the whole thing. He loves this cult as much as Alondra loves to teach ancient history. He doesn't have this much passion for being a TA. The coven is so important to him, and he seems desperate to get me to feel the same way. But I stop listening. I'm thinking about that curved knife and blood.

"Trust me," he says finally, rubbing my hand more sensually than protectively. I blush a little.

I pick up my wineglass, and I'm surprised to see my hand shaking a little.

"Cadence," he says, watching my hand, "you must believe me. I won't let anyone ever harm you. I swear it."

And I look into his eyes and he means it. I force down some wine.

"What...what did you mean water? You called Alondra a water personality."

"The whole universe," he explains, opening his hands— again quite passionately, "is made up of four elements: fire, water, air, and earth. And then there is another energy binding it all. Everyone's personality can be described based on these elements. Alondra is very sensitive and empathetic. She's also psychic. It's what makes her such an amazing leader. She's like water."

"What am I, then?"

"You are," he says with a chuckle, "an earther. Your personality includes pragmatism. And you're also very stubborn."

I laugh too. He's right about that.

"So these elemental personalities are like astrology signs?" I ask.

"Yes, exactly. In fact, an earth element corresponds to Taurus, Virgo, and Capricorn. What sign are you, Cadence?"

"Capricorn."

Bryce extends his arms in a gesture meaning *see?*

"Okay, genius, what are you, then?"

"Hmm, what do you think I am, Cadence?"

"I don't know all this sign bullshit yet."

He shakes his head. "I really wish you believed a little more in magic, Katie. But that also goes with your sign... Anyway, I'm like fire and my sign is Leo and, accordingly, we are totally incompatible."

We both laugh again.

The waitress brings our food. It looks delightful, with some lovely garnishes embellishing the steak sauce. I bite into the tender steak and it's delicious.

"The tarot cards corresponding to earth are Pentacles and Coins," Bryce says with his mouth full. "Your corresponding card would probably be Queen of Pentacles, but really Wizard Reardon is the expert in cards."

"Wizard?"

"Yeah. He's the leading wizard, or warlock, of the coven."

"Oh," I say.

He chuckles again. "Alondra will expect you to know all this like the back of your hand. You'll need it to cast spells."

"Cast spells?" I raise my eyebrows.

"Yes. Spells. We're witches. We cast spells."

"So you're a witch?"

"Yes, and after you get initiated, you will be too."

"Fantastic."

He laughs. Then he scoops up some potato, swallows it quickly, and says, "Cadence, I've been dying to ask you this. Your last name is Hawthorne. Are you related to the Hawthorne family?"

"Dad probably was, but I don't know. But it helped in my admission interview."

"I'm sure it did."

"We don't really know our family tree for sure."

"Hmm. Maybe...maybe he's a descendant of Escoba's?"

He laughs, as if acknowledging how silly this is, but I have a feeling he's been thinking it.

"Or maybe Abigail, Bryce. I really don't know."

"You should check. Being that you'll be a graduate—and if you continue in the honors program, I'm sure Alondra will want to keep you as a graduate student—you should find out your connection."

"I don't know where to look."

"The archives. You could check in D.C." I think he wants to know more than I do.

I eat some more steak. It gives me a break from Tall, Dark, and Handsome. But I catch a few glimpses of him chewing his steak. He keeps looking at me. My dress is a success, I suppose.

"Let me ask you something." I say seriously. I feel like now is the time.

"Hmm?"

"That night, that night you came to me. Or...did you come to me? I don't even know." My skin feels hot, and I probably brighten as red as a tomato.

All of a sudden, he becomes very serious. He nods. "I shouldn't have, Cadence. I'm sorry. I broke the rule of the coven. I used left-handed magic without Alondra's permission. Alondra was furious."

"Left-handed?"

"Yes," Bryce says sheepishly. He looks down for a moment. "Bill taught it to me. It's a manipulative and deceptive conjuring, not white magic. Of course Reardon says there is no left or right, white or black magic. To him, casting any spell that satisfies the flesh is fair game. But not to Alondra. When Alondra found out I conjured up an incubus, she threw me out of the circle for a week. She made an offhand remark about it being because I was a man."

At this point, I have no idea what the fuck he's talking about. Nor do I care. What I really want to know is—

"Actually, I didn't even know if it would work," he adds, more to himself than to me. "I thought, at the very least, it would make you believe in magic. But it was forbidden."

"I don't care about rules, Bryce. Did you... Were you ..." I can't even think of how to ask it.

"Yes. I was there, Cadence."

I feel uncomfortable, almost violated. And my mind is mixed up. Can I even believe it? If it's true, I had sex with him. And in such a weird way. I look at him and he seems uncomfortable too.

"I told you it was wrong, Cadence. I'm sorry."

"Then why'd you do it?" I'm surprised by my own tone. I'm angry. "You didn't ask me and you didn't tell me what you were doing."

"I'm an idiot. I wanted you, just like I want you now. I'm attracted to you. And I thought the magic would convince you to sign, like you did today. You're right. It was wrong. But I—"

"By fucking me in a bathtub with a witch spell?" I ask in a forced whisper. He smiles at my jab, and it makes me angrier.

"I never knew how aroused I'd get by hearing you cuss, Cadence."

I shake my hair out angrily. He touches my hand and I quickly pull away.

"Listen to me, please, Cadence, I wanted to show you our

world. I figured the magic of that night would make you want to join."

"It was creepy. It's not how people show love."

"You're right. I was wrong. Very wrong. I'm sorry. I heard an earful already from Alondra."

"Who cares about Alondra, Bryce. This is about us."

"You'll care," he says, lifting his glass of wine and pointing at me. "Alondra is our leader."

"You're a pervert. It seems all you men are." And I stick my fork into a couple of pieces of broccoli over that conclusion.

"Yeah, probably. That's exactly what Alondra said. It was wrong." Then he touches my hand, but I pull away. "Look, I won't ever do anything like that again. I promise. Please forgive me, Cadence. I told you, I thought it was a way to introduce you to magic. I thought ... it was okay because it was magic. I never thought I was disregarding your wishes. You must believe, I would never want to deceive you. God, I'd never want to hurt you. Besides, the spell doesn't even work unless it's done by mutual consent."

He has this really sad look, but he still pisses me off. I look straight into his eyes, and I drawl very distinctly and slowly, "F-u-c-k y-o-u."

I can't eat my steak. I feel too much pressure in my throat. And I can't look at him. Not even those to-die-for glorious blue eyes.

"Anyway, you didn't," I continue, "because nothing really happened. The whole thing was impossible."

Bryce puts his fork and knife gently down on his plate, leans back and closes his eyes. Then he says, "You chose a small bathroom. You covered the mirror with a large black drape. There were red rose petals along the sinks, and there was a small figurine of a goddess. The figurine was a white stone statue, covering her naked groin with one hand while holding her long hair with the other. You faced away from the door. There were two sinks, and the faucets were old-fashioned with long brass stems and bronze handles. There was a white carpet on the floor."

"You probably saw the figurine," I say with a shrug. "Or Maddie told you."

"I didn't see the carpet in the bathroom."

"A lot of houses have white carpets."

He exhales impatiently and then quips, "All right. You need more?" He talks more quietly. "First we held hands, then we kissed. You pulled at my shirt, yanking off the top button, then you took my shirt—"

"Enough," I say with my hand raised. I don't want to hear it played out. It creeps me out even more.

"I was there, Cadence. I was as much there as I am here before you. But it was a spell, an incubus spell."

"So I'm no longer a virgin?" I snap. He looks at me oddly; then he looks around the restaurant because I'm really loud. He laughs and covers his mouth.

"Really?" he asks.

"You took my virginity with a witch spell?"

"First off," he says, finally getting a little angry too but talking quietly, "I didn't know you were a virgin. That's adorable. Second of all, a virgin is someone who has not had intercourse. I did not have intercourse with you, Cadence. It was a spell. Any man would love to sleep with you, but that is totally up to you."

"I think you should take me home," I snap. I hit the table. "This is unreal."

"Jesus! Come on!" He runs his hand down his face.

"Yes, Jesus. Perhaps you and your coven should think more about him."

"*Our* coven! You know, Cadence ..." His face has reddened, and his lips are quivering in rage. "Cadence, you are the most difficult girl I've ever met. You're not just stubborn, you're completely impossible. I don't think you would believe in magic even if I pulled a rabbit out of my ass!"

He's really pissed. I just shrug.

I'm relieved. I've been wanting to talk about that night throughout our date. Now I feel like I've finally gotten everything off my chest. I don't even feel that angry at him anymore. In fact, even with his lingering rage, I'm studying his gorgeous features.

He gulps some wine and does everything possible to avoid my eyes.

"I'm enjoying dinner," I say, biting into more steak. "And my bath... It was lovely... Thank you. Are we having dessert?"

He cocks his head in amazement. "What would you like, Cadence?"

"Crème brûlée."

17

MANDRAKE

To say that I'm not nervous would be stupid. I'm sitting on one of Alondra's elegant white leather sofas, staring at the flat-screen TV on the wall. There's nothing on, but there's also no one to talk to at the moment. I'm by myself, tapping my knees and waiting. And that's making me more nervous. Meanwhile, every so often, one of the ladies from the coven walks by, gives me a nod, opens the sliding door, and takes something outside. They're preparing for some kind of outdoor event, and that's weird because it's cold and raining outside.

Every one of the girls is wearing a long black cape and short black dress. I'm not. I'm in a white sweater and jeans.

I cross one leg over another. Then I switch legs and stare at the elegant stone chimney. Then I cross the other leg back again, fidgeting with my fingers.

One of the members, Tammy—the pretty black girl with long hair like me—hands me a glass of red wine. I get up and smile. "I know it's a bit weird, Cadence, but we'll be done soon," she says with a wink. "Just sit tight, 'kay?"

"You sure there's nothing I can do to help?"

"Not unless you know how to brew cauldrons."

I laugh, but it's not really funny. Still, I like Tammy. She's a lot like me. And I suppose she's prone to saying funny things at inopportune moments too.

The wine tastes good. It's very smooth.

Tammy rushes back to the kitchen. I can hear them murmuring. I wonder if they're talking about me. Probably.

I need to pee. But I'm tired of getting up and using the restroom. I have a bad habit of having to pee when I'm nervous.

Then Mira comes in. She's wearing exactly the same black dress and cape as the others. She seems friendlier than ever and reaches out to me with both hands, signaling that I should rise. I feel really weird but I get up.

"When it stops raining, we're going to go outside, Katie," Mira says. Her auburn eyes are staring at mine. "It's cold, but the cloak will warm you. And when we go to the service, the fire is warm enough. Why don't you finish your wine so you'll be more relaxed? The rain will stop soon, and then you'll know we're ready."

"It's going to stop raining?"

"Yes. In another fifteen minutes."

That's where all the magic starts, right? Now they can control the weather?

Maddie rescues me. She walks in holding a wineglass too. "I'm so excited for you, Kate!" she says. Mira backs away and sits on a furry chair beside the fireplace. "You nervous?"

"Nah." Of course I'm nervous. I'm terrified and Maddie knows it.

She sits beside me and pats my knee. "Things might get a little weird, Cadence. But you'll be fine. Trust me, right?"

"Yeah."

"She'll help you along."

"Just ignore Dr. Reardon," Mira chimes in.

"Why?" I ask.

"He's a sick fuck," Mira says. I'm shocked by her language,

particularly since I saw Dr. Reardon a few minutes ago in his black cape, helping out in the kitchen with my to-die-for boyfriend. "His ideas are exactly what you're afraid of, Cadence."

"Even he will help you," says Maddie. She scowls at Mira.

"What about his ideas?" I ask Mira.

"Just forget it, Katie," Maddie says. She's warning Mira to shut up with a look of venom. "You nervous?" Maddie repeats, turning back to me. She looks into my eyes seriously.

"Should I be?"

"I was," Maddie says. "But things worked out."

"Sure did," quips Mira.

Maddie whirls back toward Mira, furious. "Why don't you go finish helping the others!"

Mira smiles slyly and sighs. "Okay." She gets up and leaves us, and I hear her laughing as she makes her way back to the kitchen.

Then Maddie turns to me and holds my hand again.

"Cadence," she says seriously, "Alondra is permitting me to tell you some things before we start. She thinks it might put you at ease."

"All right."

Maddie looks around and takes a deep breath. "Do you remember the July fourth party last year?"

"How can I forget?" I got more drunk at the Lambda Lambda Delta frat house than I had ever been in my life—I probably drank a full bottle of tequila. I vomited all night and wanted to die the next morning.

"Right, well," she says, looking nervous, "do you recall what we experimented with?"

"Ecstasy."

"Yeah."

"And three or four bottles of tequila."

"Yeah," Maddie says, laughing.

"And boys."

"Right." We both laugh stupidly.

"I promised I'd never go to their house again."

"Yeah," Maddie says.

"Just spit it out. Tell me, Maddie."

"Well," Maddie says, "you're gonna take something tonight. It's not ecstasy, but it's a drug and it'll make you feel weird. You're going to sweat, you may feel dizzy, and you might even vomit."

"If Alondra sent you to make me feel better, then—"

"I know," Maddie says, taking my hand. "But, Katie, it'll make you feel good too. And while you're doing it, all of us, even that bitch Mira, will be beside you helping you."

"What if I don't want to take anything?"

"You have to, Cadence. It's required for the initiation. You do want to join, right?"

"Not really. I joined to find out what the hell they're doing to *you*."

Maddie gives me a hug. Then she surprises me. She looks at me and she's fighting back tears. "I love you, Cadence. Really. You're so cute. Just...trust me, okay?"

"Yeah."

"All right. When Alondra hands you the elixir, drink it. It's required."

"I'd feel less nervous if you told me what else is required."

Maddie nods. "Nothing. Not for you. You're lucky." Then she jumps up. "When it stops raining, we'll walk through the mud to the fire. I'll be there, but I'll be under my cloak. We'll be chanting and dancing. Then we'll disrobe."

"Naked?"

"Yes."

"Do *I* have to be naked?" Alondra told me it was up to me. Would I ever want to? It's just so weird.

"No," Maddie says with a smile. "But you will have to be

sworn in. The swearing in for the coven will involve blood. It isn't required, but it's how you make your vow. No one will force you, but out of respect for me, Alondra, Bryce, and the rest of us, I really would like it if you would let her initiate you with the knife."

I feel my bowels turn. I've been thinking about blood since Bryce mentioned it. I don't want to do it.

"Think about it," Maddie says with a smile as she helps me up from the couch. "It won't be so bad after the drink... And now, I told you just enough to prepare you. If I tell you more, I might just make you more nervous."

"You already have."

Maddie lifts my chin. "It'll be alright, 'kay? I promise, Katie."

"And I'll like it?"

Maddie laughs. It must be my expression. I'm completely disgusted and baffled by the whole thing. She nods.

"Excuse me for a moment," I say. "I have to pee."

After I finish relieving myself in Alondra's bathroom (which is very chic and cool, with marble countertops, a bidet, and a fancy tub and sink), I return to the living room. The lights are off, and lit candles are lying along the floor, beside the door. The rain has stopped. It's silent. Beside an end table near the sofa are my and Maddie's half-drunk glasses of wine.

Bryce is standing by the door in a black cloak. "Come, Cadence." He reaches out his hand. "Put on your cloak. And R-E-L-A-X. Try to. Don't let the ceremony scare you. I'll be with you the whole time."

Through the glass, I can see the coven. There's a bonfire, just as there was for the ceremony for my mother, only this time they're not sitting. Everyone is slowly circling the fire in their black cloaks. I can't make out any faces, but I count twelve.

I put on my cloak and step outside. It's damp but it's not raining anymore. The clouds are moving away quickly in the moonlit sky. It's a half-moon. I put my arms around myself because the cloak is really not warm enough. Bryce sees it and puts an arm around me. He's warm enough. I walk across the field to the fire, held by Tall, Dark, and Handsome.

The witches in the circle are chanting something not in English. When I'm close, I see a single plastic chair. Oddly, Bryce directs me to sit with my back turned to the flames as they continue to walk around the fire, and they walk behind me. The fire is warm, and the cold no longer bothers me.

Then I see faces circling me. I recognize Tammy, Hannah, Hope, Gilda, and Mira. Then I spot Dr. Reardon. There are other girls I don't know well. I remember seeing them in the kitchen when I walked in. They all look at me. They don't look drugged, nor are they particularly menacing. If anything, they're friendly. They all smile, even Mira, as they pass slowly by. They move fluidly; it's more like a dance than a march.

They circle very slowly for what seems like a long time. I'm tempted to check the time on my cell phone, in my pocket, but I recall Mira's séance and that stops my hand. They continue circling, but they turn so that none of them is facing me. I understand this to mean that I am not yet part of the group.

None of them makes me nervous. Except Reardon. He just creeps along, continually watching me. I don't like him.

When he passes me for the third time, he speaks. "Turn your back on me, I still am," he says in a commanding voice. They all say "Atman," and the head wizard continues to speak. "Be it virgin or harlot, I remain. From the seed of man art thou. That is all. Do not fall into trickery. To dust you go, to the depths of hell. In such abyss, nothingness shall pass. And there, you find me. When you close your eyes, I shall manifest in front, not behind. Hide no more. In nothingness lies peace. Know this. I offer your sacrifice, your death. Give me your virginity, I shall return my seed. This offering, this exchange, done in sanctum for centuries, will allow you to end your suffering. And so, let us chant, sisters and brother:

"*In sanctum e tenebris inferni, igne sacrificii unctus. Lux tenebris.*"

Everyone around me repeats, "*Lux tenebris. Lux tenebris. Lux tenebris.*"

"Here we all gather to partake in semen and…"

Okay, *semen*? I mean, *WTF*, right?

I'm totally spooked with all this weird old language shit. I never liked Professor Reardon, and now that he's gone from being a quiet, dull man to this freak, I feel serious heebie-jeebies every time he passes behind me. Then I have my fears confirmed after looking into his hungry old-man pervert eyes. It's like he wants to have sex with me, and that makes me want to throw up.

I jump as one of the witches circling me touches my shoulder. But it's Maddie. She's looking back at me with an encouraging smile. The bitch knows me too well. She knows I'm about to bolt.

"Lux tenebris."

After a few more rounds of "lux tenebris," they thankfully stop chanting, and they stop moving. Everyone turns and faces the house. They're all standing directly behind me, and a few have their hands on my white plastic chair.

A woman with a torch comes from the side of the house. I know it's Alondra. She's the only one who hasn't entered the circle yet. I'm relieved that it's her and I don't have to hear from this freak any longer. But then, my ease is shattered and my skin crawls as I look upon her. She's completely naked, with her long black hair flowing and her jade eyes glowing beside the flickering torch. She isn't even wearing a cloak. But there is no shame in her step. She sways her naked hips, her large breasts bobbing, as she treads straight over to me. Then she adds her torch to the fire and looks down upon me with the same smile she's always given me.

"A blessed day," she says, looking at me while addressing the coven. "A blessed day. We have a new initiate, someone I've waited to welcome since she first arrived in Hawthorne." She kneels on one knee, stark naked yet still comforting me with those eyes and that soothing smile. Then she says, "Don't be afraid, Cadence. Our ways seem odd to you now, but soon you will understand."

I can't say a thing.

"Do you still want to join?"

After the chanting, I'm not so sure. But then I look at Maddie. Her face is under the hood and she's nodding, trying to encourage me again. Then I turn to Bryce. They seem concerned—concerned for my welfare. They're all worried about me, and it gives me a warm feeling inside. I know that may seem corny to you, but it's a warm feeling in my chest. All these people care about me. And then I feel a little sad when I realize that these are my friends. Throughout all of Hawthorne, these are the people who are closest to me. This coven. This coven loves me. No matter how strange they are, they're my friends. And that is why I want to join.

"Yes," I say, and I mean it with all my heart.

"Glory be to the gods," Alondra says, looking up to the sky. Then she looks at Dr. Reardon. "Bathe your white witch with mandragora, Black Wizard."

Dr. Reardon takes an old wooden barrel, opens the lid, and carries it over to Alondra. I notice a bunch of similar barrels stacked near the pyre. He walks to Alondra, but she does not turn from my gaze. As she watches me, without moving or turning her eyes, Reardon pours the fluid from the barrel over her naked body. The reddish-brown liquid sticks to her long black hair and her breasts and back. She remains kneeling.

"Soon, Cadence, I will be in a trance," she says, staring

intently at me. "Then I will no longer guide you with reason, only feelings. And so I warn you. No matter what transpires, know that you are free. If you wish to leave, go to the door. Run. No matter what I or anyone else in the coven says, this is my wish. It is my wish, and always has been, that you do what your heart tells you to do. Do you understand?"

The liquid is dripping from her hair to her cheeks and chin, but her face is serious and intense. I nod, but my body shakes a little.

"The herbs we offer you will change your perception. If you partake in the herbs ..." She pauses for a moment and signals to Mira to bring over a flask. Then she lifts it over my head and murmurs something under her breath, some sort of incantation. "If you partake in this drink, you will be bound to us and us to you. You will feel great joy. But you will also lose all reason. Do you understand?"

I nod again.

"Even now..." She closes her eyes in rapture. "I can feel the mandrake root inside me. Mandrake root, or mandragora, is a hallucinogen, Cadence. It is...powerful. It is said that when you pull mandragora from the ground, the herb screams. It has that great a power. The mandrake ..." She pauses for a moment, and one of the other witches helps her up. Alondra motions for her to return to her position in the circle. She opens her eyes, a little too wide, and then continues. "The mandrake is absorbed through the skin, Cadence. That is one reason, among many, that we witches hold ceremonies naked. Do you understand?" It's like she's giving a lecture again, only this time my professor is naked and drenched in a potion.

"Yes," I say, a little too sheepishly, I think.

"Cadence Hawthorne," Alondra says, taking a deep breath and raising her glass flask. The fluid in the flask is reddish-brown, just like the fluid that was spilled on her. "Do you wish to join our coven?" Alondra looks down, her eyes wide. I can tell she's fighting to control herself. Her hands and lips are twitching.

"Yes," I say.

"Take this flask." Alondra closes her eyes again and hands me the glass flask. "Take it to your lips. Sip slowly. But know— our secrets must remain in the circle. If you ever unveil our secrets, so you will be cursed and cast out from us forever. Do you understand?"

I simply nod.

"*Lux alba*," she says.

Everyone in the coven repeats, "*Lux alba. Lux alba.*" They say it again and again, some even whispering it to themselves. Everyone repeats the incantation, except Reardon.

I look down at the reddish-brown elixir and, under the flickering fire, the fluid looks like blood. Bryce, Maddie, and the others nod encouragingly.

I sip. It's pungent and sharp. It's like the strongest alcohol, burning my mouth. It tastes like poison. I gag and spit some of it from my mouth. The act makes many of the other witches shout something while looking up to the sky.

Alondra touches my shoulder. "Drink it, Cadence. Drink all of it. Don't be afraid. It's diluted with wormwood and charcoal, but you must drink the entire flask."

I look at her like she's crazy. Then, judging from those jade eyes and that wet, dripping face, I think she may very well be insane. But the flask is already half-drunk, so I empty the rest into my mouth.

"Blessed are you, under the stars of the night sky, and in the cradle of Mother Earth!" cries Alondra, looking up with crazed eyes. She frightens me with her outburst, and I lean back in the white plastic chair. Then she makes it worse by looking down upon me with wild eyes. "Welcome! Here ye shall be known as Windstorm, for you are born anew upon the wind and rain. I am the High Priestess. As long as I shall lead, you shall follow. And when I depart, you shall carry on my order."

Everyone starts chanting the word *windstorm*.

"Turn toward the fire, Windstorm," Alondra says.

I face the fire now. Everyone does. But they're all looking at me.

Alondra turns to Mira. "Bring her the book."

Mira walks slowly over. She pulls off her hood and places a hand on my shoulder, smiling her stupid, geeky, uncomfortable grin. Then she hands me the book. "This is your Book of Shadows, Cadence," Mira says. "You will use this to record your spells. Keep it hidden. In time, as you advance in your wizardry, you may one day understand the secrets known by the High Priestess and the Eternal Wizard themselves."

I look down at the book and flip through the pages. It's just a simple diary. I even see a small price tag on the back.

"Welcome," Mira says and hugs me tightly.

Then the others come. Tammy. Hannah. Maddie and Bryce. Each of them hugs me as they circle around me.

"I'm Mandy," says a short blonde girl. "Welcome."

"I'm Frida," says another. "Welcome."

"Natasha. Welcome."

"Marilyn. Call me Mary. Welcome, Cadence. I'm so happy for you."

And that's all of them. The whole coven hugs me. Then Bryce walks over and takes my hand. He guides me slowly around the pyre. Everyone follows in single file.

"Follow me," Bryce says. "Try to match our rhythm and movement."

I nod and walk slowly behind him.

The music becomes heavier. I seem to see it, not just hear it. At first it was like birds chirping in the trees, but it changes its tempo and pounds into my whole body. I see it as color and flashes of light: red, blue, green, and white. The sounds light the grass of Alondra's backyard.

But there never was any music. Was there?

Alondra is no longer conscious. I catch a glimpse of her eyes, and she's completely lost in a trance, bobbing up and down. As she snaps her head back, showing the whites of her eyes, she appears more like an animal than a woman.

"Disrobe!" she commands.

Everyone begins taking their clothes off. In the recesses of my mind, this was the part I remember being most afraid of. This, and the knife. I watch as they remove their cloaks and cast them aside as they dance beside the pyre. They cast off their shoes. They pull their dresses over their heads. They came prepared, not wearing anything underneath. They're naked, bobbing and weaving, up and down, around the great fire pit. I remove my cloak and cast it aside with them, but I stop at my clothes.

Bryce stands in front of me as he pulls his shirt over his head and then pulls down his pants and underwear. He too dances naked beside the fire.

I'm aroused by him. I remember feeling this way in the bath with the incubus spell. I am so attracted to this guy—his strong back muscles, his tight ass. In another place, this would be a dream for me. And yet, at this ceremony and rite, it seems wrong to look upon him sexually. But I do. I'm very aroused by his physique, and I can't stop glancing at his ass under the flickering flames.

I touch his shoulders. He doesn't stop dancing, but I walk behind him, feeling from his shoulders down to his back and back up again. He lets me.

Dr. Reardon steps out of the circle. As each naked body passes him, he splashes it with the fluid from the barrels. Each member of the circle shakes the fluid from their hair as if they're throwing off water from a pool. Many laugh and giggle.

Some drops of the fluid from Bryce and the girl behind me, Frida, touch me. But I'm still fully clothed.

That's when it happens.

That's when I rise.

I feel like all the weight is being lifted from me, and my body rises into the air. The circle moves like a train, rising and falling on invisible tracks, up and down, around the flames. Alondra turns and her face is strangely altered. Her green eyes have enlarged and are now permanently fixed orbs like the eyes of an owl, her nose has extended into a beak, and her ears are pointed back along her flowing black hair. She laughs and gestures for us to follow.

We leave the flames and rise higher. And with our ascent, the clouds clear. I look down, seeing Alondra's house from above. For the first time, I see her mansion perched on a hill, and all the trees surrounding it seem to circle around it. The house is like the fire, directing the surrounding nature to follow her. We fly over a pond. I didn't know she had a pond. It's shadowed in the darkness.

I reach down to touch Bryce's buttocks, and I feel the crack of his ass. It arouses me uncontrollably as I run my finger along the plump tightness of his buttocks. Then I fondle him some more, running my palm along his tight abs. He's so muscular and my body tingles. He turns and I cradle him as we fly, as if we're spooning on a bed of air.

We fly over the dirt parking lot, and I can see my beat-up Honda and the rest of the witches' cars below. Alondra's sleek Jaguar is parked in the circular driveway in front of her mansion.

We pass into the hills and over the beautiful nearby lake. It's shadowed and everything is dark—except our bodies. The bodies of my companions seem to glow.

Bryce takes me in his arms as we fly together over campus. His hands glide along my body, and he presses his hand inside my sweater and under my bra. He fondles my breasts and then enters my mouth with his tongue. I close my eyes and feel only the rushing wind of air passing by us.

I look down and spot his classroom. I point. He nods with a smile. Again, I've never seen it from above, and it looks so lovely with the paths lit in the dark quad below.

We suddenly descend. We land softly on a plateau and I recognize it—it's the grassy plateau I found on my run in the center of Hawthorne. We circle over the ground again. The moon from the cloudless sky lights us from above.

I touch Bryce again, and I pull my sweater over my head, touching the lace of my bra.

Bryce looks back.

"Leave it on," he says. Bryce stops moving, but it's strange. I still feel like I'm moving around in the smoke, but Bryce is standing beside me, holding my arms. "Cadence," he says, "leave it on."

I shake my head.

"No, Cadence. Leave it."

"I don't want to."

"You have to. Just keep it on, okay?"

"But *your* clothes are off."

"No, they're not. It's the mandrake."

I look down and his pants are on, but he's shirtless. I feel panic and sudden embarrassment. To my left is the fire, and we're back in Alondra's yard.

"You okay?" he asks, running his hand along my cheek with a smile.

No.

The music is throbbing in my head. It's becoming too loud. But then I remember that there never was any music.

I'm feeling sick. I walk from the circle and lean over the grass. Sweat—is it sweat or is it the mandrake? I'm not sure— drips from my forehead. The field sways as if I'm on a boat. I stumble and fall to my knees. Then I throw up all over the grass.

"You okay, Cadence?"

I look up, but there's no one there. Everyone is still circling the fire. And they seem to be blurring and popping in and out of my vision. They're moving so slow. I'm feeling dizzy again.

"Windstorm, return to the circle," the High Priestess demands, so I will myself to come back. It seems to take forever for my feet to return to me.

I look around and suddenly everyone has gone. All that is left is a smoking pyre of logs surrounded by a white chalk circle. The coven is gone. There is no music. There is no chanting. There are no witches. Everything is gone. Only silence. And the wind.

It starts to rain. Then it begins to pour. I look up as the rain comes down furiously from a cloudless sky.

It's cold, but it cleanses me. It showers over me and seems to wipe away any fear and worry. I stand in the rain, closing my eyes, enjoying the drops of water over my cheeks and eyelids. Then I remove my sweater. I yank it off, resolved to stand naked under the pelting drops. I take off my bra, pants, and underwear. I reach out my arms and stand naked under the water as it washes over me. And I feel a strange mix of peace and exhilaration I've never felt before.

"I Yatu Raven," says the coven.

I repeat the words as if I've known them all my life.

"I Yatu Raven."

Alondra, wearing a cloak over her drenched naked body, is kneeling beside me. She looks exhausted. Then she looks over me gently with concern. She reaches into her cloak and brings out her metal pentagram and a dagger.

"With this blade, Windstorm, I consummate our union. Will you join us together forever as one?"

I nod.

She smiles, takes my outstretched arm, and cuts it. The cut stings, but it only lasts a second. Then the sting bites into my arm and I scream. I feel people holding me from behind. She takes the flask that I drank the mandrake root from and drips my blood into it, filling it to the top. The crimson blood is now indistinguishable from what was mandrake. Then the pain in my arm fades. Alondra hands the flask to each of the witches as they stand in a circle around me. Each one drinks from my blood. Then she hands the flask to me.

"Drink it," Alondra says, touching the pentagram to my forehead. "Finish the flask, my child, my daughter, my sacrifice, and be reborn. Let your own energy fill you as it fills each of us, your family."

I obey and drink the contents of the flask. It's salty and sharp.

The field turns and twists around me. Trees seem like obstacles flying toward my vision. I close my eyes and swoon, feeling as if I am falling.

I open my eyes and see myself naked on a large slab of granite, my wrists and ankles tied and my body lying in the shape of an X.

"You are the sacrifice," says a voice. It's harsh and low. It sounds like Reardon's.

My heart is racing, but it's not out of fear. It's desire.

I see Bryce. He stands before me, naked, holding Alondra's dagger and looking down upon me, unsure.

"Welcome," he says.

"Oh, Bryce, have sex with me," I say. I have never desired anything more. "Please! Fuck me. I'm here for you. Please, fuck me! Take me now. Fuck me now, Bryce!"

"Shh." He kisses my forehead. "It's the mandrake." He shakes his head and drops the knife. "Welcome to the coven, Cadence."

I'm lying in someone else's bedroom. The sun is shining through a window, and I block the light with my hand. The bedroom is elegant with a mahogany dresser, a white canopy over the large bed, and a small nightstand. The window looks out on the dirt parking lot, and I can see my beat-up Honda in the distance. I'm lying in bed in a white nightgown with lace. I recognize it. It's the one Maddie made me try on at Victoria's Secret the day I went home with my father.

I jump as something touches the bed. It's a black cat. I reach to pet it, but it jumps down near the nightstand.

On the nightstand is a book. I recognize it as the one presented to me during the ceremony. It's the same size, but this one appears old. It's open, with a pen, and handwritten on the first page is one word: *BROOMSTICK.*

18

CROWLEY

So we're walking into the university coffee shop, and Maddie is saying we're truly sisters now. *Actual* sisters. Like family. She's giddy and giggly over the whole thing. I'm having this weird sense of déjà vu and berating her for not talking about what the hell happened the other night, because I can't for the life of me remember all of it. But she says she can't remember everything either. All I recall is waking up in Alondra's house, grabbing an English muffin and orange juice, and being driven home by her. No one else was at her house.

I had assumed joining their stupid cult would give me all the answers I needed. It hasn't. I feel more confused than ever. Little does Maddie know that she's the main reason I joined. Well...and maybe that boy. Was I inappropriate with him last night? Under some weird spell? God, did I have sex with him? Again!

"I'm so happy," Maddie repeats with a flash of a wry smile, which is just as annoying.

That's when she reaches out and nonchalantly grabs a small drink off the coffee shop counter. Of course we haven't ordered anything yet. Then she signals for us to get out, and get out *fast*.

"You look good, Cadence," she says, giggling, a little out of breath as we dash down a paved path. "I'm so happy you joined."

"But you don't remember anything?" I ask.

"No. I don't." She sips some of her drink. Then she gives it a funny look. "This is really gross." She shoves it into my hand. "You have it."

I shake my head.

"Here, try it," Maddie insists.

"Why do you do that?" I ask.

"Just try it." Maddie giggles again. "The mystery is fun."

I sigh and sip it. "It's...coffee. With cream."

"Tastes like shit," she says.

"Well, maybe you should order something next time. You can tell them what you want."

"Yeah," she says with a giggle. Then Maddie hugs me real close and giggles again as we walk together. She's been in a good mood all day, since we came back to the dorm.

"So...when do I get warts?" I ask.

We make our way down the cement path. Unlike last time Maddie stole a drink, the grassy hill is vacant. Pretty soon, it will be icy. It's cold and I clutch my arms tightly inside my white sweater.

"You see a wart on me, Kate?" Hardly. Maddie's one of the hottest girls on campus. I've become used to seeing boys ogling her. She's cuter than me, anyway.

"Warts?" I ask again. "Cauldrons? Broomsticks?"

That makes me think of the book. Now it's on my bookshelf, back at the dormitory, as if it's another textbook. It looks a hundred years old, and half of it is written in someone's lovely calligraphy. Maddie said my job is to finish it.

"No warts, Katie," my friend finally answers as we walk

under an ugly metal awning. She waves to an acquaintance named Bryan. Bryan's pretty cute.

I'm still in shock over last night. "Broomsticks, yeah. Remember flying? Did we fly?" I ask. I feel stupid again. Then I get mad. Why isn't she answering? Haven't I been initiated?

"Forget it, Cadence." She dumps the coffee into a trash can.

We open the double doors and, as usual, the lecture hall is packed. I can almost swear Alondra smiled at us as we walked in, although there are twenty aisles of students between us.

Alondra is wearing a sweater, gym pants, and glasses. There is such a contrast between her outfit and her witch clothes, or lack thereof, that I begin to doubt that the events of last night actually happened.

She's wearing plenty of eyeliner and lipstick, and her hair is tied in a bun. She looks pretty, almost alluring. If I were a boy I'd be too distracted by looking at her to pay attention.

"We're going to do things a little differently this morning," Alondra says through a microphone on her blouse.

Maddie and I grab seats along the long lecture desk in the fourth row.

"Open your book to page fifty-three."

I forgot my book. I look over Maddie's shoulder, and she pushes her book closer to me. There's a black-and-white picture depicting the beast: Satan. It's a classic image of a goat with a pentagram on his forehead. The goat has one hand up and the other down. He has horns and a tail, his head is hairy like an animal's, and he has breasts. And there are two snakes between his legs, of course—because Satan is a pervert, like all the witches in my coven.

"Many of you recognize this image," Alondra says, pacing along the stage. The lights dim and she presses a remote, projecting a very large image of the beast, now tinted red, on the screen above her. It's the same image as on page fifty-three of the textbook, but the dark red shade makes it look more menacing and evil. "The devil? Satan? Right?" Alondra says. "Who knows the origin? Where is the picture from?"

I raise my hand. Maddie tries to pull it down. Alondra looks over and smiles in encouragement. "Cadence?" Why I want to announce this in front of a hundred and fifty people is beyond me. But somehow, I want to.

"Baphomet," I say in a way-too-shy voice.

"Baphomet. Exactly right, Cadence." I love how she uses my name, and many students look jealous at the fact that she knows my name. "But do you know the origin?"

Now I might have the courage to call out a name, but there's no way I'm going to offer a monologue in front of all these students. NO WAY. So I squirm back into my plastic swivel chair and keep silent.

"Eliphas Levi's Sabbatic Goat," Alondra says. "Eliphas is thought to have adapted the tarot card of the devil to the goat that we now associate with the devil. This and this"—a picture of a red pentagram shines above Alondra—"are usually associated with the devil by the Christian church." Then the image of Baphomet, this time in black and white, is projected. "The origin is thought to be much earlier. Hundreds of years earlier. The inquisition of the Knights Templar involved false accusations of worshipping Satan. You are responsible for reading about the inquisition, the Templars' desecration of the cross, and the subsequent torture and death of the knights.

"Note the black and white moons. These represent the two elements of nature, light and dark. Baphomet here is a hermaphrodite. His presence represents good and evil, man and woman. Some believe that Baphomet was a mistranslation of the word Mahomet or Muhammad. Others believe the Knight Templars to have been Gnostics. Of course Aleister Crowley, the well-known English occultist, believed this image had great power in magic. Satanic? Evil?"

Everyone is silent. The whole auditorium is as quiet as

humanly possible with over a hundred and fifty students staring at my favorite history teacher with gaping mouths. Most students seem to adore her or be amused, but I can feel a negative tension about ready to burst. A few students have expressions of disgust.

"You will study the history," Alondra continues. "You will learn about this image, but more importantly, you will learn about yourselves. How does this image make you feel?" She points to the beast with an outstretched arm. "Does it make you uncomfortable?" *Yes.* "But is it possible, fellow students, that you have been told a lie? That perhaps, instead of magic or Satan, this is simply an image of idolatry? Like the worshipping of Baal by the Hebrews, condemned when Moses came down from the mount with the commandments?

"Well, I suppose even idolatry, worshipping other gods, is a sin in the Judeo-Christian world. But that could include any symbol from another religion, such as Buddha or Krishna. If I put up an image of this"—an image of a jade Buddha meditating is shown above her—"does it make you uncomfortable? Or ..." She presses on the remote again, and an image of a blue god with multiple arms among the clouds appears. "What about this one? Hmm? Do you feel at ease now?" She paces a little more, then turns her back on us and presses her remote again. The image of Baphomet is back up.

"And now back to this. Why does this bother you? Is it from years of Western Christian teachings? Does the goat here represent evil, an actual image of Satan that we so fear, or is it simply a goat, an idol, separate from the cross? Why does it stir up so much emotion in the twenty-first century? Your thoughts?"

Quite a lot of hands come up. She calls on one of them.

"It's the devil, Dr. Johansen," says a boy. "It's like putting up a picture of a vampire with blood. It's evil. Whether its historical source is evil or not...it's evil." The boy is a skinny young blond kid. I've never talked to him. He's kind of nerdy but seems nice enough. But he's very worked up at the moment.

"What makes it evil?" Alondra asks, more curious than challenging.

The kid doesn't say anything. Alondra points to another raised hand.

"I always see these things as the devil," says a boisterous girl named Claire. She's nice enough. I don't know her that well either. "The pentagram—"

"The pentagram is not always evil," Alondra interrupts, shaking her head. I'm suddenly remembering my private meeting with her. "If you turn it, it represents the five wounds of Christ."

"It's Satan, Dr. Johansen," the girl insists.

"Satan. The devil?" asks Alondra. Then she walks pensively with her head down. "Hmm. I posit there's quite a lot in this world we don't understand. And misunderstanding leads to fear. After all, it's the Buddha that teaches that ignorance is evil. Perhaps our ignorance drives our fear. Perhaps you fear this image because of a void in your knowledge."

I raise my hand. Maddie grabs it again and I tug it back up. I don't know what the hell's gotten into me, but it's like I want to save Alondra from the negative vibe in the lecture hall. I'm gonna say that it's just a stupid picture, that's all.

Alondra looks up and smiles again. "Yes, Madison."

Not her.

I watch my lovely friend turn pale. She shakes her head and mutters, "Huh?"

"What are your thoughts, Madison?"

No, me.

"Well, a lot of us are Christians, Dr. Johansen," Maddie says. "Some are taught in Sunday school to reject evil...to reject images like this."

Maddie is hardly defending Alondra. Alondra should have picked me.

"As schoolchildren," Alondra says, "you *should* hate representations of evil. But as adults, you should face them and try to understand them. Is this evil? Is it the devil? Satan?"

"Evil is evil," shouts another student. "The devil is the devil."

"Good," Alondra says with a nod. "I've gotten under your skin."

"I like it!" shouts another idiot.

The hall laughs.

"You will read the historical facts that are known about the above image and write an essay on it," says Alondra with a nod. "I want all of your honest opinions. Search within yourself. If evil is evil, as you just said, Monica, then tell me again. But read and incorporate facts into your essay. You have one week to write the essay—on Baphomet, the historical origins, and your thoughts on the subject. I want your honest opinion. Obviously, I will not judge your religious views on the matter. But I do want you to search within yourself."

"But you can't separate religion from it," says Monica.

"Then don't," Alondra says with a shrug. Then she switches off the image above her.

"But how are we supposed to be objective?" asks another.

Alondra just smiles. She's a master of getting our attention. That's why she always packs the lecture hall.

"And now for the more mundane," she says with a chuckle. The image above changes to a caricature of a man with a bird beak, goggles, and a long gown. That shocks us too, being hardly "mundane." "Turn your book to page sixty-five, and we'll start a discourse on the fourteenth-century Black Death. Soon you'll have to give me historical facts and thoughts about this too."

19

FRIDAY NIGHT

THE COVEN MEETS AT AROUND EIGHT O'CLOCK AT NIGHT. I prepare myself for another drug-filled hallucinogenic adventure but find instead an ordinary campfire experience, with the twelve of us sitting in a circle around the bonfire and just talking about the past week. In fact, the only thing particularly magical about the evening is a few introductory incantations spoken by Mira. And our clothes—we're all wearing long black robes with hoods, like ancient druids.

Mira, as creepy as always, stands up in a long velvet robe and throws colored smoke before the fire, saying things that aren't in English. I ask what she's saying, and Maddie tells me that it's a language Mira made up. She entered it in her Book of Spells. Then Tammy tells us about her new boyfriend. I feel Bryce's stare as she talks about this new student, who just arrived from Maine. I meet Bryce's eyes and he looks away, but he has a smirk on his face. And, of course, Maddie notices and nods at me with a gaping smile.

Then Alondra asks me about my Book of Spells, *Broomstick*, and how far along I am in writing it. I gulp nervously, hating to speak aloud, even to the small group in the coven, and tell her, feeling a little ashamed, that I haven't written anything yet. She surprises me with a nod and smile and asks if I read what was already written. I hesitantly shake my head. She raises an eyebrow at me and then moves on to Frida. Mira looks over and is seriously pissed at me. But before she can admonish me, Frida tells us about a sweater she's knitting. It's such a boring topic that I'm shocked at the interest everyone seems to have. Hannah's next, and she talks about her cat being sick.

I start looking around for a drink or something.

It's at this exact moment that Alondra makes me nervous again. She turns to me with her penetrating green eyes and says, "Windstorm, you're new to the coven. Tell us what you remember about your initiation."

Windstorm? I had forgotten that was my coven name.

I don't remember much of anything. Except everyone undressing. Was I undressed? I think so. And then flying.

"I remember seeing the school from above. I was flying like a bird."

She nods. "Do you remember what you felt in your chest? Do you recall an energy as you flew?"

"Uh...no."

"I flew with her," Bryce says. Then he looks at me with an encouraging smile. I suddenly remember holding his hands, soaring like a bird. But how could he possibly remember that? Was it not the drug, the mandrake root? "We flew twice over the school."

"Yeah, but not on a broomstick," I say.

"Do not joke about our sacred ceremony!" snaps Mira. "This isn't a joke, Cadence."

"I'm not trying to make fun of it. I'm just—"

"It's all right, Cadence," Alondra says. Then she turns to Mira. "Lighten up, Mira. You could learn from Cadence's sense of humor."

"Bullshit." Mira stands up. I'm surprised how angry she is. "Cadence should never have been let in. She doesn't believe."

"Sit down, Mira," Alondra says, cocking her head. "Stop it. She's a sister now."

"Fuck her, Alondra," says Mira.

Alondra stands up. "No, fuck you. Sit down," she snaps. I'm shocked by her reaction. Mira throws her hood off, shakes out her dark hair, and sits back down, folding her arms and glaring at me.

"Each of your sisters has no right to disrespect you, Windstorm," Alondra says to me, "but over the years since I started my coven, it's been common for it to take time for all of my sisters to get along. I trust you." Alondra's sharp eyes land on Mira. "And so will Mira."

"It's all right," I say.

"Since we're all pals, sister," Mira says, "why doesn't Dr. Reardon tell our new initiate about his views on religion? Then he can expound on his actions and how he helps the coven find true love."

"Really, Raven," Alondra says, shaking her head. "What are you doing?"

I learned from Maddie that Mira's coven name is Raven. And Maddie's name is Blackbird. The boys do not have coven names.

"I do not believe Windstorm will stay Windstorm, High Priestess," Mira replies. "I think she will desert us when she truly understands what we do and what happens in our ceremonies."

"What do you do?" I ask her.

Mira leans forward with a sly smile. "We sacrifice little children, drink blood, and fuck virgins."

"Get out, Raven!" shouts Alondra. "Enough of this."

"That's what the bitch thinks."

Maddie jumps up. "What is your problem, Mira?"

"I don't want Little Bo-Peep here. She's a Hawthorne. So what? Escoba's blood or not, High Priestess, she's still a goddamn Little Bo-Peep. And just because her mommy passed doesn't give her a ticket to our sacred club. The minute she gets over her mommy's death, she'll—"

"You bitch!" I shout, jumping up.

Alondra stands up. As she rises, she turns to Mira and I can swear there's a flicker of light in her eye. Maybe it's a reflection of the flames. I'm not sure. But then, under a cloudless sky, there's thunder. And Mira, of all people, looks at Alondra with sudden terror.

"Get out! Leave now, Raven!" cries Alondra.

Mira squints at me, but she rushes off into the house.

Alondra takes a deep breath and sits back down. Everyone else sits.

My heart is thumping hard in my chest. I want to fight Mira, I'm so mad. Maddie takes my hand and gently prompts me to sit back down.

"Raven's been through a lot, Windstorm," says Alondra.

"I don't understand," I reply. "I thought she wanted me to join?"

"That was what I asked her to say to you."

"Raven doesn't want anyone to join," Bryce says, looking over at me with a wink. "She's a witch—a real one."

"Anyway, Cadence," says Alondra, "you said you recall flying. Did you feel the chakra? The energy? The energy coursing through your chest and back?"

I look at her, confused.

"There are chakras within your body. The mandragora sometimes causes the chakras to become more focused. Not only might you feel as if you're flying, you can learn to control the energy along your spine, and great magic can come of it. This is why we share our experiences—so I can help you channel nature's energy.

You can take the power that is grounded below and let it rise and flow through you. This is the point of our meeting tonight. Just as I told you when you first came to my house, we study our energies. Part of our coven's purpose, besides caring for each other, is to try to understand magic and our place on Earth. When you harness these energies, you will find great power."

"Like you just did with the weather, High Priestess?" Tammy asks Alondra.

"I didn't do a thing, Tammy. I was upset. Nature did what it did. Not me."

But no one believes her. Everyone thinks the thunder is a divine example of our coven leader's power.

"What else, Windstorm?" asks Alondra. "What else do you recall from your initiation? Or what other questions do you have for me? All is open now. You are one of us. You can ask anything you wish."

I look over at Dr. Reardon. He's been rubbing the whiskers on his chin in thought, even during the fight with Raven. He always seems stoic, unemotional, and pensive. He never says anything. He just watches.

"Okay," I say. "What did Raven mean about you, Dr. Reardon?"

Dr. Reardon looks over at Alondra, and she nods as if to allow him to share his secrets. It's the first time I've seen Alondra exert her leadership over him. Apparently, he defers to her just like everyone else.

"I believe in Satanism, Windstorm. I believe in the devil and worship him."

Well, Mira was right. I develop butterflies in my stomach and feel sick. Maddie turns to me, concerned.

"Do you all believe this?" I ask, turning to Maddie. Maddie shakes her head. "Are you Satan worshippers?"

"We've already had this discussion when you first came to

my house, Cadence," Alondra answers. "You are an admitted atheist. Why should you fear a man who hates Jesus Christ?"

"Because he worships evil," I say. Dr. Reardon laughs. That doesn't make me feel any better. I turn to Alondra. "Is this why you mentioned this in class—because you worship the devil?"

"No, Cadence. I do not believe in Christianity; therefore, I hold no fear of someone who believes in an enemy of Christ."

"But Satan is evil."

"Not to Bill," Alondra says. "Is that not right, Bill?"

"In the Western world, Satan is evil." Dr. Reardon smiles at me. He's a socially awkward man, and his grin doesn't make me feel any better. "But I don't believe that, Windstorm. I worship the balance of nature."

"Dr. Reardon is the only one worshipping the devil in our coven," Alondra says. "And I let him. It's his right, just as any one of you has a right to worship anything you like. In fact, I believe that his left-hand energy balances mine. His dark magic and my white magic, my *lux alba* and his *lux tenebris*, create a very powerful magical combination. Just like Baphomet holds both the sun and the moon and represents a great dichotomy. As long as you follow the beliefs of the coven—that nature rules our lives—I allow our members to embrace other religious or cultist beliefs. In fact, I even allow Frida and Helen to continue their worship of the cross. But it is nature that rules the world. It is nature—the sun and the moon, the seasons, the stars—that ultimately rule us, Windstorm. We are animals, human animals, and when you accept this and discover the power that lies within, you will be a great witch. It is why we celebrate our nakedness in our rituals. It is why we do not eat meat until we sacrifice sacred lambs that we slaughter and eat together.

"We live in a world of plastic-wrapped foods and cold electronic devices. I consider it the height of hypocrisy when a Christian zealot argues with me about our beliefs when they happily live out their fake lives in a confused modern world. I will not force my beliefs or actions on anyone. I encourage you to eat vegetables and save consuming meat for the sacrifice. Just as I encourage you to remain celibate and only perform sexual acts during sacred ceremonies. If you follow this advice, your power will grow. But I do not force any of this on you. I do ask, however, that you allow for free thought and action from your sisters, our Great Wizard, and our Wizard Disciple."

There's a pause; everyone in the coven is silent and thoughtful. It's like they're all contemplating whether they're good witches. Not *good* as in heavenly, but *good* as in doing what the High Priestess is asking of them. Like only fucking during cult witch ceremonies.

Well, my thoughts are that I still don't trust them. In fact, she had my attention until she mentioned that celibacy and sex stuff. Maybe Mira's right. Maybe I am too skeptical of magic and the coven.

"Windstorm, Mira's doubt stems from knowing Bill's worship would disturb you," she continues, as if reading my mind. "She hoped it would drive you away from us. I hope, just as I said in class—as you mentioned—that being open about these fears will make you think. Make you stop fearing. That will make you stronger."

"I believe that worshipping Satan and the devil *is* evil, Alondra," I say.

I'm surprised at everyone's response to my statement. I turn to Maddie, but she just looks down pensively (and for her to be reflective about anything freaks me out a little). Then I look at Bryce and he looks down too. The rest of them avert their eyes. Reardon is glaring at me. It's almost as if I made a racist statement. Apparently, being a part of the coven trumps everything else. In fact, I think that if I express my distaste for Dr. Reardon's beliefs again, I'll be more of an outcast than Mira.

Alondra looks at me and smiles gently. "Let us hold hands,"

she says. Everyone does, gathered around the fire. "We have had two disturbances trying to disrupt our love tonight"—*Two? Am I one of them?*—"but our love is strong. The chain cannot be broken. We shall rejoice in our time together for the rest of the evening and stop dwelling on our differences."

And that's it.

My friends Maddie and Bryce stop looking down and seem to glow as they grasp the hands of those beside them. My hand is placed in Maddie's on one side and Hannah's on the other.

Then we sit basking before the warm fire.

By ten o'clock, our meeting is done. I'm relieved that I'm not taking any more drugs, but I'm not surprised. I'm guessing that even if they'd had another mandrake-infested party, no one would have forced it on me.

The coven isn't about drugs. It's not about nakedness or sex. It's not about devil worshipping. I realize now it's about friendship and love...I think.

Speaking of love, Bryce invites me to watch a movie at his place. I feel like it's a bit forward, but I'm still relieved over my boring coven meeting. So I accept.

But I'm underdressed. Beneath the black cloak—which I dispense with, on Alondra's couch, on my way out the door—I'm wearing a long-sleeved red T-shirt and gray pants. Of course I'd never tell Bryce, but the gray pants are workout clothes.

He drives me, in a beat-up gray BMW, to his apartment, on the south side of Hawthorne University. It's a small apartment in a building with only five flats. Bryce opens the door for me, foolishly chivalrous but cute, walks me up a few stone steps, and opens the door.

Bryce's place is simple. It's one large room, with a kitchen on one end and the bedroom on the other. In the center is a small "living room" with a large-screen TV. He points to the couch. "Have a seat." Then he rummages through cabinets in the kitchen. His apartment smells like fish or chicken or something. I can't quite make it out, but I'm guessing it's yesterday's meal.

"Want something to drink?" he asks.

"Sure."

"What's your taste? I've got beer." He opens the refrigerator. "And...beer."

I chuckle. "Beer's fine."

"Great. I got that."

He opens two and hands me one. He sits beside me and turns on the TV. The set is already turned to his game system. I see a flash of some gun shooting game. Then he switches to a TV channel.

"What were you playing?"

"Hmm?"

"I saw a game. What do you play?"

Does it really matter? No, but I really don't know what to talk about. I'm lacking the courage I had at Alondra's, and I'm beginning to ask myself why I agreed to come to his house late at night.

"Nothing, Cadence." He turns on a random movie. A bunch of guys are running out of a bank, being chased by the police. I think it's a superhero movie I've seen. He just sits near me and watches.

I sip some beer.

"Feeling better?" he asks.

Huh?

"You feeling better?" he repeats. Then he sits up straighter on his very cushiony brown corduroy sofa. "I mean, you know, when Gilda lost her brother, it was like we all did. We all felt for her. Of course Gilda was already an initiate. But your mother, I mean—"

"Forget it, Bryce." I haven't thought of her. The coven has been a big distraction. And now I don't want to.

"Okay, sorry." He falls back on the couch and watches TV.

I laugh. He looks at me with a smile.

"Thanks, Bryce, but...yeah, it hurts."

He loses his smile. "I'm sorry—"

"Forget it, Bryce." And I drink some more beer. It's an IPA, a little too sharp for my taste. I look at the screen. Then I look back, and Bryce is staring at me with a grin. "What?"

"I can't forget it, Cadence. I care about you."

That is *super sweeeet.*

He's wearing a button-down navy-blue shirt and slacks, and his curly hair is well combed. How does he do it? The minute he took that ridiculous robe off at Alondra's, he looked all formal again. This guy spends way too much time looking good —not that I mind.

I usually don't trust guys like this. But he's got stubble along his chin. And that imperfection is so like him. And he has this wise-guy look, you know, like, *Well, we all know why I invited you to my house, right?* And that's almost annoying enough to convince me to leave. But he's so sweet about it. And I feel safe with him. I like him. I really do.

"I'm fine," I say after taking a deep breath. "What about you? Have you ever had anyone close to you pass away?"

"No." Then he drinks some beer.

I laugh.

"Sorry, I really haven't, Cadence. And I don't particularly want to. But I told you, we're all affected by any loss in the coven."

I sigh again. Then I scoot up on his sinking cushions. "You know, I really wish you guys just stopped saying *coven.* It seems like you're just a bunch of people meeting together. Like a club. *Coven* sounds so weird."

"Okay. *Club,* then."

"Unless there's more to tell?"

"Nope." And he stares at the stupid movie on his screen,

stretches out his arms, and yawns. "Look, why don't you sleep here with me tonight?"

"Jesus, Bryce. I mean, really?" I ask, sitting up straight.

"What? I don't mean anything by it, Cadence," he snaps, looking defensive. Then he laughs. "I can take the couch, Katie. You can take the bed."

"In your room? In this one room, *alone?* No, thanks."

"Suit yourself." But then he cracks another stupid grin and I giggle.

He sits a little closer to me.

"What do you want to watch?" he asks.

Does it really matter? I don't think either of us cares as long as we're next to each other.

At some point, I fall asleep in his arms, and I stay there the whole night.

I wake up in the morning, still in his arms on the couch. I slowly lift his arm, and he moves listlessly, snoring a little. I grab my coat by the door, deciding to walk back to my dorm. His apartment is only a block away from the university.

It's cold. There isn't a cloud in the sky, and my phone reads 6:32 a.m. There's ice along the foliage, and it snowed last night. But it's a temperate winter. Spring will be here soon enough.

I'll go to the library and study today. I have a big anthropology test Monday. And anyway, I need to work on Alondra's essay, which is due next week. Maybe I'll throw in something about psycho witches who harbor Satan-worshipping wizards in animal-sacrificing school cults.

20

MIRA APOLOGIZES

I'M READING *BROOMSTICK* ON THE THIRD FLOOR OF THE COLLEGE library, at a table not far from where I had my first date with Mr. Handsome. I know I'm supposed to be reading about the Kung tribe in Western Africa, or maybe the Black Death, but my curiosity over Alondra's gift is overwhelming. Actually, I hadn't thought much of it until our Friday Sabbath. I felt guilty over not even having looked at the book over the past week.

The library is packed; finals are in two weeks. But I've stopped studying. I don't know what's gotten into me, but I just can't study or go to class anymore. It couldn't be happening at a worse time. So I'm going to have to do what I've never done before—cram. Or fail.

So why am I reading *Broomstick*?

There are no chapters. Actually, the content really has no organization. Passages of beautiful calligraphy are mixed with chicken scratch. The topics are as diffuse as the handwriting. For example, on page twenty-two there is a lovely and inspiring excerpt from a poem regarding sunflowers and childhood training wheels—whereas the next chapter is on studying human feces and how one's diet can be ascertained from the color, texture, and scent. And the chapter after that is even worse, discussing preparations for copulating during menstruation. By page thirty, the narrator is back to calligraphy, describing prisms and the separation of light into rainbows. The book is an eclectic mixed bag of any and every topic one could discuss about life. There is an odd charm to that. And there are charms and spells too. A lot of them. Many pages of notes are on spells, usually derived by mixing herbs and potions. There are love spells, energy incantations, and even poisons. Sometimes I find my ancient book inspiring; at other times it's disgusting.

After an hour or two, I search for a book on Wicca and read about that too. Wiccans, a group of modern-day witches who are good, warn that any harmful spell cast on another will come back to the practitioner in a way that's many times worse. It makes me think of Escoba and her fate. Then I wonder if my coven believes the same thing. Are we "good"?

So I search *Broomstick* for any such warning. There's none I can find.

Maybe we're bad? Well, some of us are.

So I'm thinking about this, procrastinating on my real studies while staring at a browned, frayed page—at around page one hundred and seventy—when a shadow runs over the blank page. I look up and it's Mira.

"Hi, Cadence," she says with a wave. She's wearing all-black makeup and has her long black hair slicked back.

"Hi, Mira."

"Whatcha reading?" she asks, but her smile gives away any doubt that she already knows.

"Nothing. Just studying."

Mira puts her hand on my arm. It's very pale and feels cold. "Sorry," she says and forces a smile.

"Did Alondra make you say that?"

"Smart girl, aren't you?"

"If Alondra sent you to apologize, forget it."

"Does it matter?" she asks and throws her ugly hair back. "Look, can I talk to you, Cadence?" She points at another chair.

I shrug and she sits down.

"I really am sorry, Cadence. I was acting like a total bitch. And, yeah, Alondra told me to apologize. She was really pissed. And she was right to be. But...I just don't think you're gonna be what Alondra wants you to be."

"Yeah? And what's that?"

"You're just too vanilla, Bo-Peep."

"Stop calling me that!"

"Sorry... I—"

"I accepted the coven whether you like it or not, Mira. So you'll have to accept me as your sister."

"I know," she says. But she looks disgusted by it. "Why do you think I'm apologizing?"

"Apology accepted."

She smiles. It's not sweet. It seems wicked. Then she squints and looks down at the book. "So, what're you reading?"

My Book of Shadows.

"Well, Cadence, do you know what you're supposed to do with it?"

"Read it and write some spells, I guess."

"You're not supposed to read it," Mira says. "You're supposed to experiment with your energies. You're supposed to write experiments, your spells, in the book. It's like a lab book, but for magic. You have to ignore the other writings... You might want to start with your experience with Bryce. Talk about what it was like fucking him."

"You're such a bitch, Mira!" I hiss. A few people turn in the quiet library.

Mira laughs.

"Just go away."

"Sorry," she says, trying to get a hold of herself. "I couldn't resist. But that's—"

"Just go. Alondra's apology is accepted. Now go."

"Well, I'm not really good with people," she says, looking down.

That's for sure.

"I really did want to welcome you to the coven. Not because of Alondra. I mean it, Cadence. I'm sorry I challenged you... And I'll stop saying 'Bo-Peep.' Will that make things better between us?"

"Maybe."

But she still has this annoying smirk on her face.

She gets up and looks like she's going to leave, but she turns back. Her grimace becomes even more mischievous. "I stopped by to give you a present." She reaches into her pocket and takes out a handwritten note. She puts it on the table near my book. Then she takes out a few hairs from her other pocket. "Here. It's"—she smiles that infernal smile again—"a way to get even with your boyfriend. It's a lock of his hair and a love incantation. You can make him materialize whenever and wherever you want. You can get back at him for what he did to you. Be his succubus. He'll be yours."

I throw the stuff back at her. "Go away, Mira."

"I'll save it for you at Alondra's." And she winks at me, picks up the lock of hair and note, and gives me the stupid smile again. "I think you'll take it back after you think of what I'm giving you. You'll find there are advantages to accepting your powers. And what better way than to cast a spell and fuck Bryce again?"

Then she blows me a kiss and walks away giggling.

Fucking witch.

21

LACEY'S AGAIN

I'm huffing and puffing, running as hard as I possibly can on the treadmill, raising the ramp and sweating so much that my eyes are blurring from stingy, salty perspiration. And I have the distinct feeling that a lot of people in the gym are watching my madness. I don't know why I've decided to make this the most intense workout of my life. My heart rate's tracking at 125 to 130, my legs are aching, my back and neck hurt, and I'm about ready to collapse, but I'm running really hard, staring at the foggy mist and trees outside the floor-to-ceiling windows of the gym. It's early, but the sun's out in the clear sky and the gym is already very busy. It's busier during exam time; a lot of other people on campus are letting off steam too. But I can bet you no one's exercising like me.

I'm listening to new age music from Constance Demby. There's the sound of a Japanese koto. It's not the most aggressive music, and it hardly fits my exercise routine, but somehow the tranquility of Ms. Demby's mesmerizing voice provides a nice balance.

I'm thinking of Bryce. I'm remembering flying with him over the school. If my body wasn't shaking from the masochistic torture of my workout from hell, I'd feel a shiver run down my spine.

Bryce told Alondra that we had flown together over the school. How the fuck did he know that? Wasn't it all a hallucination? Then I'm thinking of the last Witch Sabbath and wondering why they didn't tell me anything more about the coven. Had I not been initiated? *Broomstick* is more a diary than a book; it isn't very informative.

There are so many other questions. Why did Maddie come home looking as if she'd been assaulted? She was bruised and looking shaken. Maddie is the most carefree girl in the world, but something happened to her that night. She never told me what, even after my "initiation." And what about the candle? When I came back to my dorm after sleeping over at Bryce's house, it was lit again, and Maddie insisted she'd never lit the candle. And what of Alondra's new fascination with evil and the devil? Is that what I am now—a devil worshipper? My father's Catholic. Mom wasn't very religious, so we rarely went to church, but Dad does. He would never let me anywhere near Alondra if he knew about her.

What about Mom? Maybe all of this weirdness is a way to keep away from my feelings about her. Like this exercise.

I stop the treadmill and do my cool-down walk. I hang my head and lean forward on the rails, breathing heavily. Then I turn to the right and jump. There's a little boy sitting about ten feet from me, leaning against the glass wall. He startles me because he's so creepy. So icy. He "feels" cold. I don't know how else to describe him. And what's he doing here? Children aren't permitted in the gym.

He's a black child, wearing old-fashioned clothes: suspenders with a raggedy beige button-down shirt and baggy pants. He's maybe ten or eleven. His hands and shoes are muddy, and his black hair's curled but a little disheveled. His eyes, open wide, reflect the light in the gym, like a cat's eyes.

He's staring at me, looking scared.

I lean down on the rail again and wipe the sweat from my head. I'm wearing a pink sweatband, but it's not doing anything. I look to my left and there's an older guy—probably a professor—riding an exercise bike. Then I look back at the boy. He's gone.

I hop off the treadmill and head to a water fountain to fill my bottle.

That's when I nearly drop the bottle. I see the boy again. He's at the door on the other side of the gym. He looks so afraid, which spooks me more. I stare at him because, for a second, it seems like I can see right through him.

I wave. His eyes turn big and I watch him fade. As he fades, the glass exit door reveals a tree behind him in the mist.

Now I'm not only completely winded and exhausted but totally freaked out. I turn to the bench press and see a young man sweating and lifting a lot of weights.

"Did you see him?" I ask the stranger.

The man looks at me funny, finishes his lift, and says. "Huh?"

"A boy? Did you see a boy? A black boy?"

The stranger shakes his head.

"How about you?" I ask the old guy on the exercise bike. He just looks at me like I'm crazy.

I walk over to a nearby weight-lifting bench and sit down. I lower my head again, still breathing hard, feeling exhausted. Then I stuff my earbuds in my pocket.

The stranger puts his barbell down and sits up and turns to me. He has that jock I'm-gonna-hit-on-you-now look. I'm really not in the mood for that, so I look away.

"Kids aren't allowed in the gym," he says.

"Oh," I say, finally catching my breath. "I thought I saw a boy."

I did see a boy. No, I saw a ghost.

~

It's seven o'clock, and I'm on my second dinner date at Lacey's. I'd told Bryce how much I'd liked the place last time, so he brought me here again. I wish he had thought of somewhere different.

"You're so mysterious, Cadence," he says. I'm feeling déjà vu.

"Oh, *I'm mysterious*? What about you and your cult?"

But then we're interrupted by a waitress in a suit. "Is your steak all right?"

"Everything's fine," says Bryce.

But everything's not fine. I'm unnerved by the gym incident. And I'm upset that, even though I've joined the coven, I still feel like everybody's keeping things from me.

The waitress nods and walks off. I look around the dark restaurant. Each table has a single small candle, and many couples are holding hands or leaning in close to one another. I recognize my sociology professor in the flickering light. His wife has long gray hair. She's pretty—she was probably gorgeous when she was younger. It's cute how the older couple's staring into each other's eyes.

"The coven is not a cult," Bryce says, a little miffed, cutting into his steak. "We're family."

"Hmm, well, if we're family, it'd sure be nice if my family told me all their secrets. I've been initiated, but I still don't know what the hell's going on."

"What do you want to know?" He's very sincere and that's sweet.

He also looks really handsome tonight. He's wearing a red sweater and green shirt. It looks like Christmas, and only someone as hot as Bryce could make it look good. And jeans— blue jeans. I'm wearing a simple black dress.

It's time, I think. Since he asked, there is something I've been wondering about for a long time. I push my steak and utensils to the side. Then I look into his gorgeous blues and force myself to ignore them.

"I want to know what happened to my friend. Maddie's initiation was a lot different than mine. After hers, she came home looking like she'd been in a fight. Every time I confront her, she says she can't remember everything."

He's surprised by this. He was probably thinking I was curious about another random historical fact about witchcraft. "And what makes you think it was so different?" he asks.

"Just tell me what happened, Bryce."

He nods and pushes his food to the side. He becomes very serious, which makes me more nervous. Then he pauses for a moment. "Believe it or not, Cadence, your friend had exactly the same initiation rites as you."

I don't believe that. I don't believe that at all. "Bryce, Maddie is why I joined. I'm worried about her."

"Maddie isn't why you joined," he says with a smug look.

"Well, something happened to her that night. She had scratches all over. And her clothes were torn. Were you with her?"

"Yes. I saw everything." He hesitates.

That means he's known all along. Well, of course he has. But then...why hasn't he told me?

He looks around. The other tables are far enough away that if he speaks softly, neighbors won't hear. "Madison took mandrake too." He takes a deep breath. "Only she didn't have someone with her to watch her. She got intoxicated on the drug, something happened, and we lost her in the woods. When we found her, she had fallen in the brush. That's what all the scrapes on her skin were from."

"No," I say, shaking my head, "there's more. Tell me what happened."

But I'm not sure I want to know. I feel like I'd be relieved if Bryce came up with more extraneous facts to block the real truth. In my gut, I know exactly what happened.

I look down at the candle and it starts to bother me. It reminds me of my mother's candle, the one that keeps lighting by itself. Before it seemed so quaint in the restaurant. Now it's almost spooky. And it seems to be flickering more brightly. I'm getting anxious and upset.

Bryce shakes his head and drinks some white wine. It seems he has difficulty swallowing.

"What happened, Bryce?" I insist.

"Nothing."

"What happened?" I repeat.

He shakes his head. "I know you've been initiated, Cadence, but I'm not sure you're ready for this."

"Ready for what?"

I can feel the warmth in my cheeks. The more evasive he is, the more pissed I'm getting. And it's because I know he's finally about to tell me.

"Do you remember your fight with Mira in the circle? Do recall Dr. Reardon and his beliefs?"

"In Satan. Yes. How can I forget?"

"Well, unlike Alondra, Dr. Reardon can be savage."

"Bryce, what happened!" I exclaim, hitting the table.

A few people at nearby tables turn during my outburst. I'm a little louder than I intended. Bryce looks embarrassed. He puts his hand up to calm me down, but I'm ready to take my glass of wine and throw the contents in his face.

"Bill," Bryce says very quietly. He searches my eyes and says slowly, "Bill had sex with Madison, Cadence. Under the influence of mandrake. They had sex naked, on the hilltop overlooking the university. There was another rite up there. Sometimes we worship there instead of at Alondra's house."

I feel sick. Bryce puts his hand up again, but now there's no point. I've lost all reason.

"Why the secrets? Why didn't you guys just tell me! Why wait until now, when I've already joined!"

"Because it was done during a ceremony," he insists, almost in a whisper. "It's our rule. If something like this happens, and it has been known to happen before, it is forgotten. Everyone, including Madison, intends to forget the whole thing. It is our law, in the coven, to forget anything that happens under the influence of our sacred root. It...it's why I stopped you, Katie. You were undressing in front of me, pulling me to you. You don't remember?"

My eyes are probably bulging out of my sockets. I can't believe this.

But I can. I've known all along. I could tell that Maddie had been raped. That was why she seemed changed. Now I'm furious that my friends, my boyfriend, and my mentor have all concealed it from me. And even Maddie—she seems to have hidden it from herself.

But by Dr. Reardon? That stiff dull old gray-bearded perverted prick!

"You think by stopping me from having sex with you, you're some kind of hero!" I rage. I can't believe my own mouth. The whole restaurant is looking over. I'm furious.

Then the candle on the table explodes. Everyone looks over. Bryce smothers the fire with his napkin.

"Cadence, calm down," he says anxiously.

I stand and shout at him. "How could you! How could all of you? How could you keep this"—my voice is cracking and I'm about to cry—"from me? And...I...I joined? You're disgusting. All of you are so disgusting!"

"You don't understand, Cadence. Please. Sit down. This is why we didn't tell you." He touches my arm, but I yank it away. "Please sit down, Cadence. Please. Let me explain."

"You guys raped my friend and you want to explain it to me!"

I feel tears run from my eyes. Then Bryce, my hero, my Prince Charming, does what he always does. In the midst of humiliation, in front of the whole restaurant, this guy swallows his pride and looks at me with concern. But this time his empathetic kindness pushes me over the edge.

"Please, Cadence, let me explain," he says desperately.

"Forget you!" I shout. "Forget all of you."

I run toward the exit. Bryce touches my arm again, but somebody stops him from following me. I think it's my sociology professor.

I run out the exit.

"Cadence, let me at least take you home!" I hear in the parking lot.

I run across the street to a gas station and call for a cab.

22

OFFICE HOURS

WOULDN'T YOU KNOW IT, THE VERY NEXT DAY IS FRIDAY. AND IT'S on Friday morning that Alondra has office hours, devoting two hours to answering questions. So after spending a sleepless night wandering around the school like a madwoman, in the freezing cold, I head to her office. Of course my BFF has been sending me texts all night. She's worried sick about me. But I take a sick pleasure in making her worry. It feels like payback for keeping such an awful thing from her best friend.

Of course there's a line of students waiting for Alondra. Finals are in a few days.

I promptly walk to the front and hammer rudely on her door. My mentor, my favorite professor—who, at the moment, I want to inflict bodily harm on—sticks her head out the door. She's wearing thin spectacles, an elegant blouse, and slacks. She sees me and looks surprised.

"Cadence? What is it?"

"I need to talk."

"Cadence, there's a line—"

"I need to talk *now*."

She looks at the line, then looks back at me and gives an impatient sigh. "All right. Fine. Just a moment."

A boy—I know the guy, he's a burly football player named Tyler—comes out, giving me a grumpy look. The students in line are shouting objections at me in complete disbelief.

Alondra gestures for me to come in. I barge in and shut the door.

My teacher is leaning back, with her usual arrogance, in her leather swivel chair. She looks up at me inquisitively.

"What the fuck did you do to my best friend!" I shout. Alondra's eyes widen under her spectacles. "You could have told me before I was initiated. Now I'm initiated. I'm part of your sick sex cult. Now tell me what the hell you did to Maddie."

"Cadence, you need to keep your voice down," she says calmly.

"Why? So your little secret won't be out?" I yell, making sure the line of students hear me.

"Yes... Sit. Sit down and calm down... You look tired."

"I don't want to sit. I really don't want to do anything you ask of me."

"Sit down, Windstorm," she commands.

Oh, the audacity, using my mystic name. Is she trying to give me orders as if I'm some kind of cult slave?

"Answer me," I say, still standing.

"You already know the answer. You just don't want to hear it."

"So you raped Maddie?"

"I can't believe this," she says, removing her glasses and rubbing her eyes.

"You can't believe what?"

"Listen to me, Cadence," Alondra snaps. "You have the potential to be the leader of my coven. You have the power in your hands. You can do amazing things, but you don't believe.

You suspect us, but you don't trust your heart. You think I'm evil, but you—"

"You asked us to write an essay about Satan."

"So that you could search your heart about what evil is. Is Satan evil?"

"Yes!"

"Then write that. Write the essay and tell me Satan is evil. Don't you think I know that Satan is evil, Cadence? Don't you think I believe that Baphomet and the pentagram are evil? Of course I do. But you have to know evil to know good. The coven is not evil. Our family is based on love. Love for ourselves and love for nature. Jesus teaches love. Is that not the same? Why don't you trust me? Why don't you trust us?"

"Because your associate fucked my friend!"

"Keep your voice down!" Alondra says, jumping up. I've never seen her so angry. "I know you're under stress with your mother, but—"

"No, you don't. You have no idea what it's like to lose a mother."

"I've lost my mother, Cadence," Alondra says, sitting back down. "And my father. I've lost both my parents. I know well what it's like to lose a loved one. That is why I am so focused on magic and religion. I would do anything in my power to stop death. But I don't have the power. I know of no one who does. I once thought Mira might, but no one has such power. Not even you."

"I don't have any power."

"You're a Hawthorne, Cadence. You hold more power than any of us. But you don't believe. You believe in evil, the devil, and Satan, but you don't believe in yourself. A witch can never be whole without believing in herself. Neither can a human being."

Alondra leans back in the chair and puts her glasses back

on. Then she takes a book from a shelf. It's a Bible. She lays it before me on the desk.

"You think I can teach everything? Or you can read it from a book? Witches write a Book of Shadows as a book of discovery. You have yet to jot down a single word. You've experienced one of the spells with your boyfriend. You've experienced séances. And you've even seen ghosts. They're all real, Cadence. But you don't believe your own eyes. Well...at least read this book, then." She pushes the Bible closer to me. "If all you can do is read and not experience life, then at least read it. You think me and the coven evil? Would an evil, sinful witch hand you the Bible? Read it. Know it cover to cover for yourself. I have. Cadence, God gives you faculties with which to experience the world. Use them. But don't fear evil. Stare at it in the face." Then she recites the well-known prayer: "*As I walk through the shadow of death, I fear no evil.* Walk through it. Write down your fears. You will see evil in our coven. But the God who you don't even believe in asks you to walk through it. You won't even do that."

I sit down. As usual, she impresses me with her words. But I'm still furious.

"That was the point of the assignment," she continues. "Know yourself to be true and good, and then you can face darkness with the light of goodness that all religions aspire to."

"Bryce told me Maddie was raped." My teacher's eloquent words might calm me, but they can't sway the facts.

"I know," Alondra says quietly, looking down. "It was unfortunate. But it was consensual and under the influence of mandrake." She says it as if that makes everything all right. I can't believe it. And even with all her flowery words, she seems to be unsure of herself as she utters it.

"How could you?" I ask, having difficulty speaking. "How could you have let this happen?"

"The only thing stopping it from happening to you was

Bryce. Bryce stopped you. You were willing to have sex too. Mandrake is a powerful aphrodisiac."

"So you've raped other students before?"

"Stop it. Cadence, don't be stupid."

"Isn't that what you're saying? You've had sex with students while they were under the influence of a drug?"

And finally, as those words come from my mouth, I understand the coven's secrecy. And I know why they haven't told me everything up until now.

"I've had sex with people under mandragora." Her bright green eyes look right into mine, unapologetic. "If you consider that rape, Cadence, I'm sorry you view it that way. It was consensual."

I want to cry, but that would be weak. I'm too upset. "This coven disgusts me," I say, standing up. "I can't believe what you did to my friend. You act like it's nothing. I don't want to be a part of it. I want out now."

"This coven is Mother Nature. It is what you truly are as an animal. It is the sun, the moon, the harvest, and the stars. We are all animals. It is what you truly are as a human being."

"No, I'm not."

"You are. And as Escoba Hawthorne's direct descendant, you're more a part of our coven than any of us. I have spent a lifetime studying this. You *are* it."

"How dare you!" I hiss. "Is that it, Alondra? Did you recruit me because of my family?"

"What do you think, Cadence? Why else would I have the patience to deal with you?"

And that is the last straw. I jump up, throw the door open, and slam it shut.

"I'm done!" I cry to the students in line. "You go talk to the witch!"

They stare at me as I take off down the hallway in no direction in particular. For I have nowhere to go.

23

ALONE

I have never felt so alone before in my life. I can't return to my dorm because then I'll have to speak to my best friend. If I do that, I'll lose her. I know I'll yell and scream and only distance myself from her for good. I can't go to my other best friend, my "boyfriend," because I just screamed at him and humiliated him in a restaurant. I can't return home to my father because I'll think of my mother. I can't think of my mother because she's dead.

I'm alone.

I have no one.

Now I know why I worked out so hard at the gym.

So that's where I go. The gym. It's still open. It closes at ten, which is in half an hour.

But I don't want to be here either. So after I wander around the indoor swimming pool and weight room, I walk back outside into the gloomy night.

I walk a dirt path outside the school and into the woods. And the darkness only grows as I move away from the lights of the university. The woods are creepy at night. But I don't care anymore. I don't even care if I see that creepy kid. Hell, the creepy kid would be company.

So I'm walking alone through the woods in the pitch darkness, in the middle of the night, in a black dress and tennis shoes when my cell phone rings. It's Dad.

"Hello."

"Hi, squirt. How are you doing?"

I say nothing. Just silence on the line between me and my father.

"Hello? You there, Cadence?"

"Yes."

"You okay?"

"No. I'm leaving."

"Hmm? What do you mean?"

"Hawthorne University. I'm leaving." I start crying. It's finally the right moment to cry, you know. "I'm leaving."

"Why? What's the matter?" he asks.

"It's...it's really weird here. Everyone's so weird. I don't feel like I fit in. I want to go home."

There's a pause. Dad's thinking of what to say. I keep whimpering.

"You can come home anytime you like," he says, but he sounds really down.

"I'm sorry. I know how much—"

"Baby, I just want you to be all right," he says. "Can you tell me what's wrong?"

Then I lose it. I'm surrounded by trees and darkness—there's nothing out there. I can't even see the lights of the buildings any longer. I feel alone and afraid, even while speaking to my dad.

"Mom died," I say between sobs.

"I know," he says. But he sounds so fucking depressed about it.

"She's dead, Dad. And...if she were here, I would tell her."

"I'm sorry, baby."

"No... No, I'm sorry. It's hard enough on you. I should be there for you. I should—"

"Cadence, you're always trying to help everyone. Everyone but yourself."

I walk through bushes and trees and discover a reflective pool of water. It's our lake. A full moon is finally illuminating the clouds above and reflecting off the water, surrounded by the tall trees. It's strikingly beautiful.

"Are you still there, babe?" my father asks.

"Yes."

I stand over the dirt and moss beside the water and lean against a tree. I just sit there for a moment and collect my thoughts. My dad's still on the line. I like hearing him just breathing, but maybe I'm worrying him.

"I'm sorry, Dad. What...what did you want?"

"I didn't want anything. You called me."

I did?

I look out along the water; then I see something. It's on the other side of the lake. It's standing erect. A person. A short person. A child. I recognize the figure. It's the boy—that weird boy I saw this morning in the gym. This time he's standing still, just staring. His head is turned down, with his flickering eyes looking up at me. He's shaking, or shivering. He looks like he's being hunted.

Maverick. I hear the name whispered in the wind. Or perhaps it's in my mind. And the brown-skinned boy in dirty suspenders and baggy pants stares with his eyes wide open. He's terrified, and his fear is frightening me.

The child screams. But he doesn't move. I hear the boy's cry, but the apparition in front of me is just shaking and looking at me with a downturned head and frightened eyes.

"Daddy?" I ask. My hand shakes, trying to hold the phone. The boy is grabbed from behind by what looks like a black shadow. It's as if the blackness of the surrounding trees swallowed him.

"Dad?" I repeat in a shaken whisper.

"Yeah, squirt?"

Dad is tired. He sounds worn out, not only by Mom's death but by worrying about me. And it makes me mad. Did I call him? I don't remember calling him. But I shouldn't have. I shouldn't even be talking to him.

"I'll just go."

"You're scaring me, Cadence. What's the matter? I can...I can drive over now. What's wrong, babe?"

"Nothing, Dad." Then I cry. He comforts me on the phone, but I just cry. I fall down by the tree trunk and cry. Because I don't want to talk to my dad, but my dad is all I have at the moment.

Then I think of my mom. If she hadn't passed, I'd be crying with Mom, and she would be comforting me. But it's not Mom, it's my dad.

I touch the cold, wet ground under me and muddy my free hand. My dress is now filthy. I just plopped myself down in a puddle of mud. While holding my cell phone between my shoulder and ear, I swirl my fingers in the mud, touching pine needles and leaves. It's really weird, because I've never liked dirt, but somehow the touch of the ground is comforting, because I know it will remain still. It won't talk. It won't get upset. It just is, soft like clay between my fingers as I grip clumps of wet soil with my bare hands.

"Are you still there, baby?" asks Dad.

The earth, the sound of birds, the wind, and the leaves—it's all there and won't change, regardless of my emotions. I yearn to be like that. To forget my ghosts and become one with the never-changing Earth.

But I don't forget my ghosts. My mother. And the real ghost I just saw across the lake.

I look out over the lake and, thank God, there is no boy standing there anymore. I whimper a little. Then I turn toward the path from whence I came.

That's when I drop the phone in the mud. There, standing only a few feet from me, is the boy. He's pointing at me, and this time he doesn't look afraid; he looks angry. He's accusing me as if all of his anguish is my fault. I'm frozen. This time, I feel like a hunted animal—a rabbit or squirrel—frozen, not daring to move. I can still hear my dad on the line, in the slushy mud, but I don't dare avert my eyes. And the boy is staring at me.

Then, in my mind, he screams. And disappears.

My heart is racing. I'm feeling sick. I'm having difficulty catching my breath. I'm breathing so hard, but I just can't breathe.

"Cadence? Cadence, are you okay?"

I pick up my drenched cell phone, now caked in mud.

"Cadence!" my father yells.

"Yeah, Dad," I say, out of breath.

"Baby, what the hell is the matter?"

"Dad ..." I try to catch my breath. I rub my muddy hands along my sleeves, wiping off the grime. Then I grip them tightly, trying to control my panic. I'm still holding the phone.

"It's all right, Dad."

"No, it's not. What the hell's the matter?"

"Dad ... You told me once that we had great-great-grandparents that settled and built this town. That we were related to Gweneth and..."

"Maverick."

Maverick appears once more, this time standing right over me. He's crying. He doesn't frighten me. I pity him.

"Mother," Maverick says. "Don't let Abigail hurt us."

I drop the cell phone on the ground. I raise my hands and he falls into my arms.

"I won't let her hurt you," I say. "I won't ever let her hurt you, my boy. I promise." And I kiss him on the forehead. His skin is dirty and muddied too.

"Stop scaring me," he whispers in my ear. His breath is foul.

"There, there," I say. "There, there, Maverick."

"Bairn, bairn, Escoba," he says. "Bairn, bairn. Bairn. Bairn."

I've had enough. I'm comforting a ghost. What am I doing?

My chest seems to explode. I can't breathe. Maverick fades from my arms. I fall and all grows dark.

24

MAKING UP

"Where have you been!" Maddie demands as I walk in my dorm room.

She looks terrible. She threw on a white T-shirt and sweatpants. It's early in the morning. Maddie's been known to sleep in occasionally. But she hasn't been sleeping. She has bags under her eyes and looks exhausted.

I ignore her, like a bitch, and walk to our bed. I take off my tennis shoes, which once were white but are now very brown from all the needless wandering I've been doing over the past few days. Then, without changing out of my filthy dress, I lie down in bed. I start to cry.

Maddie is looking down at me. She's obviously been up all night, worried—probably a few nights.

But it's Madison. My best friend. She stops yelling and sits down at the edge of the bed. Then she rubs my back as I cry.

"Jesus, Katie, what happened to you?"

It takes more rubbing and sobbing before I have the nerve to look into the eyes of my friend. She has a warm smile.

How do I put it? Does she even know I'm angry *for her*? I don't know what I'm going to do if she acts like Alondra and implies that having sex with that demonic freak bastard Professor Reardon was nothing.

"I know...I know why you didn't tell me what happened to you."

"Know? Know what? What do you mean?" Maddie asks. She doesn't seem evasive. She really seems not to know what I'm talking about.

"Your initiation."

Oh, that.

Her hands shake as she lets go of me. I can tell she doesn't want to talk about it. And her countenance changes so quickly from concern to anger. Her next words surprise me.

"I can take care of myself, Cadence."

That pisses me off, but it's not as bad as I'd feared. I think I would have run out of the room if she'd said it was no big deal.

I sit up in bed. "Why did you let me join?" I ask, rubbing my eyes with a dirty arm. "Why, knowing the bad things that happened?"

She takes a deep breath. Tears are starting to fill her eyes too. Then she shakes her head. "Cadence, you don't understand. I ... I'm not even sure exactly what happened."

"You know what happened."

"But I wouldn't ever let it happen to you," she says, giving me a pained look and shaking her head. "You don't understand that we all support each other. Even when terrible things happen ... I let you join because I wanted you to join. I trust the coven. I knew you would be safe. Had Bryce not made sure, I would have. But I needed you so much. I love you, Katie. You're my best friend. I ... I know what happened was wrong, but that wasn't what bothered me. What bothered me after the initiation was that I couldn't talk to you anymore, confide in you—you, Kate. That's why I wanted you to join. You're my BFF ... I'm just relieved I can open up to you now." She scoots onto the bed and holds me, her forehead leaning against the back of my head.

"Friends?" she asks after some silence.

"Yeah," I say, but I turn away from her.

She laughs and I chuckle a little too.

I drift off to sleep. I'm so tired. But after a few minutes, or maybe even an hour—I don't know—Maddie says to me, "Cadence, please, don't talk about it ever again. Okay?"

I don't answer her.

25

DADDY

I wake up to a knock. It's dark in my room, and Maddie's gone. I'm still lying in my filthy clothes on my bed. There's a note from my roommate: "Went to eat, Katesy." I know she's in the dining commons. And she wants me to join her—if I'm awake enough. I'm not.

There are more knocks. I sluggishly turn, try to get up, then sink back in bed.

Is everything supposed to be better now? Maddie and I made up. But I still picture that little black boy staring at me. And now, in my mind, I'm wandering again through the thick mist, smelling the moisture in the air, the dirt, and the thick foliage of the wilderness surrounding Hawthorne University. I'm remembering walking around in the forest like a madwoman. I can't recall all of it. I was so distraught. I just kept making my way through the trees, not looking for a path in particular, just walking over the leaves and mud. And playing... playing in the mud like a toddler.

What the fuck is the matter with me? I was careful enough with my steps, avoiding twisting my ankle. At least I didn't get hurt. I recall the moon lighting the darkness enough to see about five feet in front of me. And after a while, I just moved through the brush with no destination. Like an animal. I remember a drizzle. But it felt warm. It was as warm as a sunny day.

I remember cupping my hands in murky water to drink. And I recall eating roots and sap from trees. I was an animal. I felt like I was drugged. Now...I'm scared. Because I wasn't drugged.

Never in my life had I given up, but last night I wanted to end everything. I wanted everything to be over. My life? I didn't care. I just wanted not to feel anymore. I wanted to feel numb. The wilderness gave this to me. And the weirdest thing about my mad break was the soothing feeling in the center of my body. I felt at ease. I even recall cutting my arm over a sharp twig and not feeling any pain. I looked down, but it was too dark. I felt the sticky trickle of blood, smeared it around, and tasted my arm, but I couldn't see the red. I felt nothing. No pain. Just curiosity. Curiosity about the metallic salty taste of my blood, mixed with the earthen taste of the caked mud-clay.

That was how I felt about everything. And it was good. No, it was wonderful. I recall walking, without direction, through the thick trees with my arms stretched out, as if I were in a dark cave, with only the shadows of the leaves of tall trees, under a white full moon and the clouds above. I even circled back to the lake a couple of times. The same place where I saw Maverick. Maybe if I saw the ghost again, it would snap me out of it. But the boy knew better. I probably looked more menacing in my madness than he did. He had asked me not to scare him. Because he wasn't the monster in the night—I was.

Someone knocks on the door again, this time really hard. BANG. BANG. BANG.

"Cadence," says a man's voice. Dad.

Shit. I look awful. Why didn't Maddie stop him!

I roll off the bed and nearly hit my head on the carpet. Then

I rise to my knees, running my hand through my hair. I pull out some leaves—gross. Not good. Then I push myself up. I turn on the lights. It's so bright that I'm squinting. I run to the mirror ...

"Cadence! Open the door. Madison told me you were here."

"I'm coming, Dad."

My eyes look straight into the mirror and, for a moment, I think I see someone else. How can I explain the figure I see in the mirror? My reflection is horrid. My mascara has run down my cheeks. My lipstick is half-faded. My cheeks are smudged with a thin brown film of dirt. Small leaves are snarled in my long curly black hair. There are cuts along my arms and dried blood on my lower legs.

And Maddie slept in my arms. Gee, she must really love me.

Well, there is no way, no way, I'm going to let my dad see me like this.

"What do you want, Dad?" I ask, trying to stall him.

"Will you open the door so we can talk?"

"Not now. I...I...need to shower." Yeah. Maybe a *few* showers.

"I just drove two hours, squirt. I need you to open the door. Open it now."

"I'm not dressed, Dad. I was going to run to the bathroom and shower. Can you come back in thirty minutes?"

"Open it now, Cadence."

"I can't. Just...just thirty minutes. We can meet in thirty minutes."

I can practically feel his anger. His caring is actually kind of cute.

"All right... I'll wait out here."

"Dad."

"Hmm?"

"Dad, the shower is across the hall. And Maddie's still washing the towels."

"Fine," he snaps. "Thirty minutes, babe. But I swear, I'm

going to stand by the exit to the dormitory. You don't know how worried I've been."

"'Kay. See you soon."

I spend the next few minutes pulling sticks, filth, and leaves out of my hair by the mirror. See, even though I know my dad will keep his word, I don't want my dorm mates to see me with this bird's nest on top of my head either. When I look passable as a human being, I open the door and run to the communal showers.

And people still stare. A lot of girls stare.

I think I smell. I clear out the shower pretty fast. The only girl left is a chubby girl with glasses, fixing her short hair beside the mirror. I know her. She's a nerdy, friendly girl named Veronica. She looks at me. Then she wrinkles her brow at the trail of muddy water meandering from my legs to the drain. "Hi, Cadence." She sounds confused.

"Hi."

I take a long shower—not too long because I know my dad was in such a state that he might run into the girls' shower and grab me if I don't meet him at the time I promised.

I run naked back to my room—see, I wasn't lying about Maddie not washing our towels.

Then I spend my remaining time fixing my hair and face. I throw on a short white skirt, tennis shoes, and a navy-blue blouse. It's a summer outfit. I don't know why, maybe it's intentional, but I'm not in the mood for gloomy winter clothes. When I'm done, I'm pretty impressed at my reflection in the mirror. I can look pretty good in a short amount of time. And it covers up the homeless-bum-whore look that I had when I woke up.

There's a knock at the door again. I straighten my skirt and open the door with the best smile I can manage.

"Cadence," he says. I've never seen him so worried. He

quickly scoops me up in his arms. But then he steps back. I think I still smell a little.

"Hi, Daddy."

"What the hell's going on?" He walks in the bedroom and looks at my muddy clothes, lying in a hamper by the door. They're caked in dirt. I can't believe I was wearing them.

"Everything's fine, Dad."

"No—no, it isn't." He shakes his head. "What happened? Where have you been? Why haven't you answered my calls? Madison's calls? Why—"

"Dad." My voice chokes up.

He stops. I'm sitting in bed, which I now realize is dirty from my muddy clothes, and I throw a hand up toward him, warning him not to say another word. After a long silence, I turn and see him leaning against the closed door, staring at me. I notice huge bags under his eyes. Sweet. He hasn't been sleeping either.

"Don't worry about me," I say.

"Are you serious?"

"I'm fine. You're the one with Mom—"

"Katie, I told you on the phone that you worry too much about others. Try thinking about yourself. I'm worried about *you*. You scared the hell out of me..." He runs his hand through his short black hair. "You were yelling at someone. You kept yelling *Maverick*. I didn't understand. You kept saying, 'I'm a maverick.' You kept repeating that. Your voice sounded changed. It was really weird. Why?"

I did? I don't remember yelling "Maverick." I remember seeing Maverick.

That's when I feel it. Deep in my chest, I feel a weight that draws me deep into the cushion of my bed. I feel really sick. Dizzy. I put my head in my hands and start bawling. But I'm not sad. I'm scared. I'm horrified because I realize that I really must be losing my mind. I mean really going crazy. I spent the last few days wandering through the dark, cold forest alone. Now my dad says I told him things I can't even remember.

He sits beside me and holds me. I weep even harder in his arms.

"What's the matter, baby?" he whispers in my ear. "Oh, Cadence."

"I'm scared. I'm so scared, Daddy. I don't know what's happening."

"It's okay… It's all right, sweetheart. Tell me. You can tell me… Are you taking drugs?"

Uh, just a lot of beer. And mandrake root—yeah, there's mandrake. Maybe sometimes nightshade… And. Shit, yeah, I guess I am.

So I do something I never do with my father. I lie to him. Or is it a lie? I don't even know. "No," I answer.

"Then what's the matter? If it's school, you can just leave. I can take you home."

I pull away from him, angry. "I don't want to go home!" I snap. "The last thing I want to do is go home and see Mom. You made the whole house a fucking memorial for her."

"Cadence!"

"It's true. I can't go there. I don't want to ever go back home, thinking of her day in and day out like you. I…I can't—"

"Fine, Cadence. Fine. Then…what do you want to do? You told me on the phone you wanted to go home. You can come home for Christmas break."

"I don't know. I just don't want to go home. But I can't be here either. Everybody's so weird. I don't have any friends except Maddie, and they took her. Even she's been changed by them. They're everywhere in the school. It's like evil, you know. It's totally fucked up here."

"Watch your language, Katie."

"Whatever." I take a deep breath.

"Who took her?"

"Look, I just can't go home, 'kay?"

"You were fine here last year with Madison. Can you tell me what's going on?"

"No." And I clam up. I'm not going to tell him anything.

"I got a call from the provost," he says after a long silence.

Shit.

"You failed every class except metaphysical history, whatever the hell that subject is," he says. "And that was considered incomplete. You didn't take a single final exam this week. I don't understand. You're a straight-A student. I can't even remember a time you got a C." Then he rubs the thin whiskers on his chin. "No, I do understand it, baby. It's Mom. You're always so strong that I didn't realize how much her death affected you."

I shrug and force a smile.

I don't want to tell him what's really going on. Would he believe it? That I've joined a satanic witch sex cult? My father is neither a prude nor a zealot, but I know he wouldn't be happy about Alondra's coven. And there's something about his expression that tells me he knows—it's like he knows I'm hiding things. Just as I always knew the coven was hiding things from me.

"So, what do you want to do, squirt?" he asks. "Maybe... maybe you could stay at Jane's house if you don't want to come home. Then you could leave school for a little bit. How would that sound? I've already spoken with the provost. He's okay with you taking a break. He even offered to forget the semester, considering that you're grieving. He's attributing everything to what's happened."

I shrug.

"Whatever you want, Cadence. I just don't want to see you like this."

I look down and stare at the red-and-brown carpet. I've always found the dormitory carpet so fluffy and ugly. Now it's a comforting escape from my father's worried look. "I think I need to see a counselor, Dad."

"Yeah? Well there's Father Dayton. Why don't you talk to him about Mom?"

Mom. He has no idea it's not Mom driving me insane. Am I insane? Well, normal people don't live like animals for days.

"No." I shake my head. "No, I need to see a shrink, Dad. Serious. At least the school counselor."

His frightened expression makes me feel worse. Then I look at the window. The light peeking through the sides of the red drapes has darkened. Night is falling.

"Can we go out to dinner, Dad?" I ask, really wanting to change the subject. And, actually, I'm really hungry.

"Sure."

"I love you, Dad."

"I love you more, sweetheart."

He holds me and I almost fall apart again, crying. But I don't. I just sit there, looking back down at the carpet with my dad still holding me in his arms.

We go to a buffet restaurant. We talk. It's mostly about Dad and how he's holding up back home. He tells me he has no inclination to move, despite how much I hate the house now. I eat lots of servings of everything and wash it down with Coke. I do my best not to show dad how much I'm starving, but he gives me a weird look after the fourth plate. Then I'm sorry to see him leave. He offers to stay with me at a hotel, but I refuse.

Maddie comes back to our dorm room and acts like her jubilant self. She's so convincing that my dad and I seem to forget all about my breakdown, my need to seek a psychiatrist, and my failing out of school. Then Dad gives me a long hug, runs his hand through my hair, and kisses me on the cheek. I adore him. Then he hugs Maddie and goes home.

I log the whole thing in my Book of Shadows, called *Broomstick.*

26

MIRA

SO A MONTH PASSES AND I DON'T LEAVE THE SCHOOL, I DON'T move out of the dorm, and I don't see a psychiatrist. I don't even give up on my studies. I work harder than ever. My classes were all fails, not only because I missed final exams, but because I didn't bother to attend any lectures over the last three weeks of the semester. I was too busy staring at ghosts or wandering around the school like a weirdo.

After I hang my head in shame—and add a little begging, mixed with some help from the provost because of my bereavement—my teachers are willing to give me a C if I retest and earn As on remedial tests. That means I'm studying harder than I've ever studied in my life, because I have to cover this semester *and* last semester at the same time. I know I can do it —except in Alondra's class. I don't ask her to remediate and, of course, I avoid Bryce like the plague (no incidental reference intended).

Right now, I'm in the dining commons, eating tacos. It's Taco Tuesday. I'm sitting with an old friend I met my freshman year. Her name's Catherine. We met in an English lit class because I walked up to her and said, "You know, my name's also Catherine, sort of." And wouldn't you know it, people call her Katie. Well, Katie is the most vanilla girl I've ever met. That is so refreshing. Her father's a preacher. But she's really nice.

I snicker inside as I crunch on a taco, imagining her expression if she visited Alondra's house during one of our ceremonies.

"Are you going to the dance?" Catherine asks.

What? Are we in high school again?

"There's a dance at the church," she explains. Catherine's an Asian girl, really cute with a big smile. I always liked her. Maddie can't stand her. "Oh, I forgot you don't go to my church."

"Yeah," I say, smiling back; then I sip some Coke from my straw.

On my right is *Wuthering Heights*, opened to page 132. I'm reading the novel for an English class. I'm glancing at it while she's speaking. Talk about multitasking.

"Well, I met a boy," Catherine says.

I'm reading about the Catherine who is the main character of *Wuthering Heights*, another nomenclature coincidence. So I'm completely ignoring the prissy Catherine across the table. Then I look up as I dip a chip in some beans and notice that my cute friend is staring at me. She looks a little upset. I think it's because I'm not listening to her.

"Huh?" I ask.

"I met a boy," Catherine says. "Kurt. He's really cute."

"Oh. Where? In class?"

"No. At church. You should come, Cadence. You should come to church with me."

"No, thanks." But I flash her a sweet smile. I'm trying to be nice. Honestly, I really like Catherine; it's just that I'm realizing I have to finish this novel and write an essay by eleven tomorrow morning to complete my English literature retest. I've never dealt with procrastination. The whole thing is new for me. I realize I don't even have time to talk to my friend.

But she looks hurt again.

"Sorry, Katie," I say. "I'm really busy with my studies."

"I know. But ..." Then she giggles. "He's really cute."

I sigh, close the book, and lean back in my plastic chair. "Tell me about him."

And can you guess who shows up and stands over me and my old friend? Mira. Mira with her black lipstick, her stupid superior smile, and her nasty penetrating eyes. She's looking at Catherine with disgust. I guess she can't recognize a girl who's innocent and pure.

"Is this seat taken?" Mira asks me. She puts a tray with a taco salad on the table beside Catherine. The table has four chairs. Catherine nods and scoots over. Mira completely ignores her and directs a sly grin at me.

"As a matter of fact, it is," I say.

Mira ignores me. "So, how are things?" she asks, holding a chip, turning her back on Catherine.

"I said the seat is taken, Mira," I say. "Maddie and one of her friends are coming to join us."

"Yeah, well," Mira says with a shrug, "I'm Maddie's friend."

Fucking bitch.

I look away from Mira and say to Catherine, "Kurt? Tell me about him."

"Well, he's really tall," Catherine says. She's giddy. "He's got a beard and he's like always smiling. I used to just look over at him on Sunday mornings during prayer. And we'd like"—Mira chuckles, and Catherine gives her a funny look—"meet each other's eyes. I know he likes me, Cadence. He's really nice."

"How cute," Mira comments. Then she eats more of her lettuce.

"This is Catherine, Mira," I say—mostly to get the bitch to finally recognize her existence.

"People call me Katie," Catherine says.

"How confusing," Mira says with a laugh. Then she lifts another chip, waving it in the air. "You know, *Katie*"—now she's talking to my friend—"I used to know a cute man in church too. His name was Jack. He was also tall with a beard."

"I'm sure Catherine doesn't want to know about your boyfriends, Mira."

"No, I do," Catherine says. "What about this Jack?"

"Well," Mira says, "see, Jack liked to drink. He used to drink so much that he'd sneak a couple of those small bottles—you know, the ones you can get at the gas station, pull out of your pants, and chug down. Vodka, bourbon, whatever."

Catherine giggles, and Mira waves her hand and winks like they're the best of friends.

"Of course," Mira continues, "he was only sixteen, but he had an older brother as a supplier... Well, Jack used to look over at me too. And I'd just kind of slip down my top a little, not enough to be noticed by others on the row, but enough for Jack to see. I'd dip down my top just enough to show my nipple. I used to laugh, 'cause the priest would look over in complete shock. Of course, I got Jack to notice. I mean, I might be big, but that has the added plus of giving me really big boobs. So as the priest is talking, I'm rubbing my cunt—"

"Shut up, Mira," I snap.

"She gets to tell her story, but I don't?" Mira asks, acting hurt.

"No one wants to hear your whore stories. Especially at church."

And this time, I was right. Catherine has her head in her hand, quietly scooping up some beans.

"Anyway," Mira adds. "I fucked him during confessional, Catherine. First, I sucked his dick real hard. Then I fucked him. He was the best fuck—"

"You would," I say, throwing my fork on my plate. "You're so cold, you'd have to be a whore in order to get any boy."

"Yeah, but Cadence, I didn't fuck the boy." Then Mira turns and winks at Catherine again. "I fucked the priest."

Catherine jumps up, disgusted. I do too.

"Where are you going?" Mira asks us.

"Tell Alondra she can talk to me herself!" I say. "I don't need her messenger."

"Who said Alondra sent me, Cadence?"

Catherine is already making a hasty exit from the dining hall. Mira sees her going too. "Sorry 'bout that," Mira says, snickering. "Some people just don't have a sense of humor."

"You're disgusting."

"Well, you're hanging out with Bo-Peeps," she says with a chuckle. "You asked me not to call you one, but if you're gonna hang with 'em, you might as well know what they are. That one's a closed-minded Barbie doll that thinks a date is a man and a woman slow dancing two feet apart."

"Catherine is one of the nicest girls I've ever known."

"Well," Mira says with a shrug and relaxes back into her plastic seat. "She's a sheep. A Little Bo-Peep, Cadence."

"What do you want?" I grudgingly sit back down.

"I want you to come back. Come back to us. *I* want this, not Alondra. Alondra's really pissed. She's tired of you. She couldn't care either way. And anyway, she's got other things to worry about at the moment."

"Well, I don't care for her anymore either."

"Right. But *I* want you back."

"Why? You asked me to leave."

Mira shrugs, twirling her chip around some salsa. Then she cracks the chip in her teeth and points at me, her finger covered in salsa. "You running away really fucked up the energy in our circle. Everyone, from your best friend to your boyfriend, is really down. It's not the same. I can't perform spells with everyone moping about. Even Alondra, who claims she doesn't care, is down about you. You need to come back to us. We're family."

Then she smiles and eats more salad. She's a pretty messy eater.

I look away from her. The flat-screen TV on the wall has a cartoon playing. I stare at it. I stare at anything but Goth Bitch. Then I think how amusing it is that doom-and-gloom girl is concerned with people in the coven being depressed.

"What'd you learn from your Wandering?" Mira asks. "Did you write it in your grimoire? Did you discover anything you can share with us?"

"What?"

"Your Book of Shadows. Did you write down your Wanderings? Your best friend told me you were in the forest for days."

I don't want to talk about it. I've tried to forget it. I've tried to bury my face in my books. In fact, it's because of that weird "Wandering" that I'm in this terrible predicament in school.

Then, thinking of books, I remember *Wuthering Heights*, so I move the book back where I can read it instead of listening to this witch.

"What was it like?"

"What, Mira?" I'm reading about Heathcliff.

"Your Wandering. Everybody has one after initiation. Usually it happens immediately after the trauma of intercourse and the loss of virginity. That's what happened to me. I wrote fifty pages after I was fucked. Dr. Reardon ceremonially fucked me too, and I kept trying to come to grips with it."

That's it. I grab my book and quickly make my way to the exit.

But she grabs my hand. "Wait, Cadence." Mira thinks she's being funny. The sick thing is she's also being completely truthful—probably about the priest story too.

"I already told the coven that I want to leave. Forget it, Mira."

"You're in way too deep, Cadence." She's holding my wrist tightly, actually hurting it. A couple of students look up from their tables.

"Let go of me!" I snap and yank my hand back.

I rush out of the Dining Commons and head straight to my dorm. It's not far, just two buildings down along a paved walkway.

It's humid outside—actually hot, even though it's around seven o'clock in the evening. It's early February and the hottest day we've had in a while. I look back and Mira is on my tail. I'm sure she intends to follow me wherever I go, so I reluctantly stop.

"Just leave me alone!" I yell.

Mira still has a big grin on her face and doesn't look deterred at all. In fact, she's a little spooky following me like this.

Then I see the real spook. The boy. The ghost in suspenders is standing still, in the shadow of one of the neighboring dormitories. It freaks me out to see a ghost staring at me. Then I shudder when I watch a student throw open a glass door and walk right through him.

I forget all about Mira, but when I turn, I see her behind me. She's staring at the boy too. There are ten to twenty students making their way to or from the dining hall. None of them see the specter. Only Mira and I do.

"Maverick," Mira mutters. For the first time, she isn't smiling. She seems afraid. Then her mouth and eyes open wide when the boy lets out an inhuman scream. No one turns; no one notices, except Mira and me. Then the boy vanishes.

"You saw him?" I ask Mira.

Mira nods slowly. But it doesn't seem like she's seen him before. Maybe it's the first ghost she's ever seen. I see the boy almost every day. But this is the first time he's yelled using his mouth. Usually I just hear it in the wind. I wish he hadn't. It reminded me of the scream from the animal sacrifice. I keep telling him not to scream.

Mira seems to forget what the chase was about. It's the perfect excuse for me to ditch her. I run across the lawn to the other building. I look back and, unfortunately, my pursuer is back to following me.

I open the glass door and head inside the dark hallway of my dorm. I hear the door close, then quickly open again. It stays locked, but it's not unusual for someone to let in a stranger. I'm pretty sure that's what just happened, and Mira's still following me.

I walk up the stairs, wave to an acquaintance of mine from last year's American history class, then rush into my hallway. It's even darker upstairs. I walk faster, remembering that Mira has never been to my room and probably won't know where to knock. But Mira's in better shape than I would have guessed, and she's huffing and puffing behind me. I cock my head back and see her familiar long trailing black dress, which fits more like a druid's cloak. I literally can't ditch this girl.

I'm mad. I'm angry that this coven is ruining my life, ruining my grades, and embarrassing sweet friends like Catherine and that now I can't shake the High Priestess's crazy noxious assistant. So I turn around, more furious than ever, ready to shout at her. And I see Maverick. For the first time, the ghost is not facing me; he's facing Mira. When Mira sees him, she falls right on her butt in horror. Again, Maverick lets out a bloodcurdling scream; this time he's staring at Mira and pointing at her. The whole floor shakes. The lights flicker and two of the ceiling lights go out.

Then the ghost disappears.

I have my keys in my hand and am about to open the door

to my room, but I don't. As much as I hate Mira, she's not getting up. She looks terrified.

I sigh deeply and walk back to her. I reach out my hand and help her up.

"What's the matter?" I ask as I help her up. "Never seen a ghost?"

~

Mira stumbles into my dorm room. Maddie's lying on the top bunk, reading something. She jumps down as she sees me help Mira inside our room.

"What happened?" asks Maddie.

"She saw a ghost," I say.

Honestly, I'm feeling really happy about her suffering. I know it's wrong, but I can't help but be amused at our so-called paranormal expert being terrified of a ghost. I've been seeing Maverick every day, and I'm pretty used to him. It does surprise me that she saw him, though. No one has ever seen him when I've pointed him out.

We help Mira sit down by the desk near our window. The shades are open. The sun's down and many of the windows in Krunner Hall, the high-rise dormitory across the street, are already glowing in the bright yellow light.

Mira is drenched with sweat. She looks sick. Maddie hands her a bottle of water, but she pushes it away. Then Maddie sits beside me on the bottom bunk.

Mira looks up to me. Finally, the famous smugness I detest returns to her face.

"That's why I want you back," Mira says.

I roll my eyes.

"I couldn't shake her," I say to Maddie. "Bitch followed me to our room."

"Then you sent your little helper, didn't you, Cadence?" asks Mira. "Casper."

"Who?" asks Maddie.

"Apparently, our Little Bo-Peep is actually Wendy. You know, Wendy and her friendly ghost, Casper."

"Fuck you, Mira!" I snap. "When you feel less dizzy, go home."

"Shh." Maddie jumps up and puts an arm around her. I turn back to my window, brush my long hair back, and rest my head in my hands. Then I remember my studies. This fiasco is already costing me half an hour. I have to get back to *Wuthering Heights*. I need every second I can get.

"What're you gonna do?" asks Mira with a smile. Her color returns. "You gonna summon back your friend?"

"Mira saw your ghost?" Maddie is kneeling beside Mira, still trying to comfort her.

"Yep."

"She's been telling me about him for weeks," Maddie says to Mira as she annoyingly rubs the witch's back. "I keep telling her I don't see a thing."

"All true witches, when their emotion is high enough, can manifest magic," Mira says. "Apparently, Maddie, your friend's hatred of me is just enough to summon Maverick."

"I don't hate you," I say. But I know I'm saying it with a scowl and a look of disgust.

Mira just shrugs. Then she opens the bottle of water and drinks it. Her hand still shakes.

We're quiet for a moment. The excitement is waning, so I lie on my bed, pick up the paperback still in my hand, and start reading about Heathcliff again.

"I told you, Maddie, I need her back," the bitch finally says to my BFF. "She has great power. Alondra was right."

"Katie needs to work on her studies right now, Mira."

Yeah. So fuck off now, please.

They start laughing together over some secret séance shit they were involved in a few days ago. That takes me over the edge. I feel like they're keeping things from me again. So I whirl around and go crazy on Mira.

"You said Dr. Reardon had sex with you! Why'd you let him?"

"Cadence!" Maddie says.

Mira's staring at me in shock. She laughs nervously and says, "Careful, you might summon your ghost back."

"How could you remain in the coven after fucking him?"

"Cadence," Maddie says.

I look at my friend and my old sickness returns. I remember that Maddie "fucked him" too. God, I just want them both to leave me alone.

"Dr. Reardon has sex with me, Cadence, as part of our ceremony," Mira says, as if explaining the obvious. "In satanic witch rituals—"

"I don't want to hear it. Just leave me alone." And I turn to my friend. "You too. I...I need to study, Maddie."

"I know, Katie."

Then Mira drawls on, practically talking to herself. "The initiate is taken into the circle blindfolded, with her hands tied behind her with a rope. The coven then watches as the initiate copulates with the Great Wizard. In this case, Dr. Reardon. It's ritualistic—"

"It's disgusting! I don't—"

"Just calm down, Katie." Mira raises a hand. But the witch has a sly grin on her face. Then she cackles nervously. "I don't want Casper to come back."

"Get out!" I shout.

"Cadence," Maddie says again.

"What do you think, Cadence?" asks Mira. "You think I'm not ashamed? Why do you think I asked you to leave? Reardon's a sick fuck. I hate him."

"Then why do you want me back?"

"Let me finish," snaps Mira. She jumps up. "I hate him. But he's part of the coven. We have to allow him—"

"No, you don't."

"Yes, we do," says Maddie. I turn to my BFF, surprised. "Katie, I didn't want to talk to you about it, but I agree with Mira. I wasn't raped. I allowed what happened to happen."

"But why?" I ask my friend.

"We believe in nature," says Mira, now leaning against my desk. "Witches believe in eating and sleeping in the woods. That's why you had your Wandering. Your inner being, Cadence, is nature. That's who you are. You're wild. You're nature. And sex is also nature. But... Reardon's a major asshole. Sometimes I wonder if he's a part of the circle just to fuck virgins."

Maddie looks at Mira in irritation. My best friend is trying to convince me of something, and she doesn't seem to think Mira is helping. But what's she trying to say? That it's okay to let an old man have sex with us in the name of witchdom?

"Under mandragora," Mira further explains, "my joy was to be a part of nature. Cadence, that also involved sex. In fact, when you were deep under the influence, you asked Bryce to have sex with you too. I remember. Under normal circumstances, he would have. But we know Bryce. He's a Bo-Peep like you. And he knew you better than most of us. He knew that even with your vows, if he had taken you, he would have lost you."

So this sounds great to me and all, but I'm still picturing this old professor fucking my friend. I'm completely disgusted. And I still think it's rape under the influence of a drug.

The two girls know it. So they give up and look everywhere but at me.

"Let's get rid of him," I say.

Mira looks surprised, as if no one ever suggested this.

"He's the Great Wizard, Cadence," Maddie says.

"Then he needs to go."

"He's also Alondra's husband," Maddie adds.

Oh, God.

"I think that ghost is gonna be here any moment," Mira quips.

I'm going to be sick.

Then Mira chuckles nervously again.

Now I'm really sick. I feel dizzy and nauseous. So all I do is turn to the window and stare at the high-rise dormitory across the street. Then I say, "I need to read my book now. Please, please leave, guys."

Mira mutters, "Cadence, I really—"

"Stop it," interrupts Maddie. "Sure, Cadence. We're leaving."

And the two of them leave my dorm room.

Far across the parking lot—over a block away, barely visible—a translucent boy in suspenders stares at the ground. He has a grin on his face. I jump up and throw the drapes closed.

27

THE ESSAY

Another month passes. I stay home for spring break. Maddie gets really pissed over that, but all my energy is directed toward my books. I read and breathe history, English, and anthropology. I'm a history major. I never told you that, did I?

I actually manage to improve my grades. Then I complete all the extra work given to me by my professors during the break. I write three reports and two essays. I get very little sleep, and my eyes feel blurry and buggy.

I'm prepared to finally stop and rest for two days before the restart of the semester when I remember Alondra's class. I had an A at the start of her course; now I'm about to fail. I wonder if my final grade will be an F. Maybe Alondra will find satisfaction in doing that. Then I remember her essay on Satanism and evil. So before I'm done with everything, I decide to complete her class by finishing this one last assignment.

Dear Dr. Johansen,

You asked us to reach deeply within ourselves, within our souls, and write an essay on Satanism. You asked us what we thought of Baphomet, the pentagram, and the fallen angel. You asked us to discuss the Knights Templar. And to write about evil.

The Knights Templar urinated on the cross. That is the extent of my research on this topic. I won't dignify it by pursuing it further.

Jesus Christ died for our sins. His suffering was meant to reverse the fall of man. When Adam tasted the forbidden fruit with Eve, Adam was cast out of the Garden of Eden. The forbidden fruit could represent sex. Or it could represent Adam's awareness of sin.

The human condition causes suffering because we think. We are aware and we do bad things. We sin. The sins of our animal nature prevent us from seeing the glory of God. But Jesus was flagellated, tortured, and carried the cross, dying for those sins. And if you are Christian, you believe Jesus was God. So God was willing to suffer for us. For me. For you. There is nothing more beautiful than that.

This suffering, this willingness to kill oneself for another, is what I believe is good. Those that worship the taste of fruit and live simply to enjoy sin, caring nothing for anyone but themselves, are evil. Satan is evil. He is fallen. He represents the beast that offers fruits to blind us from the light. And so, if your assignment asks me to reach deep within my soul and tell you what I think of Satan—he is evil. So the disgust one feels when looking at Baphomet, the goat, and the pentagram is completely normal. Satan is an idol of evil. What is so confusing about that? Why are you asking me to write about it?

I posit that you, Dr. Johansen, obviously carry some hang-up about God and religion. You believe that Satan simply represents nature and its dichotomy of the sun and the moon? That witches and the like, dancing around a pyre, are merely worshipping humans as animals? You have so little faith in the human soul. Can we not transcend what lies in the forest for a better world? Can we not reach out to God? Will he not take our hand and help us out of our affliction?

Satan is evil. Witches and demons are evil. There are Wiccans who do not practice evil, but your viewpoint as a witch is evil. If you cannot distinguish good from evil, then you are evil. I feel bad for you.

Honestly, at first I was really excited to have enrolled in your class. But now I think your teachings are the worst in the university. You entice students into listening to your twisted theories about God and religion. It's too bad, because you are really a talented lecturer.

Hellfire, the devil, pain, torture, and ritualistic sex with virgins (yes, RITUALISTIC SEX) are evil.

You asked, that's my belief.
Sincerely,
Your disillusioned former student,
Cadence Hawthorne

There.

Fuck you, Alondra. I'll drop that in your lecture box tomorrow.

I've completed last semester and won't fail a single class—except, probably, Alondra's. I lean back in my bed and sleep for twelve hours straight.

28

BOYS

Winter is over and it's hot outside. I have fond memories of spending weekends over at Maddie's house last year in the summer on days like this, and today is no different. And that's precisely where Maddie and I are now: Maddie and her aunt Jane's house.

Aunt Jane has to be the coolest mom I've ever known. She's always cheery like Maddie. Well, she raised Maddie ever since Madison was a little girl.

Right now, I'm using the bathroom at their house and looking at the lewd white statute of Venus near the sink. That's making me think of that weird sex experience with Bryce. I still can't believe how real everything felt.

I miss him, I really do, but I know that if I speak to him, it will bring me back to Alondra. So I've been walking by him in school, completely ignoring him. I'm drawn to him, but I force myself to walk away.

I wash my hands and hear my friend bursting into laughter with her aunt.

Madison is reclining in an old super-cushioned recliner. Aunt Jane is leaning forward over an expensive white linen couch, covered with smudges and dirt. But that's Jane—there's nothing stopping this woman from being carefree. It also makes her house a bit of a pigsty.

"You're looking real good lately, Katie," says Jane as I walk in.

I'm wearing a white summer skirt. It's a scorcher outside, and I see a glass of lemonade with a lot of ice on the table between my friends. They're sipping from straws. Jane gestures for me to grab the free glass.

The lemonade is amazing. Jane knows just the right amount of sugar and ice to make it perfect.

"So, Kate," Jane says with a whimsical smile, "how's your love life?"

"Excuse me?" I ask with a giggle.

I sit down on the other side of the couch. We're near a sliding glass door, and Jane's beautiful outdoor garden is blooming like crazy. I sip more of the blissful lemonade looking outside.

"Boys?" Jane asks again.

Jane has very short gray hair and a long flowery dress. She reminds me of a 1960s hippie. She's got a strong, almost mannish chin and cheekbones but very pretty brown eyelashes and eyebrows. And she's always grinning.

"I don't have much time, with my books and all," I say.

"She's a bookworm," says Maddie.

"Well, don't forget to have fun," says Jane.

Maddie gives me an annoying wink.

Jane drinks some lemonade and looks thoughtfully at the glass for a moment. She says, "Weren't you going out with that boy? That...Bryce? I remember you meeting him for a date or something a few months ago."

No, I made love with him in your bathroom under a witch spell.

"He's like all men," I reply.

"Pricks, right?" asks Jane. We laugh.

"Yeah, my first husband," says Jane, still laughing, "was an accountant. He always wore shades and grabbed his cell phone on the pretense of doing business. Of course that never stopped him from taking me to bed with him."

"Really, Mom," says Maddie.

"Then my second was a bigger bastard." Jane raises a finger with a chuckle. "He was this burly guard from Jacksonville. He was really good in the sack. But he was more of a jerk than the accountant. And unlike the first, he didn't have any money. But he had something bigger in his pants."

"Ms. Taylor," I say, embarrassed. Maddie laughs at my expression.

"Well, I've had four, my dear," says Jane. "Four husbands, Cadence. And I wouldn't have had it any other way. They were all excellent in bed."

We all drink to that.

"My advice, Cadence, is when you find a sweet man, take him. Don't let him go. There are so many assholes in this world who will hurt you that if you find one who actually cares about you, never let him go."

"Sure."

"Well," Maddie says, "Cadence still likes Bryce."

"I don't."

"You do."

"I don't."

"You do, Katie."

"Whatever."

~

Of course I call him. I know what you're thinking: *how could you?* But despite all the witch stuff over the past few months, I really like Bryce. I do. And I miss him.

He was the person who turned me away from the cult in the first place. But he was also the one who got me to join.

Our conversation is short. He asks me out on a date by the second sentence. I laugh and say maybe we should talk a little longer. He says he'd rather not, for fear of making me run away again. I laugh again. I ask him if he's taking me to Lacey's. He says no. It's too risky. We'll just meet in the library.

29

OUR THIRD DATE

I'M WEARING A JAW-DROPPING LONG, TIGHT BLACK DRESS. I'VE GOT fake pearls on my ears. And my curly hair is perfectly straightened and combed back. But I spare the makeup. It's the library, after all.

Bryce's mauve button-down shirt and black pants might look odd on someone else. But Bryce is too hot to look odd.

We're studying. The library is pretty empty right after spring break. I'm reading about Theodore Roosevelt and the Rough Boys for my nineteenth-century American history class. He's correcting papers.

I look up and his wandering eyes meet mine. He smiles. "It's good to see you again, Cadence," he says.

"I've missed you, Bryce."

"Me too." He looks up with those gorgeous blues.

"I've been meaning to ask," I say, "did you grade my last essay in Alondra's class?"

"Are you referring to the two you didn't do, or the one that Alondra personally graded?"

I bite my lip. "Yeah, well, I never got to the other two."

"Or her last test. You were the best student in her class until the last couple of weeks."

"I know."

"Well, you had an A going into it, so she probably won't fail you."

Probably won't fail. But he didn't read my last essay. I think she'll fail me after that. I wonder if it will hurt my relationship with my metaphysical history teaching assistant. No, he'll probably be more relaxed when we're not doing the teacher-student thing.

Bryce says, "I understand." Then he goes back to grading. "Don't worry so much. You're always worrying, and that's you. It's been hard for you. But I'm sure—"

And that's when it happens. I recognize my handwriting on a paper that plops down on the table between us. I was so pissed when I wrote my final essay that I didn't even type it. I handwrote it. I look up at the person dropping it on the table and couldn't be more surprised. Alondra, wearing her usual prim and proper button-down and slacks, is looking down at me. She looks pissed. Everyone in the library is staring and pointing, because everyone at Hawthorne University knows Alondra. She's infamous. And it's not often that she shows up in the library. Like never.

"Hi, Bryce," Alondra says, staring down at me. She gives us a tight smile. "Would you mind if I have a word with our *former student*?"

"Sure," Bryce says. He looks as confused as everyone else. "We were...having a date."

It sounds completely ridiculous. It's like an excuse. Or some way to explain the fact that he's with me. It's weird.

"Aha," Alondra says.

"What makes you think I want to talk to you?" I ask rudely.

"Well, it's not often that I personally meet with one of my students to give them their final grade." Yeah, she's pissed.

"I'm leaving," Bryce says. Then he walks over and gives me a peck on the cheek. Normally, I would swoon with ecstasy, but not now. I'm staring at the witch's green eyes.

Alondra and Bryce trade places. Alondra sits down and takes a deep breath. I look around and people begin to get back to their business, not visibly pointing but still gazing over from time to time.

"Take a look at it." Alondra gestures at my nasty letter to her.

I look down. There's a big red mark at the top of the page: *A–*.

"I would have given you an *A*," Alondra says, "but I thought the hostility was unnecessary."

"Was it?" I snap back.

Alondra scoots back in the uncomfortable plastic chair. "Of course you will not get an *A* in the class. You will get a *C*. You did not complete your final exam. I would allow you to remediate and change the grade, but I have a suspicion you aren't interested in anything from me anymore and more than likely wouldn't show up."

"Correct."

Alondra nods, looks around, and leans forward. "This isn't the ideal place to tell you more secrets, Cadence, but I have a sinking suspicion that I won't have another chance. So please humor me."

I don't say anything.

"I'm sorry," she says. "Your essay discusses sin. You talk about the human condition, good and evil. Surely you understand that we are fallible. We all make mistakes. I, as your teacher, was someone you looked up to. And I failed you. But I've made major mistakes in my past. My husband was one of them."

"So I've heard."

"You don't understand," she says, shaking her head. "Don't

make the mistake of thinking that the problem was only him. I've done the same thing he's done—to boys. The ceremony sometimes works both ways."

"I really don't want to talk about this," I say.

"Right. Well, I came here to tell you that you were right about me. I suffer just like you, Cadence. Maybe more. And, unlike you, I'm way too far gone to be saved by any God."

"You know I'm not Christian, Alondra. You made sure about that when you schemed to add me to your cult when you first met me. I can't help you there."

"Well, you wrote the essay like a Christian."

Then something weird happens. She stops talking. And I don't dare say a word. A few students are still glancing over.

"I'm sorry I disappointed you, Cadence," she says.

Seriously? That's a fucking understatement.

"Now to the other matter," she says. "I didn't only come here to hand-deliver your grade. I also came because Mira told me about your visions. A witch, after initiation, can receive great power. I believe you are channeling energy, but it's moving in the wrong direction. I can help you. I can help channel it so that it no longer haunts you. So that you can control it."

"I don't want your help."

Alondra raises a hand. "I know. Think it over... You are still writing your grimoire, are you not?"

"How would you know that?"

"Natural witches are part telepathic, Cadence." Then she shrugs. "And it wouldn't be a hard guess. I wouldn't doubt you'd add entries to try to understand what's going on."

"Yeah? What's going on?"

"I think you can figure it out. You're channeling the ghost because of your family's heritage. Maverick is in your blood. According to the story, Abigail tortured Escoba and her child, Maverick, in revenge. Abigail so hurt Escoba and her son that it has left a mark, like a scar, in Hawthorne. I think you are tapping into this. Their pain has become your pain, and your mind has mixed it up with your own bereavement over your mother. And Maverick's ghost manifests to you as a boy because it was at that time that his psychic energy was at its strongest."

"How do you know Maverick is my great-great-grandfather?" I ask. I've always guessed, with my surname, that I was related to the Hawthornes. I've been remembering the Wandering and asking my father, confused, about our ancestry.

She doesn't answer me. Instead she pauses pensively for a moment. Then she adds, "Abigail went mad after murdering Escoba—so the tale goes. But we don't know if she murdered her. Maybe Escoba committed suicide from the stress Abigail had caused? But both were punished with a kind of madness. Both obviously had Wanderings of their own, just like you and me. But they never seemed to recover. I think *both* Abigail and Escoba were witches.

"The same madness could happen to others who aren't helped through their Book of Shadows... It is said that Abigail wandered through the forests around our campus, haunted by visions of Escoba's ghost, after Escoba died. Does all this sound familiar, Cadence?"

"What are you trying to say?"

"Nothing."

"Are you hinting that I'll go crazy unless I get rid of Maverick?"

"Well, it's gonna be hard for your sanity if you keep seeing visions of his ghost. Isn't it? I mean, Mira is pretty open to the paranormal, but she was severely shaken after seeing your spirit. She told me you were *used to* seeing him."

"I see him," I say, looking down.

But then I'm thinking Alondra is manipulating me. She's trying to get me back. And when I look up, she seems to guess my thoughts.

"I can help you, Cadence. Unlike Mira, I've seen ghosts and I've gotten rid of them. Ghosts thrive off energy. If you can't control your energy, you might start seeing them. It can get difficult."

"I don't want your help."

"You don't have a choice," Alondra snaps. People turn again. "Cadence," she says more quietly, "you're already too deeply into this."

And isn't that what Mira told me?

Now I am reminded of it. All the times Mira came to me, it was Alondra. Mira was her messenger. Probably the last time, too, even though Mira denied it. It's another secret that lowers my respect for her. I don't feel as if I am talking to a superior anymore; I feel as if I'm talking to someone like Mira.

"I don't want this," I say, shaking my head. Tears form in my eyes.

She surprises me by taking my hand. "Cadence, I'm sorry. I'm sorry our coven hurt you. I really am. I'm so sorry. But we knew we hurt Maddie. That was why Bryce and I made sure the same didn't happen to you. I've asked you to trust me. No longer do I come to you as a professor. I am here as the High Priestess of our coven. As your sister. I'm asking you to come back...to me. Please come back to me, Cadence."

I don't say anything. I put my arm up as if to push her away, as if I'm pushing away a demon. I shake my head and jump from my chair.

Alondra doesn't run after me. I don't look back, but I don't hear her.

I run for it.

As I make it quickly down the escalator, I see Bryce. He's near the library exit. He sees me and looks concerned.

I fall in his arms and weep. I don't care if anyone's watching. I cry. I feel so confused.

See, the thing is, I still like Alondra the Witch. I feel drawn to her. But I also hate her. I hate her for everything she's put me through. She's even admitted to being evil. Am I evil?

But I like her.

Bryce holds me and whispers into my ear, "Can I take you home?"

I nod.

We run out between the glass doors.

It's pouring outside even though it's eighty degrees. It's dark because of the fog, and a yellow glow radiates from the lights lining the sidewalk. As the water rushes down my long hair, it mixes with my tears. I'm still in Bryce's arms, crying. One hand is clutching me tightly while the other is hopelessly trying to shield me from the rain. Neither of us has an umbrella this time—there was barely a cloud in the sky before I came to the library. So we're rushing down the cement sidewalk to the parking lot. Even though Bryce grasps me tightly, he's letting me guide him. He seems willing to let me take him wherever I want. I don't know where he parked—I don't really care.

Then I trip and fall to the ground. I'm not sure if it was a crack in the pavement or if I'm just too distraught. It feels like my world is collapsing again. I thought I was done with her—with him. But I called Bryce. I brought him back. Why does Alondra surprise me so much? I should have known she would follow me.

Bryce helps me up. In the parking lot he points out his used gray BMW, parked only a handful of steps away. There aren't a lot of cars parked here—we're a long way from the next major exam. But I don't go to his car. He tries to guide me to his BMW, but I don't want to go.

I turn toward my dormitory and run down the grassy hill. Bryce takes my arm and follows me without saying anything.

Even the main drag of campus is empty tonight. I want to go home. Do I? No, not really. I don't know what I want to do. Or where I want to go.

So I do something weird. I walk off the path into the trees. And Bryce is still latched on to me, trying to comfort me. I hear him saying it's going to be okay. Is it? How? How can it be okay? But I just nod.

It doesn't take long to get lost in the woods. Bryce doesn't object, and he takes out his cell phone as a flashlight. I'm still crying.

I see Maverick. I see him on nearly every corner between the trees. Flashes of his glimmering eyes between the leaves, then through the branches. The tall trees surround me and comfort me. They're like Bryce's arms, embracing me. And for a moment, I forget that Bryce is even holding me.

There's no more path. We're walking through bushes. I'm wearing boots, but I think Bryce is wearing dress shoes. It's muddy. Sometimes I feel like I'm trudging through snow. Then I feel Bryce's arm. He's still holding me. Why? Why is he doing that?

I realize I don't need him. I have the forest. The forest is my comfort. I don't need anybody.

The moon shines through the clouds, lighting our way. Then we walk toward a clearing. The rain is pouring down now, drenching my long black hair and dress. Bryce has finally let go of me. He's standing in the shadows beside a tree—I can't see his expression. I'm guessing he thinks I'm mad. Am I?

I stretch out my arms and tilt my head back. The rain is now dripping straight into my mouth and over my chest. My mascara is running as the rain pelts my face, but I don't brush it off. I stretch, arching my back as I lean back. Then I laugh. I laugh and my laughter seems to spread throughout the field, as if echoing everywhere around the trees that circle the grass. The thick trunks of oak trees circle me. They hold me just like Bryce was holding me. I'm crying now, but I'm laughing too. And I recognize this place—it's the plateau I once ran to, the highest point around Hawthorne University.

It's a wild grassy knoll surrounded by tall trees. At the center is charred wood from past pyres built by my family of witches. I stand near the charred logs and stretch myself far back again, letting the water drip down my chest, stomach, and waist. My dress is now drenched.

Then I see the familiar brown-skinned boy in suspenders standing beside Escoba. It's the first time I see Escoba, but I recognize her immediately. She's wearing a bandana, a bright ornate necklace and a long dark dress. Her smile is welcoming.

Their ghosts are not frightening. Rather, the presence of my ancestors soothes me.

Then I see Bryce. He walks over cautiously. His short black hair is soaking wet. His formal button-down is as wet as a bathing suit. And the whole thing seems more like a dream than reality. Thunder strikes. Then lightning bursts forth, casting my shadow along the grass. Bryce seems scared. And I can finally see Maverick's face, and he looks frightened too. Frightened of what? Of me?

Bryce is beside me.

"Cadence, I'll take you home," he says to me. "We need to go home."

I shake my head. I run my hand through my hair, and it feels as wet as if I just left the shower. I suddenly feel stifled in my wet clothes.

Bryce has his hand stretched out to take me home. I grab it, and then I kiss it. Then I look into his eyes—those mesmerizing blue eyes. But he looks confused.

He tugs at me again, but I pull the other way. I just stand in the hot pouring rain. Then I pull him closer. I run my hand through his hair. Then I bring my lips to his. He gasps and shakes his head, but I refuse to let him go. I won't let him go.

"Cadence," he says, finally pulling away from me. But I bring him right back into a tight embrace. I unbutton his shirt. He stops me.

"You're wet," I say. "Take it off."

"It's raining. We have to go."

I yank on each button and one pops off his shirt. Then I pull the shirt off his back. His T-shirt is taken off even more quickly. I run my hand along the wet hairs of his chest as the rain falls. Then I grasp him close again, kissing him, moving my tongue into his mouth.

Next my dress goes over my head. He's now desperately tugging at my arm, telling me we have to leave. I shake my head. I am only in a black bra and matching panties. But the water is hot. He keeps pulling me to leave the field so we can go home. I keep laughing and pulling him closer.

The thunder cracks again. Then lightning illuminates my whole body. Bryce's eyes get large, looking at me, and that makes me hungrier.

I yank his pants down and he holds me tightly as we stand close together. Between kisses, he's still pleading to leave—I think. But the words coming from his mouth contradict his actions. I feel as if we're in a warm pool, the water crashing over our bodies. It's so soothing.

I take off my bra. My breasts fall, and I can feel the curves touching the hairs of his arms. Then I remove my panties. He leans his head against my forehead and runs his hand along those curves. The other hand is grasping the crack of my ass. My nipples are hard and he plays with them between two fingers.

He's naked now. I can feel his long cock against my naked hip.

I want it. I want it so badly. I want him to enter me.

I am a virgin. In high school, I was in a heated embrace like this in the back of a boy's car, but I never let him enter me. Now I want to be entered. I want to be fucked. I want the pouring rain to wash over me while Bryce fucks me. Just like when I was on mandrake. But now I want him to fuck me so hard that I forget about everything. I just want him to fuck me in the fields, under the moonlit trees, in the pouring rain—letting the water wash over me, washing away all my problems.

We fall to the grass, and we're sitting, naked, in an embrace. I'm laughing again. He's not. His eyes are very serious. He still looks frightened by my transformation and my desire. I straddle his lap. Then I run my hands over his hair and kiss him all over his face. I touch his hard cock. He has a condom. I don't know where it came from and when he got it on, but it's there. I guide him inside me. It hurts at first, but I don't care about pain. Soon it feels incredible and satisfies my hunger.

He's not asking to leave anymore. Oh no, he's not saying a damn thing. He's slowly bobbing my nude body up and down with his thick, strong arms. And it's careful and serene—it's Bryce. And as ravenous as I feel, his kindness and care drive me even more. But I'm too wild. I'm too untamed. I'm an animal in the woods. So I bounce up and down, riding him. It hurts again. I still don't care. Mud and water splash under his buttocks as the rain pours over us. I look down into his eyes. He looks as if he's worried he'll break me. It's so nice. So Bryce. It drives me even harder.

The lightning flashes again. I see a deer behind the trees. A flash of lightning lights up the animal's eyes. Is it a deer? A cougar? A wolf? The eyes shine white. The animal is staring at us and looks afraid.

Then I turn to my lover. He's staring at me too. I can see his eyes, flashing with the bursts of lightning. Bryce looks fearful too. But he mesmerizes me with his stare as we make love, naked, in the field. He caresses my breasts and runs his hands along my wet, dripping back. I move my hips up and down on his cock. He moans.

This is when I finally realize what we're doing. We're sitting together, entwined in each other's arms—naked and drenched —in the middle of a grassy knoll surrounded by oak trees—

fucking. It's as if nature is our coven. The trees surround us like witches around a pyre. They seem to move in a circle around us.

The pleasure is beyond any imagination. I am fucking Bryce. He's not fucking me. I am fucking him in the rain in the forest. Why? Was it a spell? Did Alondra bewitch me? Or is it my spell? Did I conjure this? I don't know. But I relish holding and touching him and wish it would never end.

The rain pours harder and I push into him harder. I feel him deep inside me. I have his hair entwined in my hands, and I'm pulling it as he pushes into me. Our lips meet again, and we lick and taste each other's tongues as I bob up and down on him, again and again.

Do I love this man? He cares about me—that much is certain. I am so alone, but Bryce is here and he cares about me.

And I'm not alone. I have the grass, the trees, the breeze, the forest. I have the Earth. And I realize that when I walked through the forest in my Wandering, I wasn't alone then either. I feel like I'll never be alone again.

"Oh, Cadence."

There's an earthen smell mixed with his cologne and my perfume. I smell mud. Then I hear our naked bodies slapping against the water and dirt below him. I slam down harder. And I can feel the wind, oddly cold, under the pummeling drops of hot water.

I finally feel him climax inside me. It makes me jerk over him in a rush of pleasure. I cry out, moaning. We roll on our sides in the wild grass, my heart racing and the two of us breathing heavily. He's still holding me tightly in his warm embrace.

And then...I cry.

I'm as surprised as he is. I don't know why I'm crying. I don't feel sad. I feel confused.

"Cadence, what's the matter? Why are you crying?"

"Because it's raining."

He clutches me more tightly. On one side, I feel the sticks and mud against my naked body; on the other, I feel Bryce. He wants to get up, but I pull him back down. I want him to cover me. To stay with me.

It is sin. It's a baptism of sex under pouring rain. My virginity has been taken in this way because of who I am, because of what I am. I am a witch.

30

LATTES

It's Tuesday morning at eight thirty. Maddie and I are drinking together in the university coffeehouse. I tell her I want to drink inside so she doesn't steal anything. I have my laptop on the table. I was reading a passage on the construction of the Panama Canal before Maddie arrived. Maddie doesn't have anything in her hands. She's a known procrastinator. I've never known her to study until the night before a test. Except when she was in Alondra's class.

She's looking out the window at the lawn. There's something really morose and depressing about her. It's very unlike her. It's hot today. The coffeehouse is busy. I'm wearing a white lace summer skirt. Maddie has on shorts and a T-shirt. I see her looking at three boys at a nearby table. They're not looking at her. She could probably attract any of them if she tried, but I think she told me she's back with Nick. Is that what the doom and gloom is about? Nick?

"So..." I pause. I've been preparing how I'm going to broach the subject. Now I feel stupid about the whole thing. Of course my best friend has known me long enough to know something's on my mind.

"Do tell," Maddie says with a smile and a sip of her cup of Joe.

I look around as if it's a big secret. Of course no one can hear. The coffeehouse is packed. We were lucky to grab this small table after another couple left.

I lean forward. "I had sex last night."

Maddie giggles. She finally brightens up. "*And ...*"

"What do you mean?" I ask.

"*And ...*"

"And what?"

"Yeah," Maddie says. "*And what?*"

"What do you mean?"

"Oh, Cadence." Maddie is still laughing. I lose my smile. I feel like she's making fun of me.

"It ..." I bite my upper lip and shrug. "It was my first time."

Maddie gives me a funny look for a second. She stops laughing.

"That is *sooo* sweet, Kate." She's suddenly very thoughtful. She sips from her paper cup and touches my arm. "Sorry. I forgot. It was Bryce, right?"

"Of course."

"He's so hot. I'm happy for you, Cadence." But she doesn't look happy for me. "Really. You two make a really great couple. And anyway you've been yapping about screwing him since last year. It's about time. I'm kind of tired of hearing it. Where... where did you do it? You weren't home last night."

"I know. I didn't want to wake you."

Then she looks out the window again as if we aren't even talking.

"What's wrong?" I ask.

"Hmm?" Maddie asks.

"What's up?"

I'm a little disappointed. I thought my friend would want to know all about last night.

"It's…" Maddie hesitates. "Shit, Cadence, I guess I can tell you, technically, 'cause you're part of the coven, but then again…you're kinda not. You have nothing to do with us anymore. You don't really want to."

"Right."

"But you did just have sex with Bryce."

"Is something wrong with Bryce?" I lean forward. She laughs at my expression.

"No. I meant, you don't want to be a part of our family, but you just got really close to one of us. Now it's not just me, girl, it's me and Bryce."

"Yeah, I saw Alondra too—last night."

"I know." Maddie sips her coffee again. "She said she talked to you."

"Where did you see her? Your Sabbath is Friday, not yesterday."

"She came by our dorm," Maddie says.

"The dorm?"

I drink some of my green tea latte. I love green tea lattes—I'm a bit addicted, actually. I'm regretting choosing something hot, though. Even though it's air conditioned in the building, it's still humid and hot. Today's gonna be another scorcher. And it might rain. Like last night. Pouring rain like last night… *Pouring rain over Bryce's yummy hard body. Why aren't we talking about that?*

"Yeah, she came by our dorm," continues Maddie. "She thought you'd be back home."

"Our room? Is she chasing me now, like Mira?"

"Well, technically, Katie, Alondra is no longer our professor. Since she's not teaching us, she can come by as a friend. But our neighbors thought it was pretty weird when she visited."

"What'd she want?"

Why are we talking about Alondra? I thought Maddie'd be all over my consummated relationship story.

"Alondra's kind of down, Cadence. Haven't you noticed?"

"She seemed more pissed than down."

"Yeah," Maddie says with a chuckle; then she stares outside again. "She's really pissed at you. But she understands, Cadence. She understands everything." Maddie looks right into my eyes but seems to hesitate. Then she takes my hand in hers. "Kate...I...really."

She stops, lets go of my hand, and throws her long hair back.

"What?" I ask.

She shakes her head. Then she drinks more coffee.

"What?"

Maddie takes a deep breath. "Think about this: I need to ask something of you. I've never needed something from you so badly. Really think about it. For me. You don't have to do it, but it would mean so much to me."

"What?"

"I need you to come to our session Friday night."

"No."

"I wouldn't ask you if it weren't important."

"No."

"You know, girl, I never asked you to join."

"You coaxed me to come to her house to see Bryce," I remind her.

She's no longer sad. She's mad. She's seriously upset with me. But I'm upset too. I can't believe she's asking this of me.

"Yeah, but after that, Cadence, I let you stay away because I didn't want to hurt you. But now you're in too deep."

Not her too? What do they mean, I'm in too deep? Why do they keep saying that?

Maddie takes a deep breath, grabs my hand, and looks right into my eyes. "I'm asking you, as my best friend, to come to the session. You'll understand when Alondra tells you. You're still a part of our family. This is more important to me than you can imagine, Kate."

"Not you too," I snap. I'm surprised at how angry I feel. "I told Alondra I wanted out. I barged out of the library when she said the same shit. I don't want this."

"Babe, she came to our dorm. Do you know how weird that is? That's how important it is. It doesn't matter that she's a teacher anymore. What matters is us." She takes another deep breath. I pull my hand away, but Maddie doesn't want to let it go. "You ran away. You didn't let her tell you what she wanted to tell you."

"She told me enough. I'm a straight-A student," I remind her. I feel really nerdy saying it. "She almost destroyed my chances here."

"I know, Katie. I know. But you can study and still be with us."

"I am with you."

"No." Maddie takes another deep breath. "You're with me. But I need you with us. The coven. At least Friday night. For me. Just think about it. Everyone wants to see you again."

"Mira?"

"Especially that bitch."

I laugh at that. Then I test my BFF by being a little bit of a bitch myself. "What about Dr. Reardon?" I regret the words as soon as they come out of my mouth.

Maddie looks angrier than I've ever seen her. But then she snaps, "I don't want to fight. But...what happened, happened to me, not you, Katie. Get over it, 'kay?"

"You let that old—"

"Kate!" Maddie exclaims. Her eyes are wide and she has her hand up. "Goddamnit, Cadence, stop it."

"Sorry."

"Yeah," Maddie says, looking down at her cup. "Friday is very special. We really need you there. Friday night, that's all.

As usual, you can leave if you wish. No one forces anything upon us. But everyone wants *you* there. And ..." She hesitates again. She gulps more of her coffee. "Alondra needs you."

"Alondra needs me? Why?"

"Can't tell you."

"Oh, come on."

"Just come, Katie. Please. I'm asking you to trust me. Just this one time. Please."

I run my hands through my hair and turn from my friend.

"For me?" she implores.

Then I take a deep breath and look out the window again. "Fine." I see her out of the corner of my eye, and she looks relieved. But I'm not looking forward to another meeting with them—not looking forward to it at all. I swore I'd never go again.

Alondra came to our dorm room? That's so weird.

Maddie leans forward with a huge grin. "So, how was it?"

"Hmm? How was what?"

"Your lover?" she asks with a shrug.

I giggle and she joins me. She pats me on the shoulder. Then she raises her cup of coffee to me in a toast.

31

WINDSTORM

I DRIVE MY HONDA TO ALONDRA'S AND PARK AMONG THE familiar cars driven by the rest of the witches in my coven. I'm late. I'm often late to things. And half of me doesn't want to be here. No, all of me doesn't want to be here. Maddie said she needed to get some things and would meet me.

It's dark, but the sky is clear under a full moon and it's warm out.

So I'm walking up the lovely walkway surrounded by Alondra's flowers. I see her Jaguar in the driveway and all the poorer cars, like mine, parked behind it.

I knock on her door and wait uncomfortably.

The door opens. It's Bryce. He embraces me, friendlier than ever.

Bryce and I have been talking by phone all week since *that night*. It's so easy to talk with him. I really like him, and as much as I really don't want to be here, he has this warm grin.

"Thanks for coming, Cadence."

"I came for Maddie."

"I know," he says. "But Alondra needs you more than she does tonight."

I walk into Alondra's chic home. Not all the lights are on, but her expensive vases, travertine floors, and lovely chandelier remind me of her wealth—however she gets all that money.

We walk down the hallway past the kitchen. I look over at the dining room, remembering that first evening party where I became acquainted with my witch professor. There's no one there. There are a few trays of snacks on the island, but nobody's in the kitchen. And no one's in the living room either.

"Mind telling me what this is all about?" I ask Bryce, holding his hand.

"You'll see."

But he doesn't look happy about it. He looks really sad and depressing.

There are two black cloaks on the couch. He hands me one, and I throw it over my clothes.

"You want me to strip down naked under this?" I ask with a silly smile. He doesn't answer. "It's nothing you haven't seen," I quip.

"Stop it, Cadence," he says. He's blushing a little and it's cute. He turns to me and holds me for a moment. "I don't know what I'm going to do with you."

"Love me," I say under his gaze.

He pecks me on the lips. "Come on."

I look out the sliding glass doors and see a pyre—of course. Then I squint and see people sitting around it in chairs.

"You still look nervous," he says as he walks slowly beside me to the fire.

"Because you guys never tell me what the fuck is going on."

He chuckles. But he doesn't tell me what the fuck is going on.

We walk toward the tower of flames. I recognize Maddie under her hood. And bitch Mira too. And asshole Reardon. In fact, Reardon begins talking as we sit.

I am told to sit near Alondra. She doesn't look at me, but

she reaches out her hand. I hold her hand on one side and Bryce's on the other.

"Welcome," Reardon says. "Welcome to all who have come. Especially to Windstorm, who has once again brought her energy to the circle." *Yeah, fuck you, you pervert.* Then something really weird happens. Dr. Reardon, who is one of the most stoic, robotic guys I have ever seen, gets choked up. "We are protected, just as the darkness shades light. Through the darkness roams the hunter. The hunter brings the sacrifice. We follow truth and believe in shadows that shall guide us toward our salvation."

"Atman," says Alondra.

"Atman," say the others.

"And for Alondra, our High Priestess," continues Dr. Reardon. He looks right at me and I shudder. "Allow her to pass over to the Summerland and beyond. Let her not remain as a ghost or vapor. Let her move on to her next life."

"Atman," says Alondra.

"Atman," say the others.

"Thank you," Alondra says to Dr. Reardon.

Alondra lets go of my hand and rises. She lifts her hands to the sky and gazes at the stars.

"All things must pass," Alondra says, addressing all of us. She looks at me with a warm smile. "I have been fortunate to have been your leader for many years. It has been my honor to lead the coven... There was a recent rift in our family." Now she turns and looks right into my eyes, and I'm feeling uncomfortable. "The timing of one of our ladies' coming out could not be more difficult. With the recent loss of her mother, Emily, our sweet Cadence Hawthorne has been through more trials than many of us. So it is with heavy..." Alondra pauses, hanging her head down. The flames reveal tears in our leader's eyes. *Why is she talking about me? And all the witches are looking at me with pity.* "So recently, we have mourned the passing of

Windstorm's mother. Now we must mourn the passing of another."

Mira loses complete control of herself. And she's not one to show much emotion either. Gilda, the girl beside her, grabs her and holds her. Alondra stands straight and gestures with an outstretched hand.

"We, here in the circle, are here for the pleasure given to us by the Earth," Alondra continues. "Your High Priestess suffers from an ailment of the womb. An invasive illness that promises to take my life in a matter of months... And so it is that we are challenged with a great test. I face the greatest test. We know that the greatest illusion of life—death—disturbs our circle once more." Mira is bawling and screaming in pain. Alondra looks over but does not stop. "But do not allow it to shake our faith, girls. Death is the greatest illusion. So I face the Summerland with some trepidation, but knowing I have the support of all of you within the circle."

"Atman," says Professor Reardon coldly.

"Atman," say the others in unison.

"The coven needs a new leader." Alondra picks up a candle from the grass. It's the same type of candle as the one in my dormitory. A memorial candle. "Windstorm." She looks at me with a sweet smile, presenting the candle again. "You have the greatest power of the circle. I will my power and the leadership of our coven to you."

She gestures for me to stand. I rise from my seat and everyone looks at me.

It's supposed to be an honor. But it's not.

I'm getting angry. I mean, really, really angry. I'm feeling this mix of sadness and rage that I've never felt before, and somehow I know I'm not going to be able to control myself anymore. How dare she! How dare they all tell me this in such a contrived, weird way. It seems so cold. So cowardly. Why couldn't she just tell me like a normal person?

"Take this candle," she says. "Light it by the fire and—"

"What's wrong with you!" I shout. Alondra looks perplexed. "Why do you do this!" I yell, looking at the others. I see looks of bewilderment under their hoods. They seem amazed that anyone would dare interrupt their stupid ceremony. "Why tell me now! Like this, in your fucking freak ceremony! So you're dying, Alondra? Why didn't you tell me in the library? Why not tell me like a normal person!"

"Windstorm..." Alondra says.

"*My name is Cadence!*" I shout. I hear my voice oddly echo for miles around the forest.

"Cadence," Alondra says. "Please. Calm yourself. You must—"

"Bitch!" cries Mira, pointing at me. "You don't believe! Can't you see our High Priestess suffers? But you fight her. This is our belief. Our religion. If you don't believe in the coven, get out!" Then Mira screams, "Go away, for once!"

"She doesn't understand," says Maddie, weakly trying to come to my defense.

"You are no longer allowed to be in our sacred circle, Cadence Hawthorne," adds Reardon. It's my pleasure to ignore him.

"How long have you known?" I ask Alondra.

"A year," she says coldly. "But I didn't know it was terminal until this month."

"Why didn't you tell me?"

"Why would she tell *you* anything!" shouts Mira.

Gilda and Helen are holding Mira back. She wants to rush me. She wants to pummel me. Bryce stands before Mira to protect me.

"Everyone sit down!" Alondra orders. No one sits.

"You're so weird!" I say to Mira. Then I address all of them. "You're all so strange."

"Then leave, Cadence," Reardon repeats calmly.

"Bill is right," says Alondra with a nod. "Leave the circle if you must disturb our meeting."

"Bill is right?" I repeat incredulously. "Bill is right? And you want *me* to leave? The circle? The coven I couldn't give a shit about? You asked me to be here. You all begged. First you want me to be the leader of your sex cult, now you want me to go."

"You're obviously not ready, Windstorm," says Alondra.

"*My name is Cadence!*" My words echo once again. And this time there is a crack of thunder accompanying my words and everyone looks up, for there are no clouds. "Why didn't you tell me if you've known for so long? Why do you hide everything!"

Alondra doesn't say anything. She doesn't need to.

The flames do. The fire rises slowly over two stories high into the air. We're all stunned, staring at the pyre. Everyone is too afraid to move. I can feel the flames and smell them, and I'm wondering if it will crash down and kill us. But I can't move. I'm like a frozen animal just staring at the light. And it's real. I'm remembering that we haven't partaken in mandrake yet, which would normally creep me out even more.

But I'm not afraid. I am incensed. And thunder cracks through the valley once more, followed by a series of bursts of lightning. And some of the witches avert their eyes from me in fear.

Me? Why me? It's like my ghost. Why is everybody afraid of me?

I'm crying. My tears are flowing so hard that I can't see. Because I don't want to see. I don't want to see anything anymore. I want everything gone.

The flames blur through my tears. I feel someone holding me. Madison? Bryce? Alondra? I don't know. I don't care. I can't shake it. I can't shake them. Nor can I shake off my fury.

Alondra walks toward me, and her body is thrown back to the ground by some invisible force of air.

I look down.

Out of the corner of my eye, I see a vision of a boy in suspenders. He's out in the field, walking toward us, and there's someone beside him, holding his hand. A woman in a black cloak. The same black cloak that we all wear. They're walking over as if they're as real as we are. But I've been seeing that boy every day. I can see right through him as he fades in and out—he's Maverick, my ghost, and with him is the ghost of Escoba.

Some of the girls scream. For the first time, they can all see the ghosts too.

Then I look at Dr. Reardon. The man looks terrified. That's odd for him. His eyes are open wide, but he's not looking at the ghosts; he's staring at me.

Whoever's holding me is thrown off.

Then I face the transparent specters as they walk closer to us. I fall on my knees and my voice screams out, "Go away!"

They don't go away. They walk ever closer.

"Go away!" I yell again, between tears.

Another witch is trying to hold me back. I throw her off with ease.

"Go away!"

Maverick is only a few yards away now. I recognize his curly hair and his tattered suspenders and baggy pants. He's holding Escoba's hand. They both look as terrified as the witches surrounding the fire. Everyone is afraid. Of what? Of who?

Mira walks up to them, blocking the path leading to me. She seems to be trying to protect us. She says some incantation in a strange language, but she's thrown to the ground.

The two ghosts approach Dr. Reardon and push him toward the fire. Dr. Reardon is only a foot from the flames. He's lurching back, about to fall in. Alondra runs over to help him and tugs him away from the fire, but the specters are pulling him in.

Alondra turns to me in a panic. "Stop it, Windstorm!" she

cries, looking at me. "Stop it! This is your doing. You must stop!"

"He should be killed!" I yell, but I'm surprised because my voice sounds guttural. "I sentence him. You should have thrown him in hellfire long ago for all he's done. Let him burn in the depths of the fire he so covets."

"Stop!" Alondra yells. "Or take me! If you push him in, I swear I'll go with him! Please, I love him! Please. Please, Windstorm! Stop!"

Dr. Reardon is so close to the fire that I think it singes him. In fact, he screams. And with his goatee and terrible expression, he actually looks like Satan. Like Baphomet. If he falls in, then Satan will fall into hellfire like he deserves. I want him to fall. I want him to return to hell and never bother us again. I want to be done with him and the evil he's let loose on the world. I want to burn him in hell.

"He's the devil!" I shout, pointing an outstretched finger at him. "The devil! The devil deserves to be burned!"

"No, Windstorm!" shouts Mira. She's still on the grass. She gets on her knees. "You're the devil! You're a witch! An evil black witch! It is *you* who should be burned!"

"*Currere, agnus, sacrificium!*" I shout. I wave my hand and Mira is thrown ten yards from the pyre. If everyone wasn't trying to help Doctor Reardon, they'd be staring in amazement at this act. Even I would be in awe, if it weren't for my rage.

"*Little Bo-Peep has lost her sheep,*" I yell mockingly, but then my voice changes again. What comes from my lips is a group of children taunting her as if we are in grade school. "*Little Bo-Peep has lost her sheep. Little Bo-Peep has lost her sheep. Little Bo-Peep has lost her sheep.*"

"Please, Cadence!" Alondra pleads, still holding her husband from the flames. The two ghosts are pulling Reardon into the fire, and she's fighting to keep him out. "Please! Stop!"

"How could you do this to my mother!" I ask Alondra, but

I feel as if I've lost control of my own words. I feel as if someone else is speaking through me. "You cunt, how could you stab my mother through the heart! Take her from me and leave me to live alone! Why did you leave me alone, Abigail? Why!"

I feel an arm around me. No, two arms. I look around. It's Maddie and Bryce. They're holding me, trying to calm me.

"Stop it, Cadence," Maddie says.

"Please, Cadence," says Bryce.

There's smoke from Dr. Reardon. I look at Maddie. This man raped her. He raped my best friend. He took her when she was weak and vulnerable. How could he do that? And Alondra? She had sex with others too. Students? Unmarried men? How could she do this? They're both evil. They both deserve to be thrown to the flames.

Evil must burn. I send hellfire. The fire shall consume all to ash and cinders.

Flames are raging above us now. Dr. Reardon is shouting. It's not fear. I think it's pain. I believe he may be burning. Many of the witches are circling him, trying to pull him out. But for a second, it seems to me that they're walking around him like they walk around the pyre. They're walking around him as if he's their sacrifice. Not only him, but Alondra too. Meanwhile the two ghosts are pushing them in—all of them in. First they will burn Reardon, then Alondra, then the rest of the witches of Hawthorne. And all will be cleansed.

Escoba cocks her head back as she tugs Reardon into the fire, and the whites of her eyes stare at Alondra. Then I shout, "Why did you kill me, Abigail?"

Alondra is pulling Dr. Reardon with all her weight now. His body is completely horizontal, being pushed into the wall of fire.

"Cadence!" shouts Alondra, looking back as she pulls Reardon. "You can stop this. Maverick Hawthorne is your blood!

Your ancestor!" She's frantic. "Josiah Billington is mine. You and I are family, Cadence! All of us are a part of the same family!"

I hear her words, but they incense me more.

Why tell me now? How many secrets does this woman hold? Is not deception the greatest sign of evil? That is the core of what this family, this coven, is all about. Slithering, deceptive, unblinking, dark magic vipers. They need to be killed. And I can kill them. I can rid Hawthorne of these snakes. The whole circle must burn.

All the witches in their black cloaks are thrown to the ground and dragged on the dirt, by an invisible force, toward the flames. They scream. Dr. Reardon is closest. He remains levitating over the grass, being pulled into the fire. Alondra grips him, leaning back desperately with all her might to pull him from the flames.

"You're burning him!" yells Alondra. "My God! Stop this, Cadence! You must! Stop it now! You're hurting Bill!"

I can't.

I hear voices in my ear. I hear Maddie and I hear Bryce. They're shouting in my ears to stop.

"I can't," I whisper. I shake my head. "I can't."

No one hears me. I shake my head again. Despite all of Alondra's will to save her husband, her eyes still look upon me. But she doesn't let Reardon go. If he falls, she'll fall with him. They will both die.

Only Maddie and Bryce are standing near me. The rest of the circle is being pulled into the flames. I look at Bryce. He's no longer enamored with me. There is no care or love. He's afraid.

I read his lips. "*Devil.*"

I wake up.

I'm lying in someone else's bedroom. The sun is shining in

through a window. The bedroom is elegant with a mahogany dresser, a white canopy over the large bed, and a small nightstand. I've been here before. It's one of the rooms in Alondra's house. I'm wearing the white negligee I once wore when Maddie and I went shopping. On the nightstand is my book: *Broomstick.*

I stare at the white ceiling for ten minutes, maybe a half an hour. Then I remember the flames. In fact, there's a burning smell from my clothes—no, my body.

Someone knocks at the door. It's Bryce.

I sit up and I feel tears rush to my eyes. Bryce sits by the edge of the bed, smiles, and hugs me.

"Is everyone all right!" I exclaim. "Are you okay?"

"Everyone's fine, Cadence," Bryce says.

"I'm so sorry! I don't even know what happened."

"You proved your power," Bryce says, suddenly very serious. "You proved your worth"—he smiles—"as Alondra's replacement."

"It was real?"

Bryce nods. "Magic is very real, Cadence. I keep telling you that."

"Then I'm a witch?"

Bryce nods.

"Then I'm damned," I say, hanging my head.

Bryce chuckles. "You're human, Cadence. Alondra teaches us that it's up to you if you want to be good or not. Last night, you chose mercy." He pauses for a moment, looking out the window. "I think mercy is a sign of goodness. And Reardon... well, he's gone now. Finally. You helped Alondra and the rest of us get rid of him. He's packed his bags and left town for good."

"He deserved it for all the terrible things he did."

"We've all done things we regret, Cadence," Bryce says, looking down. He sighs. He shakes his head.

"I'm scared," I say. "And...ashamed." I feel stupid, but I

remember last night. Everything. I feel like a frightened little girl because I wasn't in control. But, in some way, I feel like I *was* in control. Maybe that frightens me even more.

He doesn't say anything. Instead, he reaches over and hugs me again.

"Alondra's sick?" I ask.

"Uterine cancer, Cadence. It's terminal. She wanted to tell you. We all knew, but we hoped to lessen your pain with the ceremony. Seems it backfired."

"It's not fair. I can't take losing her. Not after my mother."

"I noticed, Windstorm," he says dryly.

"Has she seen a doctor?"

"Of course. But she doesn't believe in Western medicine. She's a witch. She's not about to take pills or radiation."

"That's stupid. She should take medicine."

"Oh, yeah? You've got such spirit, babe. I love it. I think that's why she calls you Windstorm. Your sign might be grounded, but you have a fire burning inside you, ready to be pushed out."

He runs his hand down my long hair. Then he kisses my cheek. I lean into his hand and enjoy the sound of his breath.

"I can make her take it," I say, sitting up straighter. "I'm our new leader, right? Isn't that also what last night's meeting was about? I can order Alondra to take medicine."

"I think you should just rest," he repeats, patting my leg. Then he rises. "Why don't you go back to sleep?"

"I'm scared, Bryce. I'm...scared I'm losing it. Am I?"

"No, Cadence," he says. "You're clairvoyant. You're a witch. Your initiation and Wandering made you one with nature. It strengthened your power. You'll learn to control it. Alondra can help you."

It's then that the candle Alondra tried to present me, like the memorial candle given to me for my mother, lights up beside *Broomstick*. I don't tell Bryce—I don't want to frighten him.

"Bryce, I love Alondra. I don't think I can handle seeing her die again."

Bryce doesn't have time to respond. The door creaks open wider, and I see Maddie and Mira, who have apparently been eavesdropping on Bryce. Maddie rushes over to me and hugs me.

"Are you okay, Katie?" asks Maddie. "We were so worried. After your little show, you fainted and fell asleep for hours."

They both hug me.

"I'm fine."

Then Mira walks in. But she's got a smug smile. She leans against the door and claps. "That was the most amazing shit I've ever seen, Windstorm. I guess Alondra was right about you."

I kiss Bryce on the lips. He leans against me, forehead to forehead, and closes his eyes.

"Get a room, guys," says Mira, shaking her head.

"I love you, Bryce," I say softly, staring into his blues.

"Love you too."

Maddie is giddy watching us. Mira rolls her eyes.

"Mira, can you hand me my grimoire?" I ask. "I've got some stuff to write in it."

"I'm sure you do. But it's not your grimoire, Cadence," Mira says. "It never was. *Broomstick* is Alondra's."

By nightfall, Bryce and I are alone at Alondra's. Everyone else went home, but Bryce stayed, watching over me. He tells me Alondra went to Atlanta for some private business. He says she'll be back, but she had to take care of some things. What?

He wouldn't tell me. I can't even get all her secrets as her High Priestess.

I get dressed and he offers to take me back home. Then I turn off the light in the room, and we head down the dark hallway. I walk with him down the dimly lit hall, wrapped in his arms in an embrace. All the lights are off in her house.

He kisses me on the cheek as we walk. That's so sweet. But our romance is interrupted by two cats running across the hall. He laughs.

Bryce cocks his head. "Cadence, you forgot to turn off the light."

"No, I didn't. I just switched it off."

But I turn around and the guest room still has a yellow glow.

I walk back into the room.

That's not all I forgot. *Broomstick* is lying beside the memorial candle on the nightstand. I did switch off the light. The flickering light in the room is from the candle, which was never doused. So I grab my grimoire, and with a wave of my arm, I will the candle to blow out.

THE END

WITCHY ADVENTURES ARE CONTINUED IN WINDSTORM, BOOK 2, IN THE HAWTHORNE UNIVERSITY WITCH SERIES

THE SERIES

- WINDSTORM
- THE HAWTHORNE WITCH
- WITCH MIRROR
- RAVENS
- SHADOW CAST
- BELTANE FIRE short story prequel
- SAMHAIN WITCH short story (3.5)
- CANDY CRONE
- ALONDRA 20 yr prequel

THE BOXED SET

- THE HAWTHORNE UNIVERSITY WITCH SERIES

AND DON'T FORGET THAT THE ENTIRE SERIES IS NOW AVAILABLE ON AUDIO, PERFORMED BY ALEXA ELMY AND PRESTON GEER!

ACKNOWLEDGMENTS

I want to thank my beta readers Natalia Ramirez-Avila, Rob C. and George B. Thank you for your thoughts, particularly regarding the ending, which made for a better novel.

And to my line editor, Stephanie Ward, and proofreader, Eliza Dee. There are editors and then there are editors. These two editors go far beyond the norm. Stephanie Ward was new for A.L. and I gave her the challenge of sifting through Cadence's grammatically incorrect voice. And Eliza Dee went far beyond a proofread—as usual. That's why I keep coming back to her.

Finally, I was fortunate to have Regina Wamba, a true artist in the field, paint my cover again. A cover is the first thing a reader sees when looking at a book. And what a cover!

My work is so much better because of all of you. Thank you!

EXCERPT FROM BOOK II

THE FOLLOWING EXCERPT IS FROM "CHAPTER 1 - DARKNESS" IN WINDSTORM, BOOK 2 OF THE HAWTHORNE UNIVERSITY WITCH SERIES BY A.L. HAWKE

Some people are afraid of the dark; others can't seem to turn away. It's so weird at Hawthorne University that my friends and I are actually having a back-to-school party just to watch it. And Maddie can't stop laughing. She keeps tapping my shoulder as we meander from a dirt parking lot, across the lawn, onto a lovely dirt path in Alondra's front garden. She taps me on my arm again. By the time we reach the white-columned deck at the entrance to Alondra's house, I finally turn. Maddie thinks it's soooo funny that she's wearing these cheap cardboard sunglasses I gave her. We're also wearing damp T-shirts and shorts—I say *damp* because it's hella hot outside.

Normally my friends and I meet at Alondra's house to gather around a witch bonfire on Friday Sabbath, but we're here Wednesday the week before the fall semester because this afternoon is very special. It's special for everyone in Hawthorne.

"Will you loosen up, Cadence?" Maddie says, still laughing.

"Take those off. You look dumb."

"Yeah, well, you don't look dumb. Because you're not having any fun."

"I'm just a little nervous, that's all," I say with a shrug.

"I know, babe." Maddie loses her smile and takes off the stupid cardboard things. "You'll be fine. Everybody wants to see you again."

Do they? I haven't spoken to most of my witch friends since the night I lost control. I haven't even had a chance to apologize. I feel so terrible about what happened.

The view at Alondra's place is to die for. Every time I come here, I feel like it takes me back to the nineteenth century. It's perched on a hilltop, surrounded by the forest and the flowing sound of a nearby brook. The perfectly manicured lawn is bordered by lilies and red and yellow roses, recently planted. In the center of it all is Alondra's white antebellum house. The place is quintessentially *antebellum* (I know what the word *antebellum* means, by the way, because I'm a history major at Hawthorne U). Only Alondra knows the right way to mix Neoclassical with chic, like her swanky dark gray Jaguar parked behind an antique red carriage in the driveway.

"I invited Rock, Katie," Maddie says. We're walking up the concrete steps onto Alondra's lovely outside deck.

"Why'd you do that?"

"Because he's cute." She cocks her head with a big smile. I laugh. Then Maddie raps on the door with this really big antique brass knocker. As we wait, she winks at me.

Wouldn't you know it but Alondra herself answers. She doesn't look at all like I expected. I was half expecting her in a dark witch cloak, but she's dressed in a loose saffron blouse over white shorts and sandals. She greets us with her familiar grin.

Alondra smiles a lot. She's always trying to be happy and nice. Sometimes it's really fake. Right now her expression gives me the feeling she's not dwelling on how I nearly killed her and her husband the last time I visited.

"Hey, Maddie. Cadence. Come in."

Her house is just as stunning inside as it is outside. I'm

standing under a huge to-die-for diamond chandelier. Down the hall, I see her elegant dining room. This is my favorite room, with a window lining the wall looking out into the forest. It's next to her kitchen, with travertine floors, Viking stoves and a Sub-Zero refrigerator.

"Did you girls have a nice summer?" Alondra asks, pleasant as always.

"I had so much fun with Kate," Maddie says.

"Yes, you and Cadence stayed at your Aunt Jane's house, right?"

"Aha. How about you, Alondra?" asks Maddie. "Were you here in Hawthorne?"

Alondra is full of mysteries. I saw her practically every day last year, and I still feel like I don't know her.

"You girls excited?" Alondra says, avoiding Maddie's question.

"Yeah," I say.

"Did you bring protective shades? I don't think I have enough."

"You're talking about Katie, Alondra," Maddie replies. "My BFF has never failed to prepare for anything."

"How are you feeling, Alondra?" I ask solemnly.

Alondra has terminal cancer. You wouldn't think it, watching her agile step and cheerful demeanor, but I see bags under her eyes and a new habit of taking deep breaths. I'm guessing she's in pain. She told us the terrible news during our last ceremony. That's one of the reasons I lost control of myself. It drove me crazy that she'd been hiding that from me for so long, along with all the other horrible stuff last year. Then she made me their High Priestess, the leader of our coven. That's the thing about Alondra. See, even now, as she's walking with a quick step, she's being phony. I know she's unhappy. It's like my circle of witches. I love them so much, but I hate their secretiveness. And their deceptions. I mean, I love them all, but I hate them. Do you understand? ...If you do, please explain it to me.

"I hope everybody makes it on time." Alondra takes her cell phone from her pocket. She doesn't answer my question either.

We walk by her living room and Tammy, a cute bald black girl in our coven, is on her knees sorting through grocery bags on the coffee table. This room is just as I remembered, with the white leather sofa, fluffy white carpet, and elegant, modern stone fireplace and chimney. Through the sliding glass door is Alondra's backyard, where my coven held weekly Sabbaths last year.

Tammy jumps up and runs into Maddie's arms.

"Hey, girl!" Maddie says.

"Hey, guys!" says Tammy. She looks at me. "It's so good to see you! I missed you so much!" She hugs me.

Alondra's trying to pry open the glass door with all her weight. It's been stuck ever since I first stepped foot in her house. I walk over, lean against the bottom of the door, and pull it. It unlatches and opens. It's a trick Mira taught me last year.

"Oh, thank you, Cadence."

The door opens into her backyard. The yard is really the wilderness. It's the opposite of the front yard—no manicured lawn, tended flowers, or raked leaves—only wild grass surrounded by the dense forests of Hawthorne. In the center is a pile of logs. That's where we light our bonfires. But today Alondra has set up two picnic tables with yellow-and-red tablecloths. The tables are surrounded by the white plastic chairs we use during séances and rituals worshipping Selene, but now I see watermelons, a stack of soy patties, a few plastic bags of burger buns, red plastic cups, and a couple of glass pitchers of what looks like lemonade on one of the tables. I love lemonade. There's a Weber grill out too and a burly guy named Rocky, Maddie's boyfriend. Rocky is holding tongs, watching the soy burgers cook. Maddie runs into his arms.

"Katie," Maddie says after giving him a long embrace. "Look who's here. Can you believe it?"

He gives me a warm smile. "Hi, Cadence." I stick a palm up and wave.

"Babe," Rocky says to Maddie with a chuckle, "let me work."

"I love this guy," Maddie says.

Someone taps me on my back. I hear a quiet "hi" in a thick Brazilian accent. It's Frida. Frida is one of the shyest witches in our coven, shyer than I am. She's a petite, skinny girl with dark golden skin. Her family immigrated from Brazil fifteen years ago. She and I have always gotten along so well. As we hug, I spot Alondra walking back into her house. She just leaves us without a word.

"You stayed with Maddie in Hawthorne, right?" asks Frida. "I went home. It was hot and sweaty in New York." Frida lives in Jersey. "Awful," she says with a laugh. I'm swatting flies from my face. It's not cool in Georgia either. "Is Bryce here?"

I really wish he was.

"At least your man will be here in school," Frida adds after seeing my expression. "I'll be FaceTiming Greg every night."

We talk a little more, and Frida leaves, saying she's going to help Tammy and Mandy in the kitchen.

It's not too long before our whole coven is in Alondra's backyard. There are eleven of us (not counting my warlock boyfriend, who's still not here). Actually, twelve today as Gilda is visiting. Gilda graduated last semester.

I clam up. Large crowds turn me into a wallflower. So I sit near one of the tables in the yard, fold my arms over my lap, and do nothing. But I face the trees. The forest. I love the woods.

A butterfly lands on my finger. I'm not kidding, an actual butterfly just lands right on the back of my finger. I love that. I watch it slowly open and close its yellow-and-black wings. Then a shadow hovers over me. As I look up, I feel the butterfly

fly off. The only witch actually wearing our black hooded cloak —in the hot humidity—is my overweight goth friend, Mira. The sun shines along the red-and-black devil tattoos on her neck and glistens on her nose ring. Her face is coated in thick makeup. Her black lips curl in nasty smugness.

"Are you ready, Cadence?"

"Hi, Mira."

"I can't wait to see it." She smiles, looking around.

"Yeah."

"I'm sure your magic will come up too." I think she's the only one weird enough to actually want my magic to appear. "You know, Cadence, I did a lot of spell casting this summer. Learned a lot about tarot reading from Falconsong." Falconsong is Alondra's witch name. "The cards predict some interesting things on your horizon."

"We're going to eat burgers?"

"Falconsong is running the session. She said you wouldn't mind. You don't, right? We're gonna just talk."

As long as talking doesn't involve a two-story conflagration, ghosts, and possession. Or dancing around a pyre naked. Or taking drugs.

She surprises me by leaning over and gathering me in her arms. "I missed you, Cadence." And she means it.

"I missed you too, Mira."

"They're separated, you know," Mira says.

"Who?"

"Bill and Alondra. After your magic, Alondra kicked him out."

"I heard."

"And he's not a part of the coven anymore. I'd think that would make you happy."

"It does."

She sits down in a chair beside me. "You know…" Mira puts her hand on my leg. Then she runs her fingers over my bare knee. "I was in town two weeks ago. I texted you but you didn't answer."

The annoying thing about Mira is she knows why I didn't text her, and she's smirking about it. Yet she's not hurt, and she doesn't even look like she cares.

"I didn't get the text," I fib, biting my lip.

"Oh," Mira says with another wink. She touches my leg again. "I think it's gonna be a good year. Now that you're our leader. I can't wait for our first meeting. I'd love to try a summoning. I dealt the Magician card last night. That means great concentration and psychic powers are in our midst. There's a presence in Hawthorne and it's growing. But I also dealt the Devil card and the Death card. There's also black magic afoot." She looks around us as if searching for it. "I feel that too. Especially today. Left-sided magic."

What can I say to that? So I look at the trees again. From the corner of my eye, I see that Mira is also looking out into the forest, because she loves the trees too. She's a nature-loving witch like me.

"I also dealt the Lovers card," she continues, practically talking to herself. "But it was reversed. That means trouble in paradise. After meditating on it, I don't think it was for me." She chuckles. "I mean, I'm not much into lovers, you know. I much prefer raw sex. I think the card was for you. It came right after the High Priestess card. It was probably something about Bryce and you fucking."

"Mira!" I snap.

"What?" she asks innocently, laughing again. "I know you miss him. Is he gonna be here soon?"

She had to ask me that. But Maddie rescues me, handing paper plates with soy burgers to me and Mira. Then she gives Mira a hug.

"Hey, bitch," Maddie says to Mira. "You want to join me and Rock, Katesie?"

Yeah. But then Mira says, "I'll come too."

At Maddie's table, things go smoother. She has me talking with everyone. That's the kind of friend she is. She brings me out of my shell.

When everyone has had their fill of lemonade and soy burgers, Maddie starts clearing the plates. Mira and Gilda collect large wooden logs and throw them on the woodpile at the center of the yard. Other girls gather the plastic chairs from the tables and arrange them in a circle around the fire. Then Gilda takes a bag full of white chalk and carefully pours it around the perimeter of the chairs.

Maddie says goodbye to Rocky. She really doesn't want to, especially before the upcoming event, but she says our "club" has to meet in private.

Soon we're all sitting around a shallow fire, leaving a few chairs empty. Maddie sits on my right and Frida on my left. There's not much ceremony. It's more like a cozy campfire. But I prefer this. The only weird thing is it's the middle of the day. The sky is clear, and it's around three thirty in the afternoon. Our meetings are always at night.

Mira jumps up pointing when Alondra comes out of the house. It's like she's been waiting for her to appear all afternoon. Alondra is wearing our black cloak—the same one Mira's wearing—holding a fiery torch. Her face is covered by thick goth makeup like Mira's. By her side is another witch in a black cloak. I don't recognize this one. And following them are two other ladies in similar garb.

PARTING WORDS

What did you think of *Broomstick*? By placing a book review, you can inform others of your thoughts and help spread the word about my book.

Want more? Periodically I like to send news regarding current or new projects. If you'd like to be privy, I encourage you to sign up to my email newsletter. Your information will remain private and you can cancel any time.

Sign up at www.alhawke.com or scan the following QR code:

ABOUT THE AUTHOR

A.L. Hawke is the author of the bestselling Hawthorne University Witch series. The author lives in Southern California torching the midnight candle over lovers against a backdrop of machines, nymphs, magic, spice and mayhem. A.L. Hawke writes fantasy and romance spanning four thousand years, from pre-civilization to contemporary and beyond.

Visit A.L. Hawke at www.alhawke.com

Email: contact@alhawke.com

ALSO BY A. L. HAWKE

PARANORMAL ROMANCE

<u>WINDSTORM</u>

Believe in witches, for sometimes you need magic to ward off the evil in darkness.

It was my junior year at Hawthorne University when Mira dealt me a reversed Lovers card. That meant trouble in paradise. I thought nothing of it until Alondra introduced me to a new witch from outside our coven—Enora. Enora's precisely the sort of witch you'd call wicked. Even worse, she used to be in love with my boyfriend.

I just wanted a normal year. But as our leader fought illness, I fought with my friends trying to hold the Hawthorne coven together. I felt abandoned. And my loneliness dropped me into trances where I wandered the dark forest alone. These altered states were created by my magic, but I learned that they were spurred on by something far more sinister.

Where did this evil come from? The wicked witch? The old devil? I had to find out because it threatened the people I love.

Windstorm is Book 2 in the Hawthorne University Witch Series.

URBAN FANTASY

<u>CORA</u>

Cora has it all—wealth, loveliness—but she doesn't have a man. They just keep dying on her.

She is the immortal Greek goddess Persephone, living in a Malibu beach house in the twenty-first century. And no matter how much therapy she undergoes, nothing can ease her pain after the recent murder of her husband.

Until she meets Mr. Gabriel Cartwright, a prim and proper young East Coast realtor who's hired to arrange transfer of her things to her new home in Toronto. Cora likes him. He's tall, dark and yummy.

But Gabe holds a secret. He has Napean nymph blood, an ancestry that Imada, a despicable secret society of gods and goddesses, has been hunting for centuries. Cora knows this. That's why she hired him. She wants to be close to him. She wants to care for him. But Imada cares about him too—they want him dead.

Cora can heal wounds and move clouds, but she can't bring back her husband. Can her attraction to this new guy help her forget her loss? She has her ancient brutish lover Hades, the God of the Underworld, on her side. And Gabe has such a kind, sweet heart and is so handsome. Yeah, she'll keep her man or tear Imada apart trying.

SCIENCE FICTION

CANDY SAVANT

In 2234 men are extinct, having been deemed unnecessary.

This is the story of Candice Harlow, a brilliant young scientist arranged by Arkite's supreme ruler, Elise Jackson, to lead the Savant project. A.I. is forbidden to experiment with human genes, so it enlists researchers—Savants. Savants work to create a human being from scratch to serve as a blueprint for immortality.

Candice likes her newfound wealth and status, but she's not sure she likes Elise. Elise is unhinged. She's manic, has a furious temper, and seems to care more for Candy's dollface than her scientific aptitude. By day, Candy flies her bike to HQ laboratory. By night, she's whisked off to fancy restaurants and nightclubs.

The project's genesis is not unlike Frankenstein's creature. Though not hideous, the creation is shunned by the all-female society. Candy shelters and cares for the creation, but not before she's unfairly betrayed and accused of the worst possible crime.

Book I in the Candy Savant series.

<u>MOTHER SAVANT</u>

It is now 2244 and the all-female society of Arkite is on the brink of revolution. Only the return of the Mother Savant can hope to maintain order.

Savant Elise Jackson, Arkite's supreme leader, is stricken with terrible grief over the recent loss of her lover. She has spent the last two years with her assistant, Sara, trying to repair and genetically engineer her lover's damaged body and mind.

But the Viceroy of Pyramid City and her followers in the Savant Council have no interest in squandering the city's resources for Elise's personal gain. With the help of the mainframe AI, they will vie for power, even attempting collusion with Sara and sabotage.

And even if her enemies fail and Elise somehow manages to revive her lover, Elise knows she'll have to vie for something she covets even more—her lover's love. For Sara once loved her just as much, if not more.

Mother Savant is Book 2 in the Candy Savant Series.